THE SOVEREIGN

JAKE SUDDERTH

Copyright ©2023 by Jake Sudderth

ISBN: 979-8-88615-152-7 (Paperback)

Inks and Bindings
888-290-5218
www.inksandbindings.com
orders@inksandbindings.com

To
The Bee

CHAPTERS

BORDERS

At the end of the school day we made our way to the local grocery store. I always imagined ripping off food but never could bring myself to finish the job. The temptation was there; I just didn't have the balls. My friend Nathan taunted me because of this lack of courage. He didn't discuss the subject in front of our friends because he knew his barbs pissed me off. Nathan is like that – just when you think he is a thoughtless jerk he surprises you with a little compassion. I felt like I was shrinking when my school friends announced their tally of stolen goods. We called it "the daily." To compensate, I acted like I belonged by talking tough. But I was simply an outsider, a "wanna-be." I watched from a block or two away as friends and acquaintances combed through the aisles of Rimbo's, a shopping relic from the 1940s. The floor sags, covered with faded white and black tiles, worn down to concrete and dirt in places. Combined scents of mold and dirt wafted among aisles and dust kicked up when shoppers shuffled up and down the walkways. 7-Eleven and Safeway were also popular, as were other stores managed by people too spaced out to care.

My scene was a block or two away, spying as people left the building wearing large coats and talking feverishly, as if nothing abnormal was happening. Running meant trouble. No exit after five minutes or sprinting with goods in hand signaled emergencies because weapons or muscle created these scenarios, and nobody wants to get chased by someone with a gun when they book out the front door of the ugly yellow stucco exterior of Rimbo's. All romance evaporates. You steal because you think you are better than the neighborhood. The benefit is free food for a hungry stomach. I served as a lowly scout for these operations. When someone fled a pursuer I pretended to chase the guy, always just missing him, and then pretended to be a witness for the proprietor. By the time I finished giving my testimony there was confusion about the height, eye color, and clothing of the perpetrator and sometimes I pretended to know the identity of the person and where they attended high school. Cops are lazy and shoplifting by minors is not at the top of their list. My bullshit just sent them to the other side of town. I was only called back as a witness twice and nobody ever formally accused me of any funny business. Newspaper accounts and television really distort things. The police are not running around grabbing evidence and prints and bringing stuff back to a secret room with a hot chick and an old guy with lab coats. They don't care unless the store owner has clout or never stops calling. The guys I watched, hit locations full of apathy. If an officer ever received a call about Rimbo's he or she was gonna finish their sandwich before jumping in the patrol car. Eventually, store owners catch on and people get caught; but it takes a while.

The only person never chased down on foot by a manager, or the police, was Nathan. Too fast, slick, and skilled for his age, Nate presents a problem for everybody, from authority figures to street toughs. He can talk his way out of any conflict and his ability to manufacture charm in the presence of elders makes all of us sick. Nathan Freehold is a devious charmer.

He has never been in serious trouble during high school. His athletic feats, good looks, and a magnificent grin put people at ease. When he stretches out his sinewy 6'3 frame and raises his chin, for a confident rub or scratch, almost a thinking pose, he creates an illusion that he is even taller and more angular. Beautiful bronze skin provides a masculine glow and when he moves his large hands toward the sky and back to the center of his body, like a stretching cat, he is perfectly balanced. In appearance he is like a schoolyard preacher - a wise boy among ragged amateurs. He is the truth.

Nathan was never caught stealing because he didn't want to be. Does this sound silly to you? It did to me the first time Jasper Owens said so.

"Nate is too tall and good looking to be a thief. He sticks out," I protested.

"Exactly, but his skill is deception...he shows people something else...a confident glow." Jasper stammered as he explained Nate's special powers. "He does not fit the profile of someone doing something bad. That is why he is dangerous for the rest of us. He looks you in the eyes while the rest of us look like we are up to no good. Nathan is an escape artist." Of course Jasper was right; Nathan's confidence is his one true skill.

Mr. Deception spent most of his time with Jasper, Chirp Watkins, and me before ninth grade started, but his good looks and charm drew others to our group. Aaron Robinson and Nico Rodriguez eventually joined our crew. Nico was particularly popular because he had access to cars. He has worked as an assistant at a repair shop for years. All five of us live within fifteen blocks of each other in White Center, just outside of Seattle, a neighborhood that ceased being white years ago. When one of our peers said they were going "nowhere" or doing "nothing," nowhere was White Center and nothing meant hanging out in the "Center."

My friends vary in age because dropouts and homebodies hang out in the neighborhood. Nate is always the youngest in any crowd, he seems old, and since I am eleven months his senior, I am a natural associate. He is overly confident and I am always concerned about what people think, do and feel. When arriving for class about five seconds after the bell each day, Nathan oozes in to the room; making everybody aware he is on Freehold time. His charm is disgusting sometimes. When I was still in school he walked the gray hallways of Chief Sealth High School as if dancing on air. He always played up relations with people who could benefit him. In class he was talkative but never impolite. Smiles and silly talking out of the side of his mouth enhanced his allure. Nathan is a clown, but just an intelligent, funny goof who can make fun of himself in front of others. He comes across as a grounded kid relying on self-deprecating humor instead of a jock asshole egomaniac.

"Last night I felt pretty good about my homework until my little brother starting correcting my answers." This was Nathan in math class. "After reading my essay my mother asked me if I am retarded." Literature class, delivered to a small group of friends in a voice no teacher could decipher. And Freehold never makes such statements near people who would be offended by his language. "Do you think the Pope beats off?" This casual question, completely serious, was delivered to a random neighbor in World Affairs class. The student, probably feeling like he was part of something because Nathan was communicating with him in front of girls, laughed and buried his head in his arms on his desk like an insider.

The summer before my junior year Nathan worked at a gas station; one he had ripped off for years before applying for a job by pointing out security flaws at the facility. He mentioned the open back door near the public restroom and the lack of an auto lock on the cash register during his interview. He was frustrated he had never thought of the back door entrance. Nathan always relied on friends to make noise and create diversions while he snagged money in the register. He waited patiently to buy a soda or gum while a fake fight or breaking bottles, landing in the garage, caused a scene. The owner was an Indian woman who was widowed when her husband was shot the year before. Noise drew her to a phone in the shop, which she used to call the police while money disappeared. After her husband's tragic death, she never messed around. You would have thought Nathan was her adopted son after his "interview." I think he even gave her a hug at the end – really gross stuff. Nate has never told me how many women he has fucked but I know the number is probably staggering. Freehold is funny that way – silent about some subjects – too open about others. He tells you his thoughts without provocation and then seeps into nether land and just stays there for a while. Sometimes at school he would just talk out loud, like a big weirdo.

"Should I move to the Bay Area?" he would ask nobody in particular. "Hmmm," he demurred whether anybody answered him or not. Since he can't move anywhere without assistance, his open questions sound like wild fantasies.

For some reason, probably the fact that I do not challenge or compete with him, I am Nathan's chosen friend - his confidant. Why do I know this? He comes to me for advice and help and it never goes the other way. Now that I have graduated I will miss time spent in that disgusting school and I need to redefine our relationship. Lord knows I can't be worrying about that kind of junk anymore. I also need to get out of this neighborhood and find something to do. My plan in life thus far has focused on wasting time until something exciting comes along; and the plan is not working.

I remember attending Chirp Watkins's birthday last year in the backyard of his grandmother's house over on 26th Street. Everybody was shooting the bullshit and suddenly his father stood up and started tapping one of his mother's drinking glasses with his fork so hard that she started shouting at him. Then he made this really funny toast. "Chirp here is to your next eighteen years because your first eighteen have not been very productive."

"Oh, for god's sakes Marc, leave the boy alone for at least one day," shouted his moms. I remember starting to laugh but then I looked across the table at Chirp's clenched jaw and red face and realized it was a low blow – especially in front of all of his friends. The lesson resonated with me though. I am not very productive but, like Chirp, I would not want some loud parent or guardian making a big deal about it in front of a bunch of people.

Our whole neighborhood is that way – people spending too much time worrying about other people's business. When new people started moving into the Center in the early 1980s everybody started freaking out and bitching about rental prices creeping up. Once in a while you hear some greaseball, who never takes a bath, talking about "Rat City," the name all the old timers had for this place. Nico's father, Merton, is always blathering on about how the Center used to be the only place near Seattle where you could buy alcohol on Sundays or after a certain time of the night. He knows what he's talking about because he spends all of his time at the liquor store. If they had a club card for good shoppers he would have the most points. One time I went over to dinner at Nic's house and his dad never made it to the dinner table. He just stayed over in the corner of the living room under wool blankets surrounded by beer cans. I was pretty impressed because he had about three or four varieties in his little part of the room: Rainier, Olympia, Mickey's and one more bottle I didn't recognize. Every once in a while a hand reached out and grabbed an aspirin bottle and pulled it back under the covers. I always wonder how he managed to take the aspirin with a dry beer mouth and no water. Maybe his breath just melted everything into powder? When I go over to Nico's house I always check out the medicine cabinet when I use the bathroom. It looks like a pharmacy in there.

My mother, Wendy, claims to be "Black Irish," and my father, Richard, is black. I never understand what my mom is talking about. I figure you're Irish or not; this Black Irish thing is bullshit. My father has never been concerned with his heritage and only says one thing about my mother's genealogy: "I think she is full of shit." He summarizes everything with a bang. Pop spends most of his days in the Center talking about cities he actually likes. Seattle is not one of those places. Originally from Philadelphia, Richard Ramos bitches about local patterns, food, and the Pacific Northwest custom of cherishing the great outdoors. Whenever somebody (usually me) suggests that our family go camping or hiking, my father arches his eyebrow and stares at the offender (usually me) for several seconds.

"You want to go camping? I've got an idea. Go outside and get some pebbles and shove them down your pants. Then don't shower for a few days, get on the bus and go buy some granola at the Co-Op in West Seattle. After that, sleep in some soggy-ass place, like the bathtub, so you have an idea of fun times after a hard rain. After the granola makes you shit your pants, your wet clothes make you freeze and your body odor crackles louder than a five-piece band; you won't want to go camping anymore."

"How about a day hike then?"

"Why don't you hike your ass outside and bother somebody else. Good Lord, in Philly if I ever told my father I wanted to go hiking he would whip my ass."

I usually don't push my father in these situations because he has a temper and he is intimidating. Plus, I can make him look foolish in an argument. He is 5'11, stocky and his furrowed brow and cold eyes wear an intense glare. He looks like one of those guys that perpetually smell. He always wears jeans or painter's pants and since he is long-waisted, pop looks kind of dumpy. His eyes are wide and he turns his head with great intensity when addressing people, like he is being shocked or goosed in the ass. Nathan first met my father when he was fourteen. After we ate hot dogs together in the back yard one time he pulled me aside and asked, "Does your father ever clean the load out of his pants? Nathan is always really serious when making jokes so when I doubled up with laughter I looked crazy.

"He oughta wear shirts that cover his knees so he doesn't get pneumonia in his butt-crack."

More laughter. I always enjoy crude humor at the expense of others. And when my father sees you laughing he makes sure you know he is paying attention. "You boys have somethin' to say? I thought so."

Around my parents Nathan acts like the black Eddie Haskill. He smiles and shows interest when my mother tells endless stories about her art collection or people she encounters at the beauty parlor. The former is a grouping of oil paintings discovered in the recesses of local flea markets. He nods and smiles as she babbles and forgets to offer him anything to eat or drink. No wonder "Eddie" felt like stealing growing up. His charm never wins him anything at his friend's houses. My mother isn't much of a cook anyway. Her idea of a gourmet meal is hamburger helper or ravioli in a can. She spends most of her day humming and watching television; Ma really likes talk shows, especially 'Montel Williams.'

"The former Wendy Kennely," that is what her friend Barbara always says, has deep half circles along the sides of her mouth and is thick in the middle. She wears long, untucked, plaid shirts that never look clean. They fail to mask her fat ass, the kind of pooper that gets in your way if you want to move quickly around her in a hallway or the kitchen. In our little five-room rambler, movement near Ma requires rapid decisions. I believe my mother was beautiful years ago, I've seen old pictures, but she changed quickly. The only thing about her that remains attractive are her engaging eyes, which she turns on and off depending on her mood. When she looks at you eyelids rise, infusing her target with energy. She is hard to understand but when you tell her something she does give a shit. Nathan jokes about Ma as well. He used to say she would have a dynamite figure if you redistributed the contents of her ass up and around her body. But I can tell he cares about her and she adores him because he used to sit on her bed and talk to her while she watched TV. He could charm the balls off a brass monkey that guy. And ma loves people who watch television.

My parents met in Tacoma when my father attended officer's camp at Fort Lewis. The Kennely family was from North T-town and their daughters danced and met boys during their spare time. Dancing and booze sealed their relationship. After my old man returned from Vietnam he asked her to marry him. After receiving a tentative "Yes, I think that is a good idea," Richard suggested they elope without telling family anybody. I have heard this story a million times. After moving to Grays

Harbor in southwest Washington, Pop got a job cleaning at a pulp mill. He spent countless weekends screwing around at the National Guard headquarters in nearby Montesano. He is still very good at card games.

I was born in Hoquiam and we lived in an apartment that smelled of mold. Not the worst dwelling of decay on the "Harbor," more of an old cedar smell – like a rotting ship hull or old logs you sniff at the beach. When I was four years old I started complaining about the stench and my father told me to get a job and buy my own house. Then, as now, when pop yelled at me or shouted me down, my mother just stared out the window, the ceiling, or watched television. She is very consistent.

Eventually, moms got a job cutting hair at a local salon. That was about the time her ass began to explode. Sometimes, when I am real tired or drinking, I think of how funny it would be if my mother fell on somebody while cutting their hair and they were stuck in her butt.

"Winston…Winston…where did you go?"

I only laugh about this subject internally because my friends would unleash an impromptu joke festival if I introduced a subject like my mother's backside. Then I would laugh like a jerk, start crying, and have trouble talking. Man, I am going to miss being a kid.

Laughing at silly crap is a special talent of mine and my laugh usually prompts more of the same from my friends, who draw silliness from me just as easily. We are famous for breaking up for no reason at all. As senior year wound down it felt like we were laughing about everything. Like all high school students devoid of plans, the end of care in the loose hands of the Seattle school district leaves me wondering about the future. I feel like some outside power is destined to thrust me forward, be it a court, boss or admissions officer. And the damage is already done in terms of my grades…nothing is going to be easy. Hunger and a bright sky pulled me out of my daydream.

"Should we get some breakfast pop?"

My father pretended to ignore me one week after the highly overrated Sealth high school graduation ceremonies. I can tell he thinks I'm lazy. A story about the good old days when he managed to find a job in one hour – shining shoes or some other bullshit - was coming. At 10:30 in the morning he was ready for his second breakfast – Pop wakes every day at 5:30 and is ready for another meal about the time my mother wakes after a long night of rest. She is only cutting hair part-time these days because of poor business at Juanita's Salon. I desperately wanted to take control of our schedule before his mind wandered to my life.

"How about we go to…."

"Let's go to Bird's" interrupted my father.

I have no idea why I even tried to suggest someplace else. Richard Ramos turns up his nose at Seattle restaurants and their lack of seasoning – which he prefers. And he hates the fact that the city seems so mellow – "No energy," he shouts. "Where are the people? Ain't there any fun in this town?" He ignores the throngs of people downtown or on Capitol Hill because he never goes there…and for all his crowing about people, he does not like to go anyplace where it is difficult to park. Driving around town with him is like being around one of those cranky old grandparents that nobody likes – one of those people that always act like nothing impresses them.

Bird's is perfect for Pop because the restaurant sits in a thrashed, listing, half-abandoned brick building. Some weird Ethiopian guys walk out the front door sometimes but that is because they own the building…or at least that is what the old man told me. The woman who runs the place, Mother Bird, is from Arkansas and she puts up with food nuts coming from across the city to try her stuff and then she makes fun of them after they leave. All day long, Mother Bird is solicited for free food by starving adults. She obliges when she is in a good mood – the beggar needs a good story and Bird is the jury. My father only eats at Bird's, Denny's, all-you-can-eat places and Kentucky Fried Chicken. So I know what I am talking about when it comes to greasy joints.

When we plop down in our normal corner seat at Bird's – a card table that leans and metal chairs covered by multicolored seat cushions and blankets – it is always the same routine. I keep my mouth shut and watch everybody come and go. It sounds boring but I am constantly entertained. When Bird's business wanes and she is done cooking for the day she proclaims that the "kitchen is closed." Then she heads outside on the street and tells everyone heading her direction, customers and strangers alike. Her shrill voice makes everybody pay attention. Every phrase begins with "Hey!" Watching the stout, medium-height Bird slam the door open while yelling; apron on over a white or red button-up shirt, is quite a sight. I think she wears hair extensions but nobody has the guts to ask her. She walks in this strange sideways motion like one of her legs is pulling her entire body along a diagonal plane. She would play a good ghoul in one of those zombie movies.

Pop always gorges himself on mammoth catfish fillets, black-eyed peas, cornbread and yams. Peach cobbler is added if he is flush that day. Our last visit resulted in a short nap at the little corner table facing the television. He even started snoring, resting his hands on his gut. He awakened when forces of gravity nudged his fingers down to his lap. Fortunately, Mother Bird does not sell alcohol. If she did, my father would never leave. After intermittently snoring and performing his weird hand movements, Richard Ramos started reminiscing about the good old days in Philadelphia. "This Catfish is almost as good as the stuff I used to catch in the Schuylkill."

"You didn't catch no Catfish in the Skooykill," Mother Bird answered across the room. "There ain't no fish in that river no more, you old fool. You're an old-looking sonofabitch, but you ain't that old." My father only responded indirectly. After witnessing numerous guests sent packing for offenses ranging from body odor to debt, he was not about to tempt fate. He glanced up from his plate and, in a near whisper, stated his case to the young couple occupying a nearby table when Mother Bird waddled out of range.

"Bird, I gotta give you the facts. You've been out here in dinktown too long. My relatives still fish the Schuylkill. They set up down from the old Waterworks and fish all night. Now I know the fish is polluted, but you know a little beer will kill any poison (big laughter from Pop who was oblivious to the reactions of his table neighbors). Mother Bird, outta get some strongarm (my father's term for beer) in this fine establishment…then the Catfish would taste even better." Our neighbors on this day just smiled and pretended to laugh. They probably were hoping the loud guy with the weird son would just go back to sleep.

Every so often, people really buy into Pop's program and they start laughing - a big mistake because once he has an audience he never shuts up. Sometimes new friends are born. One time, after striking up a conversation with guy named Rocky, he shared a beer with his new friend at Uptown Tavern down the street. I waited in the car and read the newspaper while those two talked about the good old days. Pop always prepares for such encounters by wearing his most crisp hickory work shirt, yellowed in the armpits.

On the way home from treks out, pop focuses on the past. He reminisces about food, people, street energy and "atmosphere," and gets even more wound up as he talks. A favorite topic is what he terms 'signs of humanity.' He has all sorts of definitions that are hard to follow. He calls women 'science.' To him, understanding female behavior, attitudes and allure is so mystical that he chalks it up to a one large all-encompassing term: science. That concept, in his vocabulary, means the unexplainable. When discussing 'humanity,' pop is referring to people movements in and around abandoned properties or places that are shut down. Often he just cranes his neck in desolate places night or day. He likes gritty stuff and says so. "Man, when I came to this town I was confused as hell because there was no graffiti," he mentioned last time we ventured out together. When I reminded him that almost everybody in the world believes graffiti is an eyesore he whisked away my comment with a wave of his hand.

"Good graffiti is public art. Do you notice when you go out in the country you don't see any of that stuff? You know why? There ain't no demand and no place to put it. People are just blending in; they don't have to mark their territory. Graffiti in a big city is a way to communicate with people. It shows local talent; a free public gallery. It makes me comfortable when I see the orange, red, and yellow where I grew up. I feel at peace, I know that I am home." Erratic hand movements focused my attention on the steering wheel. His stories of urbanity seemed real as he turned corners with his knees and I feared for my life.

I enjoy my father's descriptions of his heritage. He tells me about his parents and grandparents and how they raised several children in a dilapidated row house over sixty years. His proud grandfather was a "cotton-picker." He self-selected public garbage, sorted and resold the merchandise. Everybody in the family contributed. Some with cash, some with food. Pop's family never made it out west and nearly everybody died by the time I reached my teenage years. I guess we visited once when I was two or three, but I don't remember anything. My Uncle Weston came through town two and a half years ago on his way to Alaska to find work. The furthest he got was a pay phone in Port Angeles where he called to borrow money for the ferry. His request was denied. Wes was the tenth child in the Philadelphia Ramos clan; my father was ninth, one of thirteen. Weston wore sweatshirts all the time and had a big laugh. He was even more stocky and compact than Pop, as if somebody took a mold and cut it down by three inches. To compensate he bounced when walking, like a human piston. Between him bouncing around the kitchen and my father doing his explosive head turning thing, it was like living with the pop-up monsters in the haunted house over at Seattle Center. I liked Uncle Wes because he was always kidding my father, who purposely ignored him while reading the sports page. He was fascinated by bugs. Wes could not believe cockroaches were hard to find in Seattle and he used to walk around searching for spiders. When he saw a big slug he freaked out and then my father spent about twenty minutes telling him about banana slugs. Now when I ask my father about Wes he always says the same thing: "He is probably dead by now." Sorry, I am daydreaming again.

"Damnit." My father was pissed when the closed sign at Mother Bird's said; "I HAVE THE FLU, NO FOOD TODAY." This same thing happened once before. On that day the sign said, "WE'RE CLOSED, GO COOK YOUR OWN FOOD."

The blaring red handwriting read like Bird's booming voice. Pop grimaced; his broad forehead furrowed and sprung deep lines. He sucked his cheeks in, eyes narrowed. A deep sigh followed. I was silently glad. I did not feel like biscuits and gravy or a catfish omelet. "If you don't like the way I drive go fuck yourself," said my father to nobody in particular. He looked angry as we searched for a replacement restaurant. As we crawled along Rainier Avenue South I remembered that Nathan expected me to meet him after his shift at Big Five Sporting Goods. Parents and schedules never work out.

After my 3-hour breakfast ordeal, which ended at Burgermaster and included a complaint-filled introduction to "Swedish Pancakes," I arrived at the sporting goods store five minutes late. "That's the last time I am going to let you talk me into eating those goddamn bread sticks. I am heading out of town tomorrow early – listen to your mother for a change while I'm away." My father dropped me off and he gave Nathan a half-assed wave…more like a swat at the air - like he was violating a bee in the car. Freehold just smiled and waved back with sincerity. He looked lost and began smoking after I sat down next to him on a bench in front of the store. My father scattered birds and cars as his rusting Dodge pick-up sliced across the parking lot diagonally; probably still shouting about the pancakes and yelling at the radio.

"Twenty-five feet boy," yelled a fellow employee on break. She was implying that Nathan was invading the non-smoking area. A solo middle finger responded to her joke.

"What the fuck am I doing here R?"

"I don't know; but you have worked here for two years. You must like something."

"This is a job for a boy…not a man." Then a broad smile crept across Nathan's face and we both laughed.

The manager of the store is Ben Rubin's brother Matt. Ben is the Sealth High School football coach and he encourages his players to work during the summer so   they don't do anything stupid off the gridiron. Matt is a successful local bookie on the side. In fact, I'm not sure he ever works in his office, a little corner job in the store with no windows and a few security cameras flashing blinking pictures all the time. His desk is littered with sports pages, legal pads and Big Five inventory reports according to Nathan. I confirmed this story while visiting Nate one time and finding him in the corner office looking at a *Penthouse* and cackling with Rubin.

There is a third Rubin brother who allegedly makes big money selling cars - he is the flashy one of the group. Ben is a real tool, but Matt is funny. Both are in their forties and are big husky loud mouths. Ben's locker room speeches are legendary for their simplicity. I never played, but numerous friends relay stories of the same tired tale, sprouted over and over.

Before road games Ben gets the team fired up for their pre-game prayer by yelling, "Gentlemen…tonight we are going to go into their neighborhood…and disrespect them." Then he poses for effect, sticks his chin out and walks around the room starring at everybody like a tough guy. When playing at home he adds a special twist: "Gentlemen… they are going to come into our neighborhood and (his voice growing louder with each word) try to disrespect you!" Sometimes Ben turns "you" into "us" when adding a personal touch, designed to tease the brain of the nimble warrior mind. Rubin teaches typing, keyboarding and computers at Sealth and he actually harms good students because of his lack of knowledge. His answers do not address direct questions. "Mr. Rubin my operating system will not support my copy of MS Office; I need online access to download a driver."

"Listen, driving, or I mean a driver, will not solve that problem…just keep typing and Mr. Graebner will work on that machine after school." Mr. G is the school's system administrator and you can tell he thinks Rubin is an idiot. He probably spends twenty percent of his time working on Rubin's personal "machine," or helping him set up a computer with direct access to high school football results. Graebner is always shuffling into Rube's class wearing a white dress shirt, some polyester brown slacks from 1973 and dragging a little cart full of equipment. Sometimes when he enters the room Rubin is babbling about the training practices of the Oakland Raiders or man leaves without a peep.

"Do we only have access to SQL here?"

"Doesn't matter, use anything you want."

"Any database?"

"Sure."

"Can we bring software from home and load it here?"

"Check with Mr. G on that one sport." Low volume snickering filled the room.

"Will the test ask specific questions about software brands and companies?" A legitimate question since *The Present and Future of Computing* is a very thick textbook.

"No, I have wanted to call this class Keyboarding for years but the school district is interested in focusing on the future… and computers are the future. Use the book as much as you wish. It is a good piece of information. But test questions will come from our time in class." After two weeks of Rubin-time everybody figured out that test questions were taken verbatim from the quiz section at the end of the book's chapters.

I had Rubin one semester and he used to walk around stopwatch in hand, beady eyes in the middle of a big red face, wearing khakis framed with a brown belt and shiny brown shoes. His golf shirts never masked his growing beer belly and if you turned your head into the seat aisle when he was coming hard around the corner   you might get the old stomach in the face routine. Rubin timed people until their fingers were practically bleeding. His methods ignored computing power and treated thinking machines like typewriters. When our time was up he yelled, "Enough," wiping his brow and moving his sandy blond hair, parted on the side, into place. His mane was never long enough to be really screwed up, but his strange hair sweep followed him to the sideline on game days. No fan could ever tell whether Sealth was ahead or behind because Matt Rubin was always playing with his hair; and he always had that damned blue stopwatch. We used to joke that he took it into bed with his wife, or Mr. G's wife, or whoever he slept with, and yelled, "Enough," when he was satisfied.

His brother's signature move is silent staring so I was relieved to see Nathan outside alone. When expressionless bookies size me up I get uncomfortable. Ben is a little shorter and slimmer than Matt. His hair is thinning and, unlike his brother, he pays no attention to the mop of brown on the top of his head and never looks in the mirror. Stained clothing and body odor follow him. Ben knows statistics and the daily schedules of every major sport and he seems to have friends in every big city. I have asked Nate on several occasions if he ever places bets with Rubin. He always claims he doesn't gamble, but I bet he sits in that building listening for tips all day long. One of his responsibilities at the 5 is to run around town, dropping off envelopes and picking them up – always unmarked and always feeling like cash. "Bookies don't take checks," says Nathan.

Ben smokes like a maniac. He also spends countless hours on his cell phone walking around the building with a little notebook, speaking in a little voice and moving his hands all over the place. The people who meet with him during the day are like characters from a movie according to Nathan. Huge guys with tattoos, little slumpy guys in their work uniforms dropping off forms, and nervous women stopping by, unannounced, to ask questions. I always wonder how he manages the store without doing any real work, but Nate tells me that his network of coaches and athletic directors, many serious bettors, purchase bulk goods for their respective teams. Maybe if you are behind in your payments buying some extra baseballs or something makes a difference.

"What happened today?" I asked Nate while sitting with him outside the store. He is the kind of guy that embellishes stories just to entertain you. I was hoping he would indulge me but on this day he had no juice.

"I've got nothing."

"What do you want to do?"

"Sit on my ass." We both laughed.

After several minutes of doing what Nathan intended we decided to walk to Kane Harvey's house. He lives with his older brother Jeremy in a small rental house. Kane is a grade older than me and two years older than Nathan, so he is long gone from Sealth. He is short, pudgy, funny and always sleeping. Working a janitor's night shift in downtown Seattle and video games occupy his time. Since K was not around we jumped the fence and shot baskets in his back yard. Nathan is so lazy he spent most of his time shooting while smoking and sitting in a hideous green lawn chair. I practiced ball fetching, half asleep in faded blue jeans and a black, Henley-style, long sleeved shirt.

After about an hour I walked down the street and bought a six-pack from some Korean guy who never asks for ID. After we drained a few, I called Kane's cell phone while walking around the block. He told me he and Jeremy were stuck in Bakersfield all weekend. I must have sounded pathetic, or he wanted someone to watch the house, because he told me where the hide-a-key was – a really stupid, obvious place - under the moldy green doormat that beckons visitors at the back door. I never saw a place with more putrid green furniture. I didn't mention Nathan was with me because the answer would have been no.

Kane also told me not to say anything to Jeremy. The latter is twenty-four and always moody. He greets me with silence and a nod of his head when I visit. He has a real stick up his ass, like everyone around him is trying to steal his girlfriend or something. Fortunately, Jeremy is usually working at Schuck's Auto Parts or his head is underneath the hood of his jeep, an old scout that somebody should just push off a cliff. He makes Kane pay rent and is always dogging him about helping out at home. When the brown grass in back needs clipping, or the weeds on the fringe of the property poke through the rotting wooden fence surrounding the back yard, he never shuts up. When we are just hanging out and J is due home we just bolt. He also looks like someone trying to escape from White Center. Instead of wearing the neighborhood uniform of low-slung jeans or shorts and baggy t-shirts and a hooded sweatshirt, he wears khaki's or slacks and slicks up short black hair. His tennis shoes look polished. When he holds his polyester work shirt the expression on his face makes you think he just ate a turd or found a dead animal in his pants.

All the fashion crap does not mask that he is a weird looking dude. Small freckles ring his white complexion and he is always putting his hands on his hips, a really gay look for a guy working at an auto parts store. He is a little taller than Kane and very slender and his habit of repeating directions back to people is really annoying. He is the kind of guy you would want operating a cash register or taking your sister on a date. And his program helps his brother. He forged a relationship with the owners of the rental house years ago while delivering papers and setting up his own lawn service at age fifteen. When the Harvey parents moved back to Bakersfield the two oldest boys remained in Seattle. Twin twelve-year- old boys, Charlie and Danny, accompanied their parents south and I sense that Jeremy believes he is the unspoken protector of Kane, the adult Harvey of the Northwest. K feels his brother takes this role too seriously, like a kid trying to be too adult-like. On several occasions I have watched television with Kane and the 80-something-year- old lady who owns the house shows up in her giant Buick to give instructions. Usually the topic is tree pruning. The oldest Harvey boy always bellows, "It's showtime Kane," and then he grabs a little spiral notebook out of one of the top drawers in the kitchen and follows the blue hair around the yard taking notes and grimacing all the time.

"Fuck dude," Kane sighed one-time when Jeremy left the house to follow orders. "You would think he understands that we do not have to start working on this project immediately. She might die on the way home."

"Do you guys do yard work every weekend?"

"Yeah…unless Jeremy is working, fixing his car or I can hide somewhere until a race is on TV. He loves NASCAR, Indy, European-style…all the auto crap." Well, enough about that asshole.

After we entered the house we perched upstairs by the kitchen and began assessing the food supply – weak. Vodka, Coke, ice, half-eaten Chinese food and random condiments. Kane was assembling an impressive used ketchup collection

– four or five different bottles. He was lucky. Nathan will eat anything and he offers condolences later with a smile and a pat on the back.

I moved downstairs onto a big couch facing a giant television sitting on the floor. Nathan decided to look around. He is the type of guy who looks at decorations and then judges the people who own the stuff. I figure that decorations consist of shit that friends and family members give homeowners.

A sharp pain awakened me as "Dumb and Dumber" blared in the background. Nathan was pinching my right nipple and giving me little slaps on the left side of my face. I tried to kick him with my right leg and he knocked down my weapon. Then he grabbed my legs and pulled me off of the couch, laughing the entire time. By the time I slapped him he just blocked his face; laughing himself silly. I gave up. I have learned not to become too aggressive with Nathan because eventually he freaks out and he is much tougher than I am. Napping in his presence is a bad idea.

Nathan grabbed the remote, looking for something to watch. "Dancing lesbians," he said softly as the "Ellen DeGeneres Show" came on and a bunch of women in the studio started running in the aisles with the host. After a while I went upstairs and discovered some stale crackers and peanut butter that I was able to roll into little balls. Nathan and I began throwing my creations at people's houses from the back porch as darkness fell. We were drinking vodka and we laughed so hard we started to cry. Nathan hit one middle-aged guy down the street in   the ass and we could see him looking all over the place through cracks in the fence. He kept saying, "What the?" over and over again. The dark bill of his baseball cap kept darting around like a little bird beak and his glasses were fogging up. Nathan mimicked him behind the fence by swiveling his head around and moving his elbows out   with a serious expression on his face, like he was doing a weird chicken dance. At 9:05 we walked up the street to the grocery store, and I saw Torrie Hopper entering the store as we crossed the parking lot. I perked up.

"You can look for food, I am going to look at Torrie," I said.

Nathan just smiled. He knows I am in love with Torrie and have been for years. After gingerly moving around the store I visually stalked her from all possible angles. She wore something tight that showed off her curves, like a body suit attached to her skin. I guess that is why they call it a bodysuit. Some women attract my attention or draw glances from me; but Torrie is akin to a work of art. Her smell draws me in, the way she moves in school hallways; the way she picks up a shopping bag for Christ sake. Everything she does is artistic and beautiful – an angel on earth. Sometimes I just stare at her for seconds on end, like a salivating dog waiting for somebody to feed him or pat him on the head. It is chemical.

Long shiny black hair rolled down a neck of perfect length and girth – slender and medium width – not too long - a perfect barrier between head and body. Her square shoulders are moderately broad, but still pointy and feminine. Her stomach is flat and Torrie's back bends inward on an incline making her ass pop out and her hips float, disconnected from her upper torso.

"John Ramos!" shouted Nathan from one aisle over. "John Ramos." As I looked around like an asshole, Torrie and her friend Jen just looked at me. Jen had busted me staring at Torrie and she was giggling. I just smiled and waved at both of them as they faced the candy bar display. I was standing near dairy when a loaf of bread landed at my feet, and as I looked skyward, and contemplated launching food grenades of my own, a cheese ball hit the top my head. I ducked and looked like a frightened turtle. Then I started thinking about the time Nathan chased a bunch of us years ago with a BB gun, shooting every kid in the neighborhood in the ass.

My fumbling caused Jen to laugh so hard that she fell down on one knee. Torrie just smiled and shook her head. She was probably thinking, "Look at that fool."

Then as I lurched toward the edge of the aisle searching for items to throw, moving toward the girls, Nathan deftly left his attack position and snuck into my aisle from behind. I was smirking and trying to move gracefully pretending I was having fun being embarrassed, covering the top of my head with both hands and crouching down. As I stupidly looked up, ready for more food bombs, he snuck up behind me and slapped me on the back without breaking stride, knocking me over. "Ramos" he said, addressing his object of ridicule. Then Freehold kept walking toward the girls at the front of the store near the checkout stands.

As I dusted myself off I watched as Nathan chatted up Torrie and Jen. By the time I reached everybody, desperately trying to saunter over slowly with a smile on my face - too cool for school - Nathan had invited both of them to come over to our borrowed pad.

"Okay, we will stop by but it is going to be a while," said Torrie. I tried to smile and act mellow while Jen continued to point and laugh.

"That was some funny shit back there."

"Yeah, Ramos is a funny guy," said the real funny guy.

"Ramos is hungry," I said. My joke drew no laughter.

"So we will see you two ladies in an hour," said Nathan. "What is your cell phone number?" he asked nobody in particular. Torrie answered to my chagrin.

"206-280-1478." As Nathan entered her number in his phone I smiled warmly. Fortunately, she was polite enough to smile back.

When my object of affection left the store ahead of us I studied Nathan's face. He was watching something closely and I sensed he was studying Torrie. I felt confused, angry and helpless all at once. My best friend is funnier, more attractive, and tougher than me and in real life, unlike the movies; guys like me do not get the girl.

Nathan knew I lusted after Torrie so I found his behavior despicable. But I also knew I would never spend time with Torrie without his assistance. His confidence is contagious. My only hope was that Nathan found beefy Jen attractive or that he was doing something for me for a change. This line of reasoning made me feel even more uncomfortable because I guessed Torrie liked neither of us. Hell, she was probably just being polite and agreed to spend time with us because her friend laughed so hard she crapped herself. My heart was racing.

2

Moving Target

We passed a couple of South Park prostitutes, collecting business and rides in White Center, on our way back to Jeremy's house.

"Hello boys," one said in a husky voice. "Ma'am," said Nathan as he nodded. I said nothing as I clenched a poorly-made turkey sandwich. After another parking lot and two more blocks Nathan put his arm around me and said, "We might have some fun tonight R. These girls are bored. Hey, do you mind if we stop by my house so I can grab some money?" It was just like Nathan to grab money in case we had to buy something in front of the girls. I had paid for the fried chicken, jo-jo's, and soda he cradled in his left arm.

"Nope."

Nathan looked ahead as if he was not paying attention to my answer…he probably had no clue what I said.

As we walked silently I played out various scenarios in my mind. In one, Nathan grabbed Torrie's ass and she slapped away his hand and came to me in tears. I then berated Nathan; and lectured him about treating women properly. In another, I punched Nathan in the face and he chose not to kill me because he admired my guts.

"Now I know you are serious my man," bellowed the noble warrior in my daydream. He then vacated the room so I could "get to know" Torrie better. In all of my crazed fantasies I cannot imagine having sex with T. I respect her too much to imagine filthy thoughts. When I daydream of Tanya Jenkins or Sadie Thompson I touch, grab, suck, lick and do every sordid thing I can think of. Torrie is different.

"I am going to take a shower," announced Nathan after we planted ourselves back inside the house. He was restless and it was early for a Saturday night – 7:35 p.m. Nathan is unpredictable in the bathroom. Sometimes he requires four minutes and once-in-a-while he spends an eternity perfecting his look. He is an opportunistic soul. I could tell this was going to be a session focused on personal improvement. Long glances in the mirror and detailed grooming were on the horizon. He even rummaged around Kane and Jeremy's stuff until he found some tweezers. When a guy starts looking for tweezers you know he is serious. While N was in the groom zone, I unsuccessfully foraged for more alcohol. I even felt like smoking a joint – an uncharacteristic craving for me so early in the evening. I could hear Nathan talking on the phone in the bathroom and I knew he was cooing Torrie. What a prick. I had to put my mind somewhere else, I started pacing.

I grabbed some scratch paper out of an old printer connected to somebody's desktop. For years I have been writing stories to put my mind at ease. At first, I thought these artifacts might be really interesting or important to me at some point, as if literary talents would take me somewhere. But now I realize it is a form of relaxation that calms panic attacks. I also keep forgetting that I am not really writing fiction because my tales are based on life stories in my neighborhood. My teachers call it reporting when I turn in some of the material. I call it assessing life.

Unemployment

Oscar found himself in the unemployment line again Monday morning. This was his fourth week in a row hitching rides or taking the bus to the place he dreaded. Why was the Washington State Employment Security Department (WSESD) so disturbing? Why had computers replaced human beings?

Computers do not answer questions, they just force you to respond and connive you into agreeing with a bunch of documentation, or else you cannot file anything. If a dispute arises a third party will always say, "You agreed you would not file if you were working one day a week… or you admit you commit fraud if you are not eligible for benefits" when you signed up.

Fraud is purposeful and willful deception. But not in the mind of a computer.

Oscar surmised these goddamn computers symbolized poverty in the unemployment line. The people waiting to sign up were treated like chumps who had to show up in person, because they did not own computers. By the time they arrived with questions they were told no humans were available for assistance. He felt as if his life were out of control, managed by someone else's ideas and controlled by machines that never empathized.

After exactly seventeen minutes of confusion and nonsense Oscar pulled house keys out of his pocket and began dismembering the keys on the keyboard when nobody was looking. He stuck some of the plastic in his pocket and left. The following day he returned to the office and cut some of the computer chords. As he left he witnessed a young man in the corner of the parking lot smashing a keyboard with a hammer. Oscar wondered if the keyboard had been taken from the office.

The following day Oscar returned for a 1:00 p.m. rendezvous. Activity was light at the WSESD because many employees took lunch. This time, he was more aggressive. He grabbed a CPU and stepped out the front door of the office picking up his pace with every step. When he moved around the southeast corner of the building he could see the bus stop in the distance. His progress was stopped by the specter of a large man blocking his path brandishing a gun.

"You are not going anywhere with that computer."

"This is mine."

"The hell it is."

"I am late! Who are you anyway?"

"I need the computer."

"Do you work for the state?" No answer. "Did you make a claim with this computer?" No answer. "This computer needs repair, I will bring it back."

One more step drew a loud shot to the chest from a .357 magnum revolver. Oscar was dead and his quest was over.

Morbid thoughts and rage continued as I furiously expressed myself on several pieces of paper.

Available

My career path has been frustrating to say the least. I worked on a fish processing boat in Alaska right after high school but my journey ended when I got in a fight on the deck with some white guy who thought he was the fish-king or something. I took exception to his comment that I wasn't doing my share, so I did my share of kicking his ass.

After returning to Seattle I felt uncomfortable so I headed south. When I reached Federal Way my mother was wearing an orange uniform.

"Why do you have an orange jumpsuit on?"

"It's required."

"What?"

"Ask them," she said as she pointed to the office at the front of the complex. The local housing authority had jurisdiction and it did not matter that federal grants were involved. Local dickheads set the standards.

"Did you happen to notice the guest badge you are wearing?"

She was right. It never crossed my mind. I am so used to wearing stupid badges around on job interviews that I had forgotten that residential entry usually does not require security profiling.

It struck me as odd that the music playing faintly in the background was replete with references to public housing kids and their mischievous deeds. This street poetry was popular music children of the wealthy. Yet I had to wear a badge and my mother was wearing an orange jumpsuit.

I felt like a zoo animal.

Who were they to decide what we should wear? My mother was glaring at me as I stared heavy at the guard booth at the front of the complex. I could feel her look as she mimed, "chill the fuck out."

"Man up bouuuy," Nathan yelled as he left the bathroom. I ceased writing and folded my papers into half pieces, then fourths, and put them in my pocket.

"Are you pretty enough yet?"

"I'm always pretty." Nathan is particularly nauseating because he makes these statements in a subdued, funny kind of way. He is able to make fun of himself effortlessly. He somehow manages to make enough eye contact to never seem pompous, he waits for you to look back and confirm you understand.

"Jen and Torrie would like to meet up and hang out tonight. They were thinking of catching a movie at Factoria or meeting up on Broadway."

I was certain Nathan used Jen's name first to understate his connection with Torrie. What a dick.

"Do you have a preference?"

"Broadway. Catching a bus to Factoria would be a pain in the ass."

Nathan nodded. "They can drive."

"Knowing you, you will convince them to let you drive."

"No license man…but you are probably right." Nathan busted out a cackling-type of laugh, and slapped my hand with his. He had amused himself and was still acting like a prick. His confidence annoyed me for a change since he had his sights on Torrie. It is just like a guy who had no trouble attracting women to entice someone else's secret, or not so secret, love.

"I think you're right about the hill. Factoria sucks."

They picked us up thirty-five minutes later. Time ticked slowly. I agonized over spending time with Nathan in the presence of Torrie. I am infatuated with her, I could just watch her walk down the street or even shop. Tuning out Nathan while spellbound is hard.

"Get in," shouted Jen. She has the manners of an ape. She sat in front and there was no way we were going to dislodge her. You can tell she is one of those girls who enjoys having a pretty friend around to draw attention. Jenny has a cute face but she is beefy. She is a lot of woman and the noise she generates with her vocal chords is amazing.

"Turn it up girl," she said as she moved the volume button skyward. She was playing some old school funky stuff that sounded vaguely familiar but my mind was somewhere else.

"How's it going gentlemen?" asked Torrie who turned to smile when we poured into the backseat.

Her skin is a beautiful bronze color and mesmerized me as her delicate jaw line sat a few inches above the front seat of the Oldsmobile. Just enough space to display a white blouse, unbuttoned at the top. Gorgeous.

"Solid," I said.

Nathan moved toward the middle and planted his forearms on the back of the long front seat.

"Would you ladies like me to drive this evening?"

"Maybe," cooed Torrie, as she slowly grasped the wheel and began to pull into the street.

"Hell no," shouted Jen.

I stared out the window wishing I was spending a quiet night reading or watching television with my parents – who usually bore me to death. Reading a sports page sounded delightful. Even smoking in front of a café and people watching sounded fascinating…just doing nothing at all.

I felt a hard push on my shoulder from Nathan.

"Hey, are you going to answer her?"

"Oh sorry, I was in deep thought."

"I'll say. Torrie just asked about your plans for the summer."

"Oh…ahh, I don't really have any plans."

"Well you better get some plans soon," piped in Jen, as obnoxious as ever. I nodded, as all three of them laughed while Jen muttered something like "You know what I'm saying."

I settled back into my haze.

"Man, I should be driving," bellowed Nathan, who wore a grin that should be outlawed. His charm really disgusts me sometimes.

"What?" said Torrie, who was giggling.

"I'm just saying."

"You should stop saying boy," shouted Jen.

"I'm just gonna pretend I'm steering."

Nathan began staring ahead, wearing a serious expression and moving with the contours of the road.

"Sonofabitch," he whispered out loud as he mimicked getting angry at another driver and shook his head. Laughter followed.

"You're crazy."

I marveled at his rap.

"Man this wheel is a little stiff."

'Like your dick,' I thought.

Nathan lightly touched Jen's hair with his right hand.

"You best keep your hands to yourself boy," shouted the beast.

"Now we've got the grease," he responded while pretending to apply lubricant to his imaginary steering wheel.

Thwack, "Owww."

A strategic blow to Nathan's right forearm was delivered by Jen's fist. A straight-down hammer job. She was fighting back laughter at the time of the attack.

"Don't hit the driver," he cooed. "Dangerous."

In one deft move Nathan had purposely offended Jennifer and positioned himself as only available for a pairing with Torrie, who was laughing hysterically.

"Girl you should let him drive if you can't keep it together."

"Yea," I added in a sad monotone.

"Oooo," bellowed Nathan as he leaned left, turning his imaginary vehicle.

I felt ill and paralyzed simultaneously. "What a disaster," I mumbled; my lips close to the window. I could have removed my clothing and nobody would notice. "Pricks, self absorbed… all of them," I mouthed.

"Yo, what's going on over there," Nathan asked gently. He gave me a little bump with his right elbow. He is one of those guys who can always redeem himself.

I smiled a pathetic smile.

"You wanna drive?" More laughter from the giggle crew. I shook my head.

As Torrie parked I noticed a dog with a couple of paralyzed legs walking alongside his owner, who navigated a wheelchair and shouted encouraging words to the dog. I began tearing up. For some reason every time I feel sorry for myself someone with a real heart- wrenching story shows up on my radar. I realized I was acting like an ass. Did I really think I was going to develop the romance of my dreams with Torrie? Deep down, I think it is possible. But I know the project will take time. Perhaps years. For me to spend time with such a spectacular catch I have to be in the right place and get close to her. Hanging out with Nathan seems to be my best chance to get close to Torrie. Unfortunately, watching them together makes me want to break things.

A trip to Taco Bell was followed by a movie. Nathan sat next to Torrie, I sat on the other side of Nathan, next to Jen, who spent most of her time talking to Jen and T and sneering at me when I made requests like, "pass the popcorn please."

"Hey, hey, hey," was all I heard from Nathan. His smooth belly laugh lit up the aisle during funny parts of the film and Torrie was so excited that I thought she was going to slide off her chair onto the floor. Both of them made me sick, and Jen made me sicker. She just kept eating – a real popcorn hog. She has strong thighs and a bulbous ass and you can just imagine the hot dogs, dots, popcorn, tacos, and root beer settling in her powerful base. I have never met anyone so focused on root beer. When they did not have any at the Bell she told them Mr. Pibb sucked and that she wouldn't return if they did not stock Barq's. When she started spilling food all over her shirt I even began to giggle under my breath.

After the flick we waited for the girls to navigate the long line to the bathroom. "How ya doin' J?"

"Great," I said, somewhere between timid and sarcastic.

"Jen is really funny."

"Are you talkin' bout that creature sitting next to me?"

"Ah-ha. Nah, she is not that bad." Nathan put his hands out in a friendly gesture and smiled, like I should mellow or chill down. With no end to the horror show in sight I contemplated several excuses and rehearsed them silently.

'My mother is sick – I should go.' Or 'I just had surgery on my heel…and even minor walking is really difficult – I'm out.' Too stupid. 'I feel like I am about to throw up.' Too gross, especially in front of Torrie. Ignoring Nathan was not helping as we meandered down the street. I glanced up looking directly at Jen's crotch – not a subject at the top of my mind. She was now sitting down at a little bench and her legs held a 40-ounce beer in a paper bag. The delightful image was enhanced by her strong right hand covering her mouth as she failed to contain a massive belch. Torrie's giggles led my eyes to her crotch where she also hosted a 40-ouncer. She was standing and casually dangled the bag and its contents, her left hand holding the bottom, her right hand the top. It is shocking how two people the same age can cause such different reactions in my mind. Jen looked like a sad, loud, sloppy gasbag. Torrie was beautiful. Watching her foist ghetto beer made her even more attractive – a hidden wild side masked by good manners and her gorgeous form.

I turned left and gazed at Nathan's face. He was glowing, staring at Torrie. She seductively smiled back while taking a swig of her beer. At that moment I adored her more than ever.

"No 40's for us ladies?" cooed Nathan.

You will have to get your own." Nathan stepped forward, slowly extending his left hand, and winked. Torrie tried to look serious and act too cool to grant his request but she could not suppress her joy. The outside of her lips quivered as she tried not to smile. In one swift motion her head dropped slightly and she used both hands as she passed her beer in a bag like a young girl would hand a found treasure to her father, simultaneous trust and exhilaration. I felt like throwing up. Temporary depression overwhelmed me and energy vacated my body. I needed to crawl away to a secret place. I was a beaten man.

As I pretended to gaze east, toward Cal Anderson Park, away from the revelry, Nathan and Torrie playfully held hands while facing each other, he standing, her sitting - the 40 resting on the ground beside them. I am sure I looked like a jackass as I posed in my best contemplative position, right hand under chin; how pathetic. Soon they would be awash in physical play, a thought too disturbing for me to bear.

"Oooph," I grunted as my body was jolted by Jen's powerful shove. "Hey," she said, a delayed reaction, the alcohol talking. "What are you doing?"

I would have welcomed her aggressive style any other night of my life. Even an abrasive person is appreciated by a lonely boy, or man, or whatever I am. For a moment, I felt like hitting her, but as I stabilized my body by grabbing her back and waist with my left arm she moved closer and slowly slid her right hand up my back. As I turned left to face her and pull away she smoothed her left hand up my back. As I turned harder she ran her hand over my ass and then grabbed the side of my belt.

I am probably seven inches taller than Jen but she had tall shoes on and her strong thighs, well-positioned hands and huge breasts made me feel surrounded. Normally, I would be excited but a quick glance at Torrie, now smiling and looking my way as if I was getting along well with her friend, cemented my emotional surrender. Nathan's wry smile as he turned his head my way while holding and facing Torrie reiterated that there never was any competition. My game plan, nonexistent as the evening began, shifted toward filling a social role, serving as an escort. I was going to look bad no matter how the evening ended. Rejecting Torrie's friend outwardly was impolite…not an option, and I did not want to pursue anything serious with the confidant of the woman I lusted after. Jen kept reaching into the left pocket of my jeans, grabbing at my dick, which was growing as her flesh pressed against mine. She had finished her drink. "That was my third 40." I think she was doing the time-honored girl thing of exaggerating consumption. Both Nathan and Torrie seemed miles away, or at least I imagined they were distant as I stood embarrassed, wallowing in misery, only slightly capable of providing comfort to Jen.

When Nathan and Torrie began kissing and fondling I slowly walked Jen into the park and asked her if she wanted to go somewhere less chilly. By this time she was smoking weed, offering me some, and too relaxed to be shrill. The transformation altered my perception of her – she was finally chill - and I hoped the inside coat pocket that delivered her relaxation held more goodies. "Follow me," she whispered. 'Good night, it's all right Johnny,' I began humming to myself. Bruce Springsteen's "Incident on 57th Street" provided a sad melody as I followed Jen onto a bus toward an unknown locale.

3

CONTROL

Twenty-five minutes later I entered a small cottage filled with too much furniture and copious video game paraphernalia – consuls everywhere. A loud television blared behind the door of what appeared to be a master bedroom. I said nothing because Jen put her right pointer finger to her lips, a call for quiet. She led me to her small cluttered bedroom; a twin bed lined with a red bedspread, old, no longer bright. Newer red pillow coverings did not match. Rap artists adorned the walls and stereo equipment was strewn across the room, as were various articles of clothing. A small window was covered by a drawn shade – the place felt like a bomb shelter. Walls were painted black – an angry room, a claustrophobic room, and a spectacular room for an angry teenager unspoiled by direct supervision. I was jealous.

"I have a question," whispered Jen as she sat on the bed and looked up glassy-eyed. Are you a virgin? I felt raw and uninhibited so I answered honestly.

"No," was followed by slow head shaking, an incredulous expression and muted laughter. When I shook my head my eyes closed for a few seconds – a purposeful look of disbelief. I had entertained this question before, even from Nathan. I am just serious and private enough, or understated, as I like to think of myself, to raise questions about sexual experiences. I never exude confidence. Jen got up and turned out the lights, moonlight, a rare Seattle experience, made everything seem the same. The shade, plain, white and old, was drawn and a stereo on button was depressed. Prince played softly.

"Good," she said as she unbuttoned my pants. I slowly helped, expressionless, like a stranger assisting with some equipment. I was an actor with no script – along for the ride – and a flaccid ride at that. I was tired and not in a sexual frame of mind. After removing my briefs Jen smiled at my soggy manhood.

"I like it when they are squishy."

She started licking and sucking the top of my penis and then she took off her black shirt, exposing a red bra that matched nothing. "Honey, you are in for a treat." Her confidence turned me on. She grabbed my member and wiggled it; I was still being exposed as the weak link, and I started panicking.

'What if she tells Torrie? Why do I care? This incident will destroy any chances with her…but she has no interest in me so it doesn't matter.' When Jennifer removed her bra and her massive breasts sagged downward I was finally able to concentrate. I had never witnessed such a sight. "Oh my," I muttered. "Hmmm," she whispered as she engulfed my prick with her boobs. Blood instantly arrived below. She was a pro – I was speechless.

After some mind blowing sliding of flesh against flesh, she turned again to her mouth. I reciprocated with my fingers feeling insecure. Suddenly, she fell back on the bed and opened a small tin box on the top of a worn nightstand. Jen held the wrapper of a lifestyle condom. "This is for you if you want it…you don't need it."

"You on the pill?"

A nod was followed by a passionate kiss. She pulled me onto the bed while heading backwards; Jen was on the bottom, turned on her left side, me awkwardly sliding my left leg between hers on the bed. As we moved even closer my cockpit rubbed against her leg and crotch, leading with excitement. I then moved on top of her and lowered myself so I strategically touched every centimeter of the outside of her moist center, which she exposed by centering and laying on her back. I pulled up again, resting vertically on her pubic bone.

"Don't tease me." Her grin was darling.

I moved back, red-faced and less hard. "I've got a problem."

"Herpes?"

"No…no STDs."

Jen looked somewhere between sad and disgusted, her expression was sobering and I started to cry. While kneeling at the bottom of the bed I wiped away tears with the corners of old blankets.

"Shhhh," she said forcefully. "What's…what the fuck is going on?" I bounced up and hugged her. She did not reciprocate.

"Get your hands off me and talk motherfucker." "I am in love with Torrie."

[Mouth agape] "Well I am not in love with you if that's what you think this is about." Her voice was soft but the tone was definitive.

Sniffling, "No, I mean I am freaked out being with her friend…even though I am attracted to you." By the end of the sentence Jen was off the bed, putting her red bra and pink panties back on. She turned on the lights.

"Please…listen to me." I started sobbing uncontrollably, grabbing her left arm with my suddenly sturdy right hand. I was unable to gauge Jen's expression because tears blocked my vision but she was stiff and cold. I sat on the bed. As I rubbed out tears she cracked the window open and smoked, throwing her pack of Marlboro Lights on the bed.

"I need you."

"You need something." She was gazing out the window.

I got up and stuck out my right hand. She ignored me. I didn't care anymore. I grabbed her cigarette and flicked it out the window with my left hand while grabbing her neck and the back of her head with my right hand and kissing her passionately. This time she reciprocated. I used my fingers to reach inside her and after I removed her underwear and pushed her onto the bed, I pleasured Jennifer with my tongue. After her orgasm she wanted to play. I came between her breasts, it did not take long. My avoidance of intercourse made me feel better about myself. We awakened simultaneously at 6:00 a.m. My lame left arm draped over her shoulder.

"You should go soon."

"Window or door?"

"That's your decision, but I would use the window." She was not kidding. Jen was no longer drunk and cuddly.

"Where's the bus stop?"

"Two blocks up, one block south."

"Up means west?"

"Yes, toward downtown…the stop is right by Torrie's house."

"I don't know where she lives."

"She's probably kicked out your boy by now."

"I doubt that…he's a charmer." I have no idea why I was defending Nathan. Natural reaction I guess.

"He's a hoe and she likes pussy."

"Are you serious?"

"She's been a lot farther than you got last night."

"Really?" I was shocked but trying to act like I was just making conversation.

"That's why your bullshit last night was so stupid. I don't think she has ever been with a man."

After five minutes of tepid hugging and kissing, I escaped out the window. "You have spectacular tits," I said as I was leaving. Jen finally looked pleased. "I've heard that before."

"John?"

After traveling only one block I heard the unmistakable voice of Lem Barnes, who was getting gas across the street on Madison. I walked over while simultaneously matting my hair down with my hands. I hoped the grease on my dome would stick to my paws so I had enough suction to tuck my undershirt into my jeans. "Dude, I am fuckin' tired. I was out with Nathan last night."

"Did you fuck him?" Lem was smoking and, as usual, his commentary began with a pause and slow breathing angled toward the sky. He always points his long nose up and the rest of his face follows. Then everything drops down and he looks you directly in the eyes before speaking.

I smiled and tried to laugh. "Yes."

"I just got off work."

"Graveyard sucks."

"Not tonight, we got off early."

"The Safeway on 15th?" A quick nod provided the answer. "Where are you heading?"

"The Center."

"If I give you gas money can I get a ride?"

"Yes, Ramos, fifty bucks." A sarcastic smile was myanswer.

Lem's old Plymouth is a mechanical disaster, but the power windows work so Barnes's smoke polluted the neighborhood. His technique was impressive. He lowered his front window just enough to draw smoke into the wild without spillage. Because of his proximity to the glass he almost hit his angular forehead against the car ceiling as he geared up to speak. Lem is so long and lean that he looks like someone took a portrait of Lincoln, de-aged him, added acne and neglected to advise him to grow a beard. His deep-set eyes look like canyons after working all night. After a scant block-and-a-half I spotted Torrie's ride.

"Hold up, that is Nathan's rig."]

"Did he steal a car?"

"...I mean Torrie's ride."

"Torrie Hopper?"

"Yes."

"Fucking Nathan...she makes my dick hard."

"I know, I had to watch her drive us around all night giggling at Nathan's jokes."

"Did you crash over here?"

"Nah, I have a friend named...Andy who lives up the road." I knew what was coming.

"Did you fuck him?"

"After I was done with Nathan."

Lem parked against traffic across the street from the driveway hosting Torrie's Buick. After he finished his smoke we discussed sports for a while. Then we both stood and leaned forward against the driver's side of his metal, leering at Torrie's house in the early morning, dreaming we were Nathan, and talking shop. Lem appears skinnier than usual in the early morning. He seems taller than his alleged 6'4 because long arms and legs carry his little torso around, like a spider. His smell was a pungent merger of smoke and body odor, mixed with the canned goods aisle; so I gave him space.

"How is Safeway?"

"Brutal, but my manager's cool. We have to join a union and listen to old vets tell us about yesteryear. I hope most of those guys die soon." Our conversation took on the rhythm of adult banter because both of us were tired. Like all high school and college dorks we just copy the cadences of our elders when discussing jobs, future plans and other serious subjects. But Barnes is never serious for long.

"Do you think Nathan fucked Torrie's mother too?"

"I hope so. Actually, I hope he only boned her mother."

I proceeded to dangerously express the nature of my blind lust for Torrie, shamelessly describing my feelings as love, starting with 4th grade, blossoming in puberty, and descending toward the absurd during third period, when every school day senior year was dedicated to staring at Torrie from every possible angle. "I would like to spend the rest of my life with her." I was in a trance, just rambling uncontrollably. If Lem felt the same way about somebody he did not say.

"Dude, anybody would want to get together with Torrie." His blank expression made me feel stupid.

"This is really embarrassing. Let's get out of here." "Okay."

Lem slumped into the driver's seat, turned the key slightly and tuned the radio without firing the ignition. He continued smoking with the door shut and the window cracked just right. I lingered and slowly made my way to the back of the car while heading around to the passenger side. The release of compressed air and a squeaky door signaled a domestic exodus across the street. I glanced up and saw Nathan and Torrie leaving the house.

"Fuck," I mouthed. I scrambled back to the other side of the car, moving my hands along the dirty Plymouth in a frog's crouch grabbing the bumper – left hand on top and right hand on bottom with a vice-like grip. Sweat glands exploded, heavy breathing caused rising steam, which I imagined to be the size of clouds. I was trying to place myself in perfect space – invisible above and below the Plymouth. Torrie was bringing garbage out to the curb and Nathan lazily stood by the driver's side door with a smile on his face. I spied them through both backseat windows from my silent crouch as I gently tugged the door handle. Nothing. The lock was depressed.

"Open the fucking door," I whispered. Glancing left, I spotted an extended hand and a middle finger on the other side of the glass and a skinny, laughing shithead in the front seat. Lem then sent the window next to him skyward with a flick of his finger and the front passenger window lowered.

"John Ramos! John Ramos!" He was screaming my name.

"What the fuck? Shut up." Lem was smiling – something never witnessed before.

"John Ramos," Torrie mouthed as she looked toward the car.

When I pounded on the car with my left fist Smiley started the rig and moved forward. I stumbled backwards, nearly falling, and stood red-faced on the sidewalk, emotionally naked. Nathan laughed so hard he nearly fell down. His noiseless guffaws punctuated by constant pointing at Lem, who shut the window and parked while listening to loud music. Barnes pointed back – only the second time he had ever smiled. What a soulless piece of shit.

"Torrie, Nathan…I ran into Lem at Safeway. We thought you might wanna get some breakfast you two." Torrie smiled and nodded. "Good morning," she said softly. "Why don't you guys go ahead."

"You in Nathan?"

"Yea sure, I'll catch you guys in the car."

I walked back to Lem shamed and in shock. He was still smiling and now standing outside on the other side of the car with his elbows up, smoking while wearing a ridiculous pair of small sunglasses. He looked like a beetle.

"You want in?"

I feigned a smile and nodded. After we were both in the car… "You are such a shitball. Not only do I look like a perverted stalker, they…think…I'm…a…freak."

"Dude, I helped you out."

"How, you stupid bastard?"

"I don't know. But that was funny."

Lem is not the kind of guy worth hitting when you're pissed. He doesn't seem very tough and I lacked the necessary energy for playful striking anyway. "What gave you the idea to yell my name by the way?"

"I saw Nathan yell "Jasper Owens" when they were both hiding from the Vice Principal in the boiler room one time in middle school. What was that guy's name? Rybinski?"

"Perfect."

Several minutes of talking and hand holding held us up. Lem fed me the play by play while I stared at his yellow teeth. When we finally left, Nathan was driving and Lem stretched out in the back seat, still smoking under an open window displaying brilliant draft technique. It is his one true skill.

"You drill T?" Words flow like poetry from Lem's lips.

"Drill?" I asked as Nathan chuckled.

"Oh, I'm sorry thesaurus man. Hey Nathan, did your penis make contact with her vagina?" I wanted to cover my ears.

"Nah, we just cuddled and then played with her stuffed animals."

"Ramos is in love with Torrie."

"He knows that."

"And she knows now." Laughter filled the car.

"Yea that car stuff was funny…especially after the text."

"What are you talking about?" I asked, unsure about the answer.

"Jen woke us up this morning with some long message about how you broke down and pledged your undying love for her."

"For Jen?"

"No, Torrie."

"Oh dude," added Lem between cackles. "That makes that car shit even funnier."

Lem was insensitive, Jen was offended by my behavior, and Nathan was being a dick. Nathan and Lem were pounding their fists together and giggling. "You should have seen Ramos's face…," I expected them to touch penises on the way home.

"Where are we going to breakfast?" I asked while staring out the rear window motionless.

"Nowhere baby, I gots to sleep…worked graveyard last night." Lem snapped his fingers for effect. Twenty minutes later I was buying Nathan breakfast at Bev's near his apartment. Lem dropped us off and was off to annoy members of his own family. I ate the bootstrapper, a glorious combination of potatoes, cheese, onions, peppers and eggs. Nathan ordered eggs "softly scrambled," whatever that means, and some other side order crap. As usual, his meal cost three times more than mine. He even added orange juice and grimaced when the waitress told us, "Sandy didn't make any fresh squeezed juice today." It was unclear whether she was kidding or not, but he was probably the only person to make such an order at Bev's in several years. In fact, he was the only person in the joint not wearing flannel – he sauntered into the diner in a smooth brown suede jacket a tight shiny blue stretch shirt, fashion slacks that matched the jacket, and leather loafers. I did not check his socks because I knew they would match his jacket and pants.

Nathan only finished half his meal – Torrie had probably already fed him breakfast. His face featured little sparkles of glitter transferred from eye shadow or makeup that T was wearing the night before. When I glanced at his face all I could think of was him making out with her all night long. When we walked to his house afterwards he turned and said, "What happened between you and Jen?" His sensitive manner made me wonder what he knew. He wasn't smiling; the tone born of concern and genuine interest.

"Nothing, just some drunken conversation, Hey." I pointed at his door because as we approached the apartment complex I saw a yellow note and I wanted to change the subject. I shrunk and slowed down as we walked on the concrete path toward his unit number, 104, because after I opened my big mouth I read the words "EVICTION NOTICE" in bold black letters. Why do people post such crap using all caps anyway? What is the point? As Nathan read the notice his pace quickened and he leaned forward as if to strike prey.

He radiated rage as he ripped the notice off the door. I stepped backwards and watched Nathan closely – wishing I could crawl away somewhere. He crumpled the paper and threw it into a rhododendron. He then opened the door with his key and stepped inside.

"What are you doing?" The noise came from inside.

I stepped forward. "Should I come in?"

"Yea."

There was grocery list tacked into the wall next to the door. *Trash bags, milk, juice, lotion, 2-cases sprite and coke, cans, snacks.* I gazed at the list intrigued by the specificity of the soda listing in contrast to the "snacks" designation.

"Look at this."

I followed Nathan's voice with trepidation. He stood in the middle of his little brother's room, now empty.

"Wow," what's the deal?"

"I have no idea. Little C's stuff is just gone."

"Maybe they went to a friend's house." I said this because I know all of Nathan's family members are in Oakland and Detroit and I did not want him to think the worst.

"My mother's stuff is pretty much all here. It's like somebody kidnapped my brother's room."

"Did Chester have a basketball game today?"

"I don't know, and my mother wouldn't know either."

After a full minute of silence Nathan turned to me with a frown and said, "I have to work at 1:00…I better take a nap

J. I didn't get much sleep last night." He clearly wanted to be left alone for a while. His tone was abrupt and angry.

"Just tell me if there is anything I can do."

On my way home I was grateful to leave Nathan behind.

4

SECRETS

Nathan disrupted my nap at 6:45. The sun dominated a benign summer sky. I managed to check my watch while knocking over a book and two pillows when answering the phone.

"Yo."

"They're at Emerald City Shelter on 1st Avenue."

I wanted to tell Nathan that I really didn't care, but I pretended to be enthusiastic. "Good news, I was worried. Are you going down there?"

"Later. Torrie's parents are out of town – her father is one of those ultra-marathon guys – he is in Northern California for a race. Jen is over and we are making some top-notch grilled cheese sandwiches."

"*You're* not making anything."

Nathan's chuckle was followed by silence. I felt uncomfortable and tingled all over. I wished I had ignored the phone. "Why did they go to the shelter?"

"My mom is an idiot. She did not want anybody scaring Chester. Anyway,"…Nathan lowered his voice… "Do you mind going down there with me later? Torrie is going to let me borrow her car and my mother respects you."

"Okay, just give me a call before you head over."

"Does he want to come over?" I heard Torrie in the background. "If you show him your titties," Jen screeched. "Shut up!" Background chaos ensued.

"K man, I will call you," click.

Of course he didn't call. After exchanging pleasantries with my mother three hours after our conversation, while I rushed around looking for shoes, he told me we were in a hurry. What an ass. He took an abnormal route – 35ᵗʰ Avenue to Alaska and then the West Seattle Bridge, which was shrouded in fog; the skyline barely visible in the distance. Bad rap pumped from the car's speakers.

"So what happened between you and Jen last night? She is cranky but I think she kind of likes you."

"She's a lotta woman."

Laughing… "Yea she is. But I bet she's good in bed."

"I don't know. When did your mother go to the shelter?" It was obvious I was trying to change the subject. Nathan looked at me with a long gaze and a smirk, like he was deciding what to ask next.

"Not sure, probably early this afternoon. She thinks the sheriff is about to come and move us out, but I don't think she has any idea what she's talking about. I know she hasn't spoken with any experts. She probably just asked one of our dumb-ass relatives."

We parked about five blocks from the shelter – an incredible feat on a Saturday night near Pioneer Square. I managed to dodge two more inquiries about the previous evening before one final attempt near the entrance to the shelter.

"So are you and Jen hanging out tonight?"

"I don't think so Nathan. Why, do you need to get rid of her?" He just shook his head, expressionless.

After checking in at the front desk we were led to Nathan's mother Laney, and his brother Chester, who seemed right at home next to his cot, sitting on the ground playing with a used Game Boy. The guy who brought us through aisles of cracked flooring and metal beds wore an orange jumpsuit like he was a space ranger or something. He had a beard and was really serious, like he just got the job. Before we followed him we had to sign some paperwork proving we understood we were not allowed to bring guests of the shelter drugs or dangerous items. When we said we would sign the thing without reading it the guy got really quiet and said, "Gentleman, I would really appreciate it if you spent a few minutes reading this entire form." So of course we had to get really serious and pretend to look at every sentence – what a waste of time. I started nodding during the process and making little humming sounds and Nate wore an intense frown like he was about to give a eulogy or break down and scream. Nathan's mother was lying on her cot reading a thick hardback with a red binder. She spotted us first and sent a little smile our way while waving, holding her right arm out while opening and closing her fingers. Then she nudged focused Chester.

"Nate!" he shouted. He jumped up and gave his brother a dramatic hug, hitting him in the sternum with his forehead. The console made a big sound as it landed on the concrete floor. Chester is strong and quick for a nine-year-old; I am sure he will be an outstanding athlete like his brother someday. Little C wore hammer pants, sweats, and shorts. I doubt he owns a pair of trousers, jeans or slacks. His bright red Adidas tracksuit featured white stripes on the side. Aqua blue sneakers, Nike, were more fashionable than his top and bottom, adding a cocky veneer to match his buzz-cut haircut with tidy lines etched into the side, above the ear, curving downward toward the back of his head.

They both looked uncomfortable at the shelter. Laney wore a multicolored scarf around her neck, black hair flowing in the back. Her intense gaze furrowed her brow, making an indention above and between her perfectly spaced eyebrows. I think she looks better with her hair down (something I have only witnessed once), but I think that about all women. Laney's sinewy body demands clothing that fits tight or else she disappears in her outerwear – she is of medium height so Ms. Sweet blends into crowds. A black leather jacket was folded on top of her duffle bag and her ensemble was colorful. An orange t-shirt fell to her denim, rope-weave belt, slightly askew in front of aging jeans, designed more for a young woman than a mother. She looked kind of like a yoga instructor after removing her reading glasses and standing up to give her son a hug.

"How are you doin?"

"Been better."

"What's the plan?"

"I don't have one. That is why we are here baby." A smile crept over Laney's face and she turned to me and shrugged, reiterating that her presence at the shelter should answer his basic questions.

"Why aren't you home?"

"I didn't want to deal with any conflict right now. They could have called me. Talked to me. Foster didn't have to post that junk on our door. We've lived there seven years. Paid a lotta rent. Kept to ourselves. We haven't been troublemakers." I guessed Foster was the landlord.

"Should I talk to him?"

"And say what?"

"Tell him we'll take care of it."

"Take care of what?"

"The rent."

"Nathan-baby, we are three months behind. The only way you are going to make any headway is to give him some money." I pretended to look away and there were plenty of characters to check out in that place – sad sights but also some people in tattered clothing coming down from drunken revelry and a few drifters who seemed to be part of the traveling semi-homeless; single men with giant duffel bags and messy hair seeking shelter from the weather.

"I have a little money."

"So do I. If you want to talk to him, bring some money honey," another smile. She sat on the cot and reached into her purse. I was asking Chester about his schoolwork and his video games by this time. Chester didn't give a damn about his assignments. We all told a few jokes and said goodbye and then the video game was again the primary attraction. Laney bid us adieu by saying, "Thank you for stopping by our new place." Then she laughed and sat back down on her cot.

When we arrived back at the car, and his face was visible among the streetlights, Nathan grimaced, like he tasted something sour. "I just want to wash my hands. Did you see some of those people in there?" I was amused because Nathan looked like he hadn't showered and his old gray sweatpants and blue tennis shoes had far less sparkle than his yellow t-shirt. I wondered if he had borrowed the sweats from Torrie's father's dresser.

"She only gave me 300 dollars…what the hell is she doing? She doesn't even have a bank account for Christ sake."

"I think your mother is just scared."

"No shit, but I can only add $75 today and the rent is $695 a month."

I knew he wanted help so I offered to talk to the landlord. Me, just an eighteen-year-old dipshit, but a more confident soul than Nathan in the ways of adult communication, and that includes understanding his mother.

Laney Sweet never married Nathan's father, Tru. She works part-time at the West Seattle library and for a maid service called Shine Time. Laney is only 34 years old but she seems wise, cerebral and thoughtful. She is always reading so the library suits her. I have never witnessed Nathan's mother with anybody besides her two boys, sired from different fathers. She's one of those rare loners who interacts well with crowds.

Sometimes she uses her Muslim name, which I never remember. She is the daughter of Black Panthers in Oakland and she grew up spending countless nights selling baked goods with her parents, who were always on the move, in the city's airport, outside Oakland Alameda Coliseum and along busy 'arterials.' That is her description. If I were telling the story I would just say 'roads' or 'highway.' Her ability to remain quiet and observe fascinates me. Laney's mannerisms are nothing like her boys, who froth with pent-up energy. Laney is thoughtful and quiet; waiting for life to turn in her favor. She never rushes and acts emotionally invisible. Even Nathan's games don't draw her in. She eschews clapping, cheering and even smiling. Support of her sons is limited to her arrival because Laney loathes boastful behavior on the gridiron or the basketball court, or anywhere.

"What are you reading John?" she once asked me during a stressful Fourth Quarter drive, completely uninterested in the action on the field. "Do you think some of these coaches have homoerotic tendencies?" she wondered out loud during a time out in another game. "Jesus, this is a waste of time," is my favorite. Laney was there to watch Nathan but her opinion that football is an outdated waste of time that takes advantage of people with few resources and turns them into gladiators for short-lived glory never wavers. I think she overdoes it with the anti-sports thing, but it is hard to argue with her examples since she always trots out people I have never heard of from her old neighborhood.

"Mike Stringer still cannot walk after his legs were mangled playing football. Jody Mutton had a neck injury and was paralyzed. Narbell Lewis was such an ass on the field that somebody shot him after one game. He was much less aggressive after that incident." Laney has a nice full laugh, one you don't expect from such a serious person; she cracked up good thinking about old Narbell.

"I hope he is learning something out there," she answered when another parent congratulated her for giving birth to such an athletic son. The lure of scholarships and free tuition did little to brighten her mood.

"Those kids are just cattle in a pen. Even when their coaches force them to go to class I question whether they learn anything. It's just like an exaggerated summer camp…girls, alcohol and yelling…a short-term fantasy world. Those that get paid just ride the fantasy train a little longer."

I tried counter analysis. "Don't you think they learn how to be leaders?" I was treated to a long pause, Laney stared straight ahead while crafting an appropriate response.

"There are many styles of leadership but I prefer the informed and wise. I question whether athletics teach anything more than group discipline, just like the army. We are such a simplistic species." Her comments on the subject continued that Friday night. By the time Sealth scored a touchdown Laney was comparing modern football coaches to dictators and decrying the lack of focus on education. I decided not to bring up my stories about Mr. Rubin and computer class. Her entire evening would have been ruined.

As we reached the driveway of my parents' small house Nathan handed me a piece of paper that contained the name and phone number of his landlord. John Ramos, advisor to the wise and beautiful. I knew the project would require some serious thought.

"Better get the car back." No mention of Torrie, no discussion. What an ass. At least we were finished with our sparse dueling over any prior contact with Jen. "Thank you buddy," Nathan said. He shook my hand through the driver's window before waiting to back up in deference to the Road Pig, who was entering the street from the other side, heading out with a roar on a Harley that rattled your teeth if you were outside. 'Road Pig' blared in bold black letters across the back of our neighbor's jean jacket. He is massive. When I watch him from across the street I feel myself shrinking.

Once safely situated in the street Nate sped off without paying any more attention to the neighborhood – he was on a mission and probably developing a story to deploy about his family situation once Torrie's parents were back in town.

I sat down in our cracked driveway and started smoking while imagining calling landlord Jim Sunday morning. I figured landlords didn't go to church. The lights on the back of the Road Pig's bike and Torrie's car flickered in the distance.

5

HOWLERS

After greeting my mother, who sat in her customary position on her bed reading while the television made pictures dance among the shadows of her room, I drank a tall glass of milk. Our kitchen leads into the living room and aimless pacing, a bad habit of mine when I am   trying to think, resulted in spontaneous glances outside,   where I peak between hideous white curtains, circa 1987. Mrs. Olson, a doddering older woman was dropping a bowl or plate on the other side of the Road Pig's fence. Her movements were slow, but precise and the pit bull on the other side of the barrier howled. I figured she couldn't hear the dog.

I was intrigued so I turned off the lights in the living room and the kitchen. Mrs. Olson has monitored me for years through her front window. She taps short stubby fingers on the glass whenever somebody encroaches upon her dingy yard. Nightmares featuring a strained face and a severe scowl topped by floppy white hair have menaced me for years. Violent head shaking and Olson's mouthing of the word *no* are so notorious that everything else about her is ignored. Her long peasant dresses, usually adorned with blue or yellow flowers, and a decrepit white apron, usually escape my mind. For the first time I really noticed her outfit and her stout body as the tables turned and I spied on her for a change. I always thought of her as this gigantic woman. Years ago she loomed large in the picture window, which sits a few feet above yard level. When I was eight she had levitating witch-like intensity. As an 83-year-old Scandinavian woman with her hair pulled back in a bun wearing glasses she reminded me of one of those people that bring a bunch of coupons to the grocery store and hold up the line. I know her age because my mother keeps track of such information.

Confusing behavior by the pit bull made sense when a stooping Mr. Olson emerged under the glimmer of a 1960s metal streetlight, firing an uncoiling hose attached to the Olson home. The dog continued to freak out but gave considerable ground. Mrs. Olson retrieved something from the garage and slowly made her way back to her initial point of contact at the front edge of the fence. As she approached the spot her husband leaned forward, peppering the cautious pit bull until the animal was in the opposite corner of the yard. Mr. Olson, who appears to have died years ago, was suddenly spry and aggressive. He even looked cute in his black and white checked flannel shirt and overalls. He labored in canvas work boots, a tuft of white hair in the middle of his head thrust in the air. He was concentrating so hard that I thought he was in a trance – like a zombie movie or something. When stepping forward he grasped the hose with both hands, like a firefighter. Both Olson's were stoic, like they were auditioning for an elderly ballet company. As the dog circled the other side of the yard, Mrs. Olson poured something into the receptacle placed earlier. Then she shuffled away. Mr. Olson continued occupying the bewildered dogs' attention with one final blast of sustained water, he squeezed that hose like it was his last drop of life. As his wife entered the garage and turned out the overhead light, he methodically turned off the hose and unscrewed it from its faucet. His coiling skills were impressive, as precise as a sailor.

I wanted to investigate, but the Road Pig's dog was really agitated. I was worked up as well. Pacing, my heart raced and I thought of Torrie and Nathan. My breathing slowed when I realized that Nathan was hardly ready to settle down. Then I wondered why a knob like me would be so arrogant. Why should I believe that Torrie should be with me? Presumptuous thoughts fueled by daydreams, fantasy and Mountain Dew made my heart race again and I wondered why I pulled away from Jen. She was treating me well and I had run away. I don't even deserve her. The howlers interrupted these circular thoughts.

Portable sirens and yelling reverberated in local streets and pierced ears. For years, Delridge has been besieged by youths on Friday and Saturday nights. The police don't care; they have bigger issues to worry about. Neighbors no longer complain; they accept the noise. Newcomers and migrants just move away if they are bothered. This small group of howlers (seven or eight) wore dark clothing and skulked back and forth across the street. They stepped in rhythm, as if their movements were choreographed. Relaxed chaos; confident marching, knowing their arrival sparked fear and attention.

I lost interest in the howler's years ago. Nathan and I tried to follow them a few times but when we noticed other kids walking the same trail we bolted. One night I looked at these boys closely. Two young men closest to the house, who looked anywhere from eighteen to twenty-five, were fascinating – I could not turn my head. The front guy had poofy hair and moved it up with a red or maroon (I couldn't tell) headband. He was shirtless and wore droopy shorts, heading in the opposite direction of his hair. He was skinny, muscular and grimaced as he walked, like he was trying to stare someone down. His chin jutted out further than the rest of his face and he was banging a pot with a ridiculously large spoon. Not ten seconds after I started watching him he violently threw something into the pavement just in front of his feet. *'Whap'* was the sound. A small plastic object, perhaps a key chain, exploded in the dark.

"No, no, no, No, NO!" shouted the stocky guy behind him. Then he screamed with clenched fists and made a hideous sound. "Yahhhhhhhhhh." His screech was more disturbing than Roger Daltrey's blast near the end of 'Won't Get Fooled Again.' Wearing a white tank top and saggy jeans, his bugged out eyes met mine. A small black cap with initials I could not read sat on a shaved head. As he sucked in his cheeks he turned and faced me and opened his arms wide, palms out as if to say, "You want some of this boy." His head bobbed downward but also forward toward me. Growing up in Delridge taught me to never appear scared even when you are. I just kept staring with no expression. He finally grabbed his crotch with his right hand, pointed at the place where the object exploded with his left, and yelled, "That's right motherfuckare." Then he moved on with another hellacious scream.

"John?"

"Hi mom." I turned around and spoke to a closed door.

"Are you hungry?"

"Nah."

"I'm going to bed."

"So am I."

Two hours later I was wide-awake and staring at an old Sonics media guide. Surrounding my twin bed with no head or bottom board were pre-read sports pages, magazines and random books. Nothing conspicuous to me occupied the room. No mirrors, magnets, or glass frames. An old John Coltrane poster, a distant treasure courtesy of my father, graces the worn, dirty white painted wall above my head when I read. My closet is half full of clothes and partially full of junk – old car parts, a keyboard, books that should not quality for space on a rickety shelf and uniforms. Two dressers, one only a couple of years old, the other faded and brittle, hold the rest of my worldly possessions. I always crack the single window to my right as I lay on my back on the bed. The practice serves two purposes: fresh air and the illusion that paper-thin walls are not the only ventilators of noise. The roar of the Road Pig's bike announced his arrival across the street.

"What the fuck!" The distant sound of the rarely heard voice of the Pig was deep. A low inquisitive rumble.

When I looked out the window he was petting and placing his head against the face of his dog, now laying prone on his side and convulsing in spastic motions. Consistent wiping of eyes and rubbing his temple followed. He propped up his head in stunned silence, shaking it slowly, cementing his grief from a stranger's perspective. I was certain the Road Pig was crying. He looked helpless, in a state of shock.

"No, no, no baby," he cooed as he picked up his furry beast and carried him into the house. The bowl was missing from the yard. More perusing of the media guide and reading of an old *Post-Intelligencer* sports page followed. I fell asleep with newspaper covering my dirty t-shirt and boxer shorts.

After fumbling around while waking at 9:30 a.m. I managed to get into the cereal cabinet and satisfy a mighty urge to eat until bloated. After casual staring and cursory glances at old clippings, a faint voice beckoned me from the other side of our home's most popular door. I opened the gateway to my mother's conscience and asked what I could do for her. The answer was bacon and mint tea. She held a ten-dollar bill in her right hand as she lay under the covers.

"Where is Dad?" I asked before leaving the room. She shook her head while lighting a cigarette in bed.

"I haven't seen him since he hit the road last night." It was my turn to nod as I shut the door.

Ten minutes later I pulled into the local Safeway parking lot, aimlessly wandering toward the store focused on locating the random items that would satisfy my mother's urges. The bacon was easy. Five minutes and discussion with a customer service expert were required to find something actually titled *mint tea*. I know how particular my mother can be. If it doesn't say 'mint' there would be a lot of back-and-forth and analysis about whether it was the proper packaging or product.

As I settled myself into Mom's messy Pontiac I noticed the gigantic, and familiar, Buick Park Avenue being loaded with groceries by Mr. and Mrs. Olson. The later wore a lavender dress so long it dragged on the ground. After his wife eased her way into the passenger seat with a grimace Mr. Olson, now wearing a crisp blue button- up and white slacks, his church outfit, re-opened the trunk. He then tossed what appeared to be *the bowl* and a container in a trashcan. I froze, hoping they would not see me or notice the car. After a while I slunk down below the dashboard to be invisible. Even an old crust can make rapid movements with their eyes sometimes.

The old Olson's spent four more minutes leaving the parking lot. After they vacated I hurried over to look in the open, metal-wire can. The bowl sat underneath a used container of antifreeze.

6

SYMBOLS

When I returned home the Road Pig was tacking up a wooden sign on the facing of his fence. I parked in the front of our house as if disinterested, my blood pressure rising. While pretending not to look I read 'What is life worth?' in bold black lettering. The sign was tightly fastened to the giant metal spikes on top and to chain links on the bottom with wire, fortified by black electrician's tape. The apparatus looked like something from a working garage, hand-made with a drill and a sturdy board.

The massive, red-faced man wearing a Mr. Bubble t-shirt and tie-dye shorts disappeared into his dark, crowded garage as I entered the house, carrying mother's bounty. Warm weather necessitated a closed screen door and an open primary. I noticed the old squeaky entrance needed about 3 coats of stain and I naturally ducked going into the house pleased to shy away from the activity outside.

After setting the groceries on the kitchen countertop and going to the bathroom I heard the most grotesque sound possible; a squishy, splattering heard when a delicate object is smashed or torn. I imagined a giant cockroach being slowly crushed, guts splashing everywhere. I bounced over to the front window just as the great beast pointed both arms toward heaven and screamed

"Ahhhhhhhhhh!"

His puppy oozed blood and painted a sickening picture impaled by medieval spikes on the fence. The tops sliced through his skin and he sat limp; suspended awkwardly by steel. The Road Pig's art installation was disturbing. Watching his dog choke to death in his own home sent him into emotional free fall. I turned abruptly and no longer cared whether the Road Pig saw me watching him. I kept going back to the window and taking in the gruesome scene. The conductor of this crude fest was walking back and forth in little circles – his body language signaled anger. Arms were thrusting and his beefy legs were like pistons, violently vaulting up and down while his mouth formed words – he was talking to himself. It was like a never-ending freak show. I was frozen with anticipation and did not know how to react.

After sharing a silent breakfast with my mother and her television set I spent a few minutes clipping my hair in the bathroom, I hate sideburns. Then I grabbed our ancient wireless phone, the kind that works well from the house next door. Landlord Jim did not answer. After setting the phone down on the concrete slab in front of our front door I did some dishes. On her way to the bathroom my mother asked me if I caught the previous night's Mariners game. "Yes, amazing comeback," I lied. Radio announcers had described the dramatic 10th inning homerun over radio waves on the way to the grocery store. Smoking outside and pacing in our plebian yard inspired a planned message, recited for landlord Jim's enjoyment.

"Mr. Foster, I am sorry to trouble you on a Sunday morning… my name is…" my weak cadence was interrupted by Peter's ringing, which forced me to concentrate and sit down obediently on the slab. My mother named the phone four years earlier one evening when noting that the bland color of the device matched the color of Peter Falk's raincoat on *Columbo*.

"Hello."

"I think somebody called me from this number." The voice was strong, confident in tone and manner.

"Isa…this a Mr. Foster?"

"Yes, who is speaking please?"

"Hi sir, ahh this is John Ramos. I am a friend of Nathan, actually Ms. Freehold (Nathan's mother had bestowed her maiden name on her boys). They are very frightened about the impending eviction and they would like to pay you back and stay at the, I mean their current place… your place."

"What is your name again?"

"John Ramos…I realize you don't know me but I know these people – I have for years and they will pay."

"It doesn't work that way, I can't make a deal on their terms – or under the understanding that somebody shall pay. Frankly, I shouldn't be talking to you about their affairs."

"Ms. Freehold asked me…"

Interrupting, "Listen, I know she is a little weird…a long pause…but I require some extra money, a deposit if you will, to cease the eviction process that is already in place. Let me check something in my notebook; I will be right back."

"A renter?" asked someone in the background. Probably Foster's wife I thought.

"Yeah, an eviction notice got somebody's attention."

The wait was lengthy. I smoked to relax while gazing across the street at the dead dog, wondering what the Olson's were thinking.

"They are three months behind, rent is only $695 a month… so if they can get me a deposit slash late fee of $500 by Tuesday and catch up on rent by the end of the month everybody can move forward."

I could not tell him the truth about the Freehold money situation. "Mr. Foster is there anything Nathan and I could do for you…some work or something? We can pick up trash, mow lawns, paint…you name it."

"Son, this is not the Millionair Club."

I had no idea what he was talking about. "I just can't let Ms. Freehold lose her home. I just can't…[my voice trailed off but I regained my composure as the sun navigated the clouds and hit me in the face]…she has done too much for me over the years and she has a young child." My voice was now high and gaining emotion. I felt like I was having an out of body experience, making an adult argument to a stranger.

"Listen, why don't you make a proposal to me that includes catching up on rent and paying me the $500 over a period of time and I will have my lawyer review the document. Or better yet, stop by my office and drop off the materials Monday morning."

"Yes sir." Oh, ahh where is the office located?"

"321 Delridge. If nobody is there just slide the materials through the mail slot to the left of the door."

"Thank you sir."

"Righto." Click.

"John?"

I had no interest in doing anything besides smoking outside as I plotted a scheme to work off a debt and be the big hero. My mother is always surprising me.

Wearing a green robe she moved into discussion position on our dusty brown couch in the living room. Glasses framed her expressionless face; she was more vacant than usual, discreet. Before speaking, her bottom lip quivered and her chin jutted forward. No tears were visible but I scanned my memory, trying to recall what I might have done and who knew about my transgressions.

"Johnny, your father sent me a letter. I would like you to read it."

After taking a seat on the floor next to our green metal coffee table, the finest army surplus piece in the house, I reached over and took the letter from her shaking hands. She forced a smile as we exchanged the paper.

"What is this thing?" It was a white piece of paper in a yellow envelope that was dated the day before.

"That is a note from American Telegram. Your father has wasted money on those things for years…the fax revolution missed him and you know how he is about phones."

"I thought he said some of the truck stops he visits have CompuServe machines."

"Can you imagine your father sitting in line to send email?" I laughed and then turned back to the letter.

Will be in Lancaster for a while – job offer working for Sight and Sound Theatres. Pay is $900 a week until the end of the summer to move equipment and live on site – on call 24 hours. Can't believe. Call me 215-441-1567 for details. Act religious over the phone! Tell JR to get a job.

The job reminder at the end of the note was my least favorite part. Even when he was on the road, and in trouble with my mother, he was on my ass.

"Well, he definitely wrote this letter, he is a man of few words." I said this to a woman of fewer words.

"Telegrams are charged by the word – he was just saving money. Do you think he is coming back?"

"Oh yeah, he says so…just for the summer," I pointed at the note now resting on the table. Her wide eyes just stared back at me.

"Why would he stay there for so long?"

"He told me he had a delivery back east. It sounds like something better came along. He sounds pretty excited to me."

"Your father has delivered cars all over the country for twelve years. Why would he suddenly stop coming home?"

"He just got a better job…temporarily."

"Did you read the area code?"

"What are you talking about?"

"215 is Philadelphia."

"Mom, I know he is always yapping about Philadelphia, but he is not there – he is in Lancaster and he is getting paid! Hell, if he asked me to come help him I would do it…I would only do it with your blessing, but this sounds like a great opportunity. Don't you agree? He never makes this kind of cheese."

She started to cry. "Mom, I have a good feeling about this." I jumped onto my feet and sat on the couch next to her, sandwiching her left hand with both of mine. "Pop thinks this is the best move." She nodded with tears in her eyes and broke my heart. I kissed her forehead and kept my arm around her through five minutes of silence; finally rising to make soup for both of us.

After sharing some crackers and Campbell's in front of the television in mom's room I moved back to the smoking hole by the slab. I forgot my buddy – the wireless phone – and my mind wandered across the street where three young boys chatted about the rotting animal. There is something really weird about people who sit and gawk at a scene. What losers. I imagined the dog coming to life in separate parts and chasing them around the block, the mouth biting at their asses. Then in my daydream the Road Pig ran out in his underwear and danced in place, thrusting his gut and crotch out as he swirled, like a man with an invisible hula hoop. I was smiling like a fool when my cell phone rang. I knew it was Nathan because I had to extinguish a new cigarette because I was holding a can of Nestle Iced Tea as well. Mr. timing.

"Yo."

"Mr. Ramos, any luck with Foster?"

"Yes and no. He will deal but he wants a proposal in his office by Monday morning."

"What a cunt."

"I was going to suggest we do some work for the guy."

"Well listen, you don't have to do anything for him. You're already helping by talking with Foster."

Classic Nathan, a half-ass compliment following his own pathetic effort. He is one of those guys who will only put himself on the line if he knows he is going to win. There was a long pause – I didn't say anything.

"He wants a proposal at his office on Monday morning?"

"Yeah."

"Shit, we don't have the money."

"Like I said, I think we ought to offer to do some work for the guy. Even if he pays five bucks an hour we can do something."

"Why don't we find some little kids to work for $1.50 and pocket some dough." I could tell Nathan was not taking this very seriously.

"Do you have a better idea?"

"Not a legal one."

"Do you even have a good illegal plan?"

"Let me think about it. Yeah, I might." "Was that you thinking?"

Laughing, "Yeah."

"I would like to hear about your plan that you obviously have thought about for a long time later, but we do need to stave this guy off and keep him off your mother's ass."

"Maybe my mother can sleep with him."

"Maybe we should attack him with hammers."

Laughing – "Or we could have Stinkbreath get in his face." Nathan was referring to Howard Riley, who does have horrifying breath.

"I am going to put some stuff on paper and hopefully we can get some dialogue with Foster…something that will slow down the eviction. Do you think you can come up with $500 to show him something…a deposit on the plan?"

"I think I can do that. My mother already has $375." I instantly knew he would borrow money from Torrie. I did not offer to help, which made sense because I didn't have any money anyway. "Well, I've got to go to work. Where do we have to go tomorrow? That place on Delridge? I have had to drop off checks in the past."

"Yeah."

"Can we meet at 9:00?"

"Sure, I don't work until 1:30. JRab, I'm talking to you later."

"Hey, I need to get this guy something early tomorrow. Can I show you a letter tonight or read it to you over the phone?"

"Sure, just call me anytime. Going." Click.

I worked on the letter while watching a Mariners game. I was having trouble concentrating but I wanted to get everything out of the way before embarrassing myself in front of Foster and I sensed time was critical. My decisive action surprised me; but appearing competent and adult- like to Torrie is all I have left. I was in a race with my own pride after my juvenile meltdown the night before.

I called Nathan; then called again. I finally reached him at 9:45 p.m. He probably was playing with Torrie or looking at himself in the mirror all night. As he chewed in my ear I read him the draft.

Dear Mr. Foster,
June 23, 2002.
We appreciate your patience as the Freehold family focuses on rebuilding their credit and good name with you. We sincerely

apologize for any inconvenience we have caused and wish to continue living in our current apartment. Enclosed with this letter is $500. We are sorry for delivering the sum in cash but please consider it a deposit and a statement of good faith.

Two months of rent can be satisfied by the 15th of July, and by the 15th of August we can pay two additional months. By September 1st we should be back on schedule. We are hoping the $500 deposit will be credited in the form of past due rent. In fact, we think there was a small deposit paid at the beginning of our first lease and we forfeit that money to help with this debt as well.

In addition we offer to work for you in the interim. We have various talents in landscaping, cleaning, and general office work, which might be of assistance as we repay our debt.

We hope that you will also make a good faith effort by immediately ceasing the eviction effort and will work with us as we try and rebuild your trust after 6 years of residence.

"A little gutless don't you think?"

"No question, but I wanted to make it weak so he works with you and everybody continues to get along."

"I was talking to a guy at work today and he said that tenant law in Seattle is pretty strong. Foster would have to spend some serious money to get us out of there."

"Yeah, but it looks like nobody is there now…like you abandoned the place."

"You're right. I am going to ask my mother to move back immediately. You didn't say anything to Foster about us moving out did you?"

"No; and he didn't bring it up. I doubt he has any idea; he sounds like he owns a ton of stuff."

"Do you think he will sleep with my mom?"

"Maybe we can package that with some office work and ask for some more time. So what is your illegal plan?"

"Ramos, it involves returns and getting cash back."

"I don't get it."

"When somebody buys something from a department store and then decides they do not want the merchandise… they can return it."

"Yeah, so what."

"Some stores do not require receipts."

"You're talkin' about Nordstrom."

"It's right in the slogan bro. That's their thing."

"What are you going to do…borrow a couple of fancy suits and then try and pocket the money?'

"I'm not going to do anything – we'll talk about this some other time – no more phones."

"Got cha."

Nathan called later in the evening but I didn't answer. I was in no mood to discuss more nonsense about Jen and Torrie, who continued to dominate my waking thoughts. She was no longer a fantasy; she was real and sharing time with someone close to me. I smoked three cigarettes in a row and just sat on the slab watching the Road Pig's decaying dog. The howlers had not rolled by and it was pretty early. So I grabbed the rest of my pack, locked up and put on my non-smoke-smelling coat, red, black and thin. Not much protection for a summer evening in Seattle but my heart was racing and the cool air curbed rising body heat fueled by adrenaline and embarrassment. I headed over to the local skating rink to check out the talent. After stepping into the street - I hate sidewalks – my path followed cracks in the road shifting east and west. I looked like a drunk after a rousing gathering. The rink is about ¾ of a mile away but it felt like a marathon. After making the three necessary turns and reaching the road to Skate World I felt exhausted and depressed at the same time, too tired to continue, too bored to stop.

Approaching the long-neglected, pock-mocked concrete parking lot of my destination was depressing. I imagined an uncovered underwater sea bottom, and one of those movies where some bad ass returns to earth after nuclear destruction or aliens have invaded. As I moved closer to the entrance, a large, double-sided red door, surrounded by a rectangular stucco-facade, loud techno music pulsated in the background, interrupted by inaudible announcements.

Every new step uncovered another zombie behind a car, dressed in low-slung jeans and a dark hoodie. Smoke from the chain artists rose into light showered on the lot of shame by three large florescent street lamps. A fourth was rendered useless by a rock or some other projectile long ago. I lacked cigarettes but was in no mood to negotiate with one of the zombies. Many never entered the skating rink and, since I was marching forward, I was an obvious interloper within the confines of their parking sanctuary. It is a perfect place to hang out because most of the guests don't have cars.

As I reached for the heavy wooden door, two rough looking teenagers – about sixteen or seventeen years of age – pushed through the entrance/exit and brushed past me, narrowly missing my face with the door. The leader wore gray sweats tied with a heavy string at the top, black high tops, his white flannel underwear top was adorned with a large neck chain. He wore the heavy undershirt over a regular white-t, a neighborhood staple. A jean jacket completed his look. Short dark hair on top and a little bit of length in back was indelicately masked by a black baseball cap with a plain white front – as if the lack of a slogan was making a point.

"Hey bro," said the stocky friend who followed his taller buddy. I nodded and said, "Hey," in response to his crooked grin and strange expression. His wide eyes were open and communicated louder than his voice. They blinked wildly and his teeth were clenched. His outfit of choice was flannel – a checkered shirt. The fading black studded belt pulled tightly on his wide waist, adding gladiator appeal to black jeans. One of the sad streetlamps shone brightly on his mug as he turned to make his greetings; a conspicuous scar dropping from his left cheekbone down to his jaw line glistened. Black Doc Martin shoes clacked against pavement as he turned and walked away, military haircut bobbing in the darkness as he followed his leader to zombie land.

On the other side of the door a young cashier with a sneer put out her hand. "Student."

"Uh-huh…$4.50."

"4.50?"

"Yah."

Her crazy pigtails, one red, one black, bounced to the music. Black eyes covered by dark eye shadow. She was communicating with someone else in the booth; small lights from a cell phone or some other device flickered in the background. In the darkness her striking white skin made her the rink vampire queen, allowing entry to anybody; no security in sight. I wondered if the joint even cared about who entered.

Expectations of danger and intrigue collapsed after twenty more yards of walking. Once bright, now-faded, Vegas-style red carpeting with squiggly blue lines showed well-worn paths to the rink. The rug was lined by zit-faced teenagers, nearly all boys, standing near the entrance, too uncomfortable to leave until nerdy friends with cars suggested they do so – not confident enough to venture to the rink. I smiled and laughed internally as I viewed people only a couple years younger than me as "kids." Some of the faces I recognized, freshman and sophomores encountered in hallways, parking lots, buses and lunchrooms. I felt their gazes and tried to appear brash and intense.

"Hey bitch tits," someone yelled and a heavy boy in sweats started chasing some skinny kid in red jeans. Turning the corner along the long, sad hallway, brighter and uglier than the rest of the rink, lined by long fluorescent bulbs, the confused and subtle were replaced by the confident. Lights danced and inaudible cadences of the disk jockey reverberated. "Nowwww, bigbaw ardart, nowtown, go." Anybody who pretended to know what he was saying was full of shit. Long lines at the snack bar and skate return desk included faces of relief, concern and sadness – some people were ready to bolt. Standing aimlessly, waiting for service, masked their true desires.

In my glassy-eyed state giant 1970s wood blocks, covered with more red carpet, serving as dual chairs and skate fitting stools, were the only objects coming into focus. The slalom course I charted navigated tens of people, mostly small kids darting and giggling toward restrooms with disco ball reflections dancing across their faces. I had a strong urge to slap some of them out of the way and fly out onto the skate floor like a lunatic. The giant room felt claustrophobic.

Finally, Alice Cooper's "No More Mr. Nice Guy," blared from the speakers, making my journey to skate land worthwhile. Sweet nostalgia filled my veins and my shoulders tingled as I hastily sat down on a red box near the rink bobbing my head, leering at young girls, smiling like a fool. It was pure heaven; my trip was worth it – even the cover charge.

"Ramos! Dude what brings you to this fine abode?"

"Alice Cooper."

"I'm not sure Alice Cooper is worth $6."

"I told them I was seventeen so I weaseled in for $4.50."

"Dude, YOU'RE A LOSER!" Skeeter laughed and slapped hands with an unknown acquaintance. I grimaced through clenched teeth.

"Who is your confidant here McCoy?"

"Confidant? Dude this is not the library." More laughter as the two stallions covered their mouths with their right hands and Skeeter stomped his feet and clapped his hands a couple of times. Skeeter's real name is Jamie but he adopted his new name years ago, about the time his balls dropped. He is opportunistic by nature so I knew, as a fellow graduate of Sealth, he was not hanging out at Skate World for the conversation.

"Hey, do you have any cigarettes?" I asked, finally remembering why I went skating in the first place – to relax.

"Nah, but we've got something else you'll like," Skeet said while motioning to his friend, who took his task very seriously, nodding and turning abruptly with tight lips. The silent errand boy exuded strong features – a square jaw and square haircut to match - short-cropped, no sideburns. Wearing a burgundy rugby shirt with only two buttons on top, faded jeans and dark brown loafers; the guy moved in one big motion, arms and legs in unison. I knew he was younger but he looked older than both of us – one of those guys that starts shaving at age eleven.

"Who is that guy Skeet?"

"That's Mark Diffenbach. He is going to be a senior next year and his sister, Carrie, is right over there," he said pointing. She will be a junior and I hope her family stays here for a long time. He-he, he-he." Skeet's laughter was not infectious, but when my mind finally made a connection with the young woman he referenced, wearing tight white jeans and a yellow shirt with long sleeves I understood his fascination. She, like her brother, appeared older than a high school student and her dark, tanned skin and black hair stood out in Seattle – land of the pale.

"Service is here my brother." A wide-eyed Skeeter held two paper bags. Gin and juice and some real cigarettes, rolled by yours truly."

Diffenbach stood behind his master with his arms folded; his head on a swivel.

"I…I just require some regular old fashioned tobacco tonight Skeet. I appreciate the offer but I have to work tomorrow morning," I lied.

"Just more for us lightweight. Hey! I'm up baby." A quick turn of his head directed his assistant to retrieve skates from their locker along the back wall. Skeeter works at the local lumber store; I have seen him in the Aldo Brother's warehouse before with my father. He makes an uncommonly high wage for a recent high school graduate with no serious plans besides late night skate outings. The gold earring he wears on his left lobe matches the red and gold skates he laced up on our giant seat block. That thing has dangled from his ear since he was twelve. In one swift motion he jumped to his wheels and slid to one of the cutout entries to the skate floor. After a couple of turns around the rink he sidled up to Carrie and skated next to her backwards. Then he started feathering his hair back with one hand and then both hands…I expected him to beckon Mark to come out and play with his hair as well.

"What the hell is he doing?"

"They are about to do a slow skate." Diffenbach had the personality of a dead animal.

"You mean the DJ?

"Yeah."

"What is McCoy doing?"

"I think he is going to skate with Carrie."

"Your sister?" I asked, trying to make conversation, or at least check the guy's pulse. He just nodded so I gave up. He probably goes home and masturbates thinking about his sister and Skeet twirling around the rink.

We watched in silence as kids and young adults of varying shapes and sizes turned in circles while holding hands or embraced in the conventional hands on hips, hands on shoulders pose. Some backward skaters deftly performed the same move and made smaller circles while their partners faced forward. Skeeter did a little of both with some ass grabbing added. His mangy look and wild grin added to the drama as his target playfully slapped away wandering hands and looked at her friends with her mouth agape. She enjoyed the attention. I was certain her friends were grossed out, but too polite to say anything. The juvenile soap opera unfolding before me pricked my social bubble. My $4.50 had been stolen… even at a discount.

"Oh-no," said Mr. Personality. I expected him to tell me the corndogs at the snack bar were on fire. Instead, he was looking at the two goons I encountered when entering the building. They were being asked to leave by an older manager and the shouting and pointing was intense and inaudible, overwhelmed by music. A crowd was gathering to watch the show. The taller boy picked up a random pair of skates and launched them onto the rink, narrowly missing some 13-year-olds. The music stopped. His partner flipped off the skate policeman, a thirty-something guy with short brown hair, a mustache, corduroy pants and a yellow t-shirt covering a beer gut. He was telling one of his employees to call the authorities. Young followers of the goons with nothing better to do gathered and bounded toward the exit. "Those guys are real troublemakers," drawled Diffenbach, who sounded like a character from a 1930s movie. I started wondering what I was doing with my life. A heavy-beat techno song started up again.

"Yo."

Skeeter was back on the sideline after tantalizing all the girls with his active hands and amateur rexing. "You should get out there Ramos."

"I think you need to calm down."

Diffenbach laughed but it was unclear whom he thought was funny.

"I am going to get me a cigarette," I interjected why they stared at each other.

"Score one for me too bro." Skeet was getting more amped by the moment.

"Will do. Do I need a stamp to get back into this hellhole?"

"Yes," said Mark, the only one of us who knew what was going on. I was transfixed by the dark smoky nature of the room since no source was in sight. I surmised rising dust and dirt from floors and rugs created the sensation. The same yellow-shirted manager at the scene of conflict stamped the back of my hand, armpit sweat marks prominently displayed. "Fifteen minutes," he said. He scanned ahead for impending danger while stamping. His work was so sloppy that he put the marking on my wrist.

"Okay." I had no idea what he meant but his jumpy persona indicated he was on watch for troublemakers. He looked smaller and older up close. His deep brown eyes darted back and forth between stamp line and the entrance. Once outside, I targeted a group of rejected skateboarders wasting time on the fringes of the parking lot. They had smokes and were not talking – perfect targets – no conversation. I gave them a quarter for their troubles. "Thanks dude," said the fifteen-year-old with long hair, a heavy red winter jacket, gray sweats and a green headband. He was so stoned he never picked up that my name is John.

"Later." I lifted my hand, too lazy to wave goodbye. Noise was rising from a gathering of young men on the other side of the lot – the same direction as home. I was intrigued so I zipped back inside and gave Skeet a cig and then booked back outside, saying my goodbyes on the fly. Nervous laughter and weak conversation ruled the night inside the magic skating building – I was ready to leave after being convinced life was too short to spend any more time on the red carpet. Back outside the group of hooligans were still stationary, but growing louder.

"Let's find a party!"

"We'll make a party!"

The gang of fourteen followed the ubiquitous tall boy and the stocky bodyguard - the rock stars of Skate World. With nothing better to do, I trailed the crew at safe distance. The pack traveled in a group descending by age. Eleven and twelve-year-olds with mop haircuts, hooded jackets and sneakers followed behind the loudest grouping, a few thirteen and fourteen-year-olds edging closer to the leaders, speaking confidently about women and mischief caused by older boys. This gathering was the most fashion conscious, stuck in a world where brand names and shoes attract the attention of older school chums. In front strutted the leader, his pal and a few rugged-looking fifteen-, sixteen- and seventeen- year-olds. The ages of the two wizards is still a complete mystery to me, but they were boys of the streets – not generic kids in hallways.

Slowing movement halted to a stop and the little crowd circled outside two small white cottage-style homes, no porches, just flat patios stepping to non-descript doors, one dark green job spotlighted by an outdoor light and the second, a faded brown color in darkness. In the former a lone indoor lamp was visible through curtains; nobody was stirring. The other home was full of life inside; people standing, making shadows in worn shades – loud enough to hear outside over the din of the gaggle of boys. A television with a massive screen was beaming something exciting – perhaps wrestling or a boxing match. Viewers were animated; yelling, competing for airtime. I migrated across the street to work on my dying cig. The only people looking my direction were the youngest boys, which was equivalent to nobody.

As the tall boy straightened between the two homes I noticed he was smoking. I was jealous since my supply was gone. "Fuck it," he said, throwing down his butt with authority. He walked diagonally across the small, flat yard to the loud zone and pounded on the door with both hands, fists clenched. Mr. Stocky was right behind him, as were two of the older boys, one wearing all black sweats and red sneakers, the other outfitted in a green sweatshirt, jeans and black hiking boots. This guy was moving his feet and rolling his neck as if he were preparing for a big football play and he was the middle linebacker.

A middle-aged man with a worn purple sweater opened the door swiftly. "What the hell is going on out here?"

His question was answered with a straight right to the face. As the man disappeared from view the leader stood silently on the patio, standing tall, fists clenched, while his nutty friend ran into the house. "Hey, what   the fuck!" Yells and grunts followed and I instinctively loped across the street to investigate. The group was gawking, scattering and laughing, everybody moving back a few paces. One young boy started to run toward the parking lot, probably peeing his pants. The giggling was a frightened reaction.

"Oh my god," and "Did you see that?" were coming out of gaping mouths. The two positioned close to the house joined their man on the   patio and the green sweatshirt boy bounded inside while screaming like a crazy warlord. Shocked, I walked toward the sight of the attack…by this time all four boys were inside and a huge ruckus was taking place; furniture was breaking. My heart was pounding and I felt like helping and laughing – both options seemed like appropriate responses.

As I peered into the home a young woman upstairs screamed "Help police!" Two college-age boys, perhaps the son of green sweater man and a friend, were punching and kicking at the black sweats boy, who was swinging wildly and keeping them away by swinging a fireplace poker. The stocky boy was locked up in a wrestling move with the father and another middle aged man was kicking the crap out of the green sweatshirt kid; holding him down on the carpet with his left hand and punching him in the side of the head and his ribs with his right fist. The tall boy was returning from the kitchen with a bunch of food in a large plastic zip-lock bag. He saw me in the entry way, smiled and said, "Hey dude."

"What is this all about?"

"Just having some fun John."

How did this kid know my name? I was becoming more confused by the minute, and a little pissed.

"Let's get out of here."

"Okay." He left abruptly. The stocky boy disengaged and grabbed at my left shirtsleeve – "Let's go!"

"Wait."

As I stepped forward the father lunged toward me and I high-tailed it out the door. He was gasping for air after his tussle and he looked crazy, full of anger. My odd acquaintances headed back across a yard and into dark shadows up the street.

As sirens blared in the background I ran home. Cold air and heavy breathing added little clarity to the experience. I was a punk among punks… too cowardly to assist anybody and possibly viewed as an accomplice. Once plastered in my bed and secure behind a closed door I listened to bad sports radio, failed to masturbate (my mind was too cluttered) and restlessly fell into light sleep. Ninety minutes later I awakened, still confused and sweating. Only the morning light indicated it was safe to begin another day.

7

THE DEAL

I don't wear watches so I am not really sure what time I arrived at 321 Delridge, but I know it was a few minutes before 9:00 a.m. Nathan was missing. I waited for about five minutes, burned one outside, slicked up my hair a little bit in the bathroom at the service station across the street and crossed back between spurts of traffic. The place was 40% nice and 60% shit. You can tell Foster picked up the property for a steal and is slowly building it up for resale. I knocked and there was no answer so I walked in the main area, which looked like an old dentist lobby. Everything was part plush and part old. There were three cubicles and a front desk where an office manager placed some family photos near the door. I spied hot coffee in an old percolator in the corner, the fumes were enticing.

There was an open hole bored in the interim door, where the knob goes. Lights were on everywhere. I poked my finger in the opening and ran my pointer along the sides of the rough edges. A new doorknob was on the way but if the rest of the place was any indication, time was not a priority for small repairs. My thoughts turned to childhood when I used to look through holes in doors at my parent's apartment when the doorknob to their bedroom fell off. I peeked through the hole and saw a long corridor with an open door at the end of the hallway. As my mind wandered, a clumsy sound came from a distant bathroom.

"Ah-hew, huh."

Coughing followed a flushing toilet and running water. Somebody sounded like they were dying or waking up next to a toilet after a long night. I scrambled back to the front of the office, just inside the door. Nervous hands patted down wayward hair on the back of my head.

"Hello? Mr. Foster?"

"Yes."

In seconds a tall heavyset man with a beard and a big red nose opened the door.

"Can I help you?"

"Yes sir, my name is John Ramos. I spoke with you on the phone yesterday."

"Right, you were trying to help out the Freehold family correct?

"Yes, and I brought a letter for your review." Since Nathan was missing I decided to call the shots.

After taking the letter Foster paused, turned toward a brown leather couch in the main room, and then turned back around. "Do you want a cup of coffee?"

"Yes, thank you."

He started to move toward the percolator, as did I. "I can help myself."

"Very well. I will be right back. I need my glasses for this stuff."

"Jesus Christ, how many pairs of these things do I need to buy? Unbelievable." It sounded like the search for eyewear was going badly.

By the time he returned I was refilling my Styrofoam cup. "Would you like a cup sir?"

"No, I would probably just lose the goddamn thing." The comment made me wonder why he made the coffee in the first place. "Hey, is anybody from the family you are protecting going to speak with me?"

"Nathan should be here any minute."

"I will believe that when I see it," Foster said while creaking into the middle of the couch. He squinted and quickly scanned the letter.

"Okay," suddenly his voice was booming, as if something had awakened in his brain. "This is what we are going to do." He leaned toward me, standing near the door, and removed his reading glasses in one ferocious action. "Son, I own a number of properties and have a pretty sizeable yard at home. I am not in the business of making rent deals, but Laney is fortunate in that I do have a lot of work to do and adding decent help to help pay down a debt is acceptable to me if the people involved work hard and I oversee their progress."

"We can do anything you need to do sir, I have…"

"Who would be doing the work?"

"Me…Nathan and I believe Nathan's mother would   assist as well." It dawned on me that Foster might be interested in getting out of some yard work himself. Maybe my timing was good for a change.

"Okay, I am going to initial this paper and we can begin monitoring the progress on a weekly basis. Can you work this Thursday?"

"Sure."

"I will make a copy of this basic agreement, oh wait you should initial this as well. I trust your style of communication more than Laney's." After I started writing on the paper he continued, "As you must know this is no contract, this is a bullshit handshake deal, but I hope this works and the family can get their cash flow back in order."

"I do too sir."

He made a copy of the paper, shook my hand and provided directions for the Thursday rendezvous, slated for 9:00 a.m. at his home. I was not really paying attention since he wrote down the address. He is one of those guys who talks too much when you are ready for him to stop. After leaving the meeting I was relieved to be back on my own schedule. After walking about a mile toward home I spotted Nathan waiting for me across the street while listening to music in Torrie's car. She sat next to him, in the passenger seat. When he saw me he jumped out and bounded over.

"Hey man, I am sorry about that...I forgot where that dude's office is."

"Here ya go." I handed him a copy of the document, a decision I instantly regretted because he loses everything.

Nathan skimmed over the piece while sitting on the sidewalk on my folks' side of the street. He wore one of those heavy black jackets, so puffy he looked like a marshmallow. His pants were brown, stylish, likely remnants of a shopping excursion with Torrie. She waved to me and looked content in the car as if she was watching her man conduct business. I responded with a little nod and an embarrassed smile, paralyzed and unsure of what to say, if anything – so I began staring at Nathan again. The bright yellow sneakers on his feet were clearly his choice. No self-respecting girlfriend would let their man leave the house with such colorful footwear. By the time one's eyes reached the bottom of his outfit he looked like a banana split.

"Okay, what next?"

"We have to do some work at his house on Circle Drive Thursday morning."

"What time?"

"Nine."

"Hey, I really appreciate all you are doing for my family. Are you sure you want to help us out so much? What can I do to repay you? I can give you a little money as I pick up checks at the Big 5."

This was the Nathan I expected after he failed to show at Foster's office and left all negotiations to me. I knew he was uncomfortable when placed in a role requiring requests for assistance, but I still felt taken advantage of. After a deep breath my eyes veered toward his; his expression was equivalent to a puppy begging for food.

"No worries, I will help. Your family would do the same for me." Jesus, I hate it when I utter movie lines like that one. I sounded like some jackass who was going away to war or something.

"My mother is going to make you some fine dinners, I can guarantee you that." What a guy. After idle chat about Skate World, smelly customers at Big 5 and commentary about the rotting dog across the street, we slapped hands and said goodbye. Torrie did not make any weird comments about the animal on the fence, she was content draining the car battery and listening to CD's. Maybe she thought it was some strange art, a sculpture of some kind. Nathan promised he would be at Foster's house on Thursday. I was skeptical. He also asked me to stop by his mother's temporary place – she was living with a friend on South 27th in the Central District - so I could personally give her the good news. His excuse was that he did not know the phone number or how to contact her. I figured he did not want to answer all of her questions. She was full of them and he has the patience of a flea. After asking and receiving the copy of the letter, which relieved me, and taking a handful of change from Nathan for bus fare, I went inside to eat cereal and rest before heading east.

8

ADVICE

⊷◆⊶

I left for 627 South 27th Street as Nathan requested. I surmised he was excited about his mother's new location because it was really close to Torrie's neighborhood and I thought of her as I comely searched for other figurines of human beauty while the bus creaked up Jackson Street. At 25th I escaped the vehicle, but my dreams continued. Sitting on public transportation is therapeutic…my imagination is never interrupted by anybody; I feel more alone than ever.

One of the runts who sat in the last row, a little tyke about eight or nine-years-old, tossed pebbles at the bus as it wheeled away. His feeble arm would strengthen in due time and I estimate that within twelve to eighteen months he will rattle rocks off the side of the bus with gusto.

"What are you looking at?"

"You," I responded.

"Why dat?"

"Because I want to little man."

"Go look at someone else."

"Chill out." I stuck out my hand. "My name is John."

"Chuck," he said, as he looked me up and down. He met my hand with his and stepped forward, making eye contact, pupils darting from his shoes to mine. At four or four and a half feet tall he wore hideous white sneakers and long droopy jeans that slung down to the pavement, frayed at the edges. Chuck's plain white t-shirt was dirty on top, the collar a suitable napkin. A weathered Oakland Raiders jacket hung from his shoulders and practically covered his entire body. His skin was coarse and black and his expressions were serious.

"Eh," we both turned to view a lighter skinned, taller, more graceful boy strutting toward the site of the great bus attack.

"You gonna come to the park, or did you lose your nerve?"

"Is that your older brother?" I asked, pointing. "No!"

Chuck tilted his head and moved the top of his body backward while conceding no ground. His spine was a fulcrum for his emotions, he moved like a puppet operated by some secret electronic force. I had not intended to offend him.

"Listen, I'm just making conversation, I just figured this guy was your brother."

"Let's go," said the other kid.

"I need to go home first." As he reached the end of the sentence Chuck's voice grew louder.

"Hurry!"

I started walking toward my destination and realized Chuck was shadowing me. "Where do you live?"

"West Seattle. I am just visiting a friend over here."

"Where?"

"627 South 27th Street."

The boy stopped. "That is my house!"

"Is there a woman named Laney staying there…or just visiting by any chance?"

"That is my mother's best friend!" For some reason Chuck shouts his way through common conversation. Relief came over me since I had come close to big-timing the kid in front of his friend when he came on strong outside the bus. My history with kids throwing rocks at buses or anybody that I feel is inappropriately talking smack is random. Sometimes, I lose my temper and act like an asshole. Other times, I just shrug it off. My dreamy state during the bus ride saved me. The world was hazy when I encountered the little tyke, the burdens of Nathan and his family were long gone, so I managed to stay mellow.

"Do you know Nathan and Chester?"

"Oh yeah. Nathan is in college, he plays for the Huskies. Chester is sweet too!"

I didn't tell the kid Nathan was still in high school. There was no point. Then he started running as we arrived at the corner of 27th. I always crack up when kids start sprinting for no reason – it seems like half of them have rocket boosters in their pants.

"Come on, let's go!" I slowly jogged behind, acting like we were racing up the street, which sloped at an incline as both of us charged southbound. With no warning the little man curved into an indention in a small white fence and bounded up steps leading to a small two-story house with a picture window downstairs in front of a living room and one rectangular window upstairs peeking out from somebody's bedroom.

He yelled "Mom!" and started knocking and ringing the doorbell like a madman. The kid has attention deficit disorder something fierce or he is just happy to be part of the action. I would hate to be his younger brother.

"All right, all right, what is a-matter?" Chuck's mother wore a long beige dress and a matching hair clip, placed in the middle of shiny black hair. She opened the door with a huge gush of wind so the little guy was knocking air and making little screaming sounds. Then she put her hands on her hips and glowered down at Chuck like he should ask permission to enter her home. "This guy knows Nathan and Chester." His little right hand pointed in my direction and he was starting to hyperventilate. His legs were bobbing up and down.

I was smiling and standing halfway between the little fence and the front door. The little walkway, a miniature barrier in front for some dog and the little boy, made me feel like a character in *Gulliver's Travels*. My droopy brown coat and giant backpack that carried the Foster paper furthered the illusion. Sweat caked my face because Seattle summer had finally arrived. It was in the low-70s, the temperature range that causes locals to start complaining it is too hot.

"Hi. What can I do for you?" Her voice was stern and her expression questioning. I felt uncomfortable on her property. Relief quashed concern when I spied Laney waving at me through the picture window. Her voice was garbled from outside but she said something like, "I know that boy." Laney is not someone who ever shows much emotion but her word is golden, so everybody believes her. I stood at my post in littleville, waiting for the go ahead to enter. The beige woman moved out of the doorway and Laney emerged. Chuck was long gone, probably jumping on the dog's tale or screaming at inanimate objects.

"Come in," beckoned Ms. Sweet with a characteristic mellow expression on her face. Her demeanor always starts off low-key, almost catatonic. She relies on other people to feed her emotions and draw her personality outward. Her long-sleeved red shirt barely covered her midriff and white pants exposed her curvy muscular form. Nathan favors his mother's sinewy body. After being introduced to Barbara Hollingbeal, the homeowner with the glare, and reintroduced to her son Chuck, I had to tour the house and pretend to give a damn about the family pictures on the wall in every room. The little man kept right on yelling and the family lab spent most of his time ramming me with his giant head and putting his smelly paws all over my jeans and jacket.

"Why don't you take your coat off son?" Mrs. Hollingbeal looked at me like I was an idiot for wearing anything other than a swimsuit since I was sweating all over the place. The back of my wrists were sopped as I wiped moisture off my forehead. Her reaction came four minutes after telling her son not to lose track of his jacket because it would be cold that afternoon. She is a woman who gives a lot of advice.

"This is my Uncle Robb," yelled Chuck after he showed me a picture of his father, Earl, and his brother. I did not have to ask about the relationship because they looked like twins fishing. The uncle was grimacing, like he was fighting a shark on his hook or had gas or something, and the father was laughing his ass off. The picture reminded me of the soggy river bottoms across the state my father has dragged me to over the years.

"Lower your voice son," shouted Mrs. Hollingbeal. Family obligations saved me so I was not forced to entertain Chuck for long. Chester was at basketball practice and Chuck went to the park after his mother busted him trying to watch television. Then she left to pick out morsels at the local farmer's market, which she explained to me was only open a few days a week – like I gave a shit. If she had taken the stupid dog with her my day would have finally brightened. 'Marvelous' the mutt remained however; and he continued to hound me. His stupid name added insult to injury. I felt like kicking him in the teeth. After Laney prepared some weird hippie tea from Eugene we sat down facing each other, me on a couch, her on a plush seat, around the coffee table, the lab jumped in the air between us and randomly chose which one of us to harass.

"Nathan told me…well these were not his words, but he said he delegated the communication with our landlord to you. I hope you understand John that I had no intention of you being burdened with this nonsense." I kept silent during her long pause as she sipped her tea. "Putting this work on your shoulders is not fair to you and it is not your responsibility.

However, I can understand why he turned to you. His skills in such matters do not match yours."

"Thank you for the compliment…but as I told Nathan, you guys have fed me on several occasions and I want to help out in any way I can. Plus, I think it is unfair to harass people." The answer bothered me as soon as it left my lips. That crap about being fed sounded weird but I did not know what else to say. I hate it when people give you compliments to your face.

Laney smiled. "I think you would have a hard time finding many people who agree with you about that last part when bills are not being paid. But I like your thinking."

"We met with Foster this morning and he agreed to let us work off some of the debt. He said there is plenty of work to do at his house and at other properties he owns."

"I think you mean you met with Foster. There is no way Nathan made it to his office on time…I know because I saw when he left this morning." Now Laney wore a frown. I just nodded and opened my eyes wide. In moments like these my mouth forms into an open circle – a general expression that mirrors a stick-figure face from "Ziggy" or "Peanuts" cartoons. To divert the discussion I grabbed my backpack and reached in to grab the beaten-down copy of our non-agreement.

"Here is a sample of, er…what we discussed…Mr. Foster and me. He thought work could be…or at least he wants work to be done beginning this Thursday at his house at 9:00 a.m." I stood and handed Laney the two- page offering and initials across the span of the coffee table, which glistened in the sunlight among heavy glass, coasters and two cups of tea. I pretended to drink the stuff because it tasted like old balls and it would have been rude to ask for a bunch of sugar. Later, when I went to the bathroom before leaving the house I carried the cup with me and poured most of it out so it appeared like I actually drank the stuff. Of course, in situations like these you never want to pour everything out or else the guest will insist that you have another cup.

"This looks good John, I assume you wrote and presented this plan?"

"Yea."

"You are a very talented and I am concerned that Nathan takes advantage of you." Her response caught me off guard – I was more concerned about the decisions I was making that affected her life.

"I just think he feels comfortable…relying on other people." Laney finished my sentence for me.

"Since he is my son I see his faults and behaviors more clearly than anybody and he is really taking your friendship to a new level – one of support – not mutual, but a one-sided beneficial thing for him." I was getting more uncomfortable by the minute. "You are smart and I know you manage him in your own way but I never want you to feel that his requests for help are driven by me or our family. He respects you and is clever enough to understand you have skills he lacks." She paused for effect. "But you cannot stifle your schedule and creativity to please someone else and I have watched Nathan exude an incredible aura that affects his friends and acquaintances in strange ways since he was a little boy."

I almost smirked because I wondered what Laney would do if I told her I wanted to fuck her son. However, this was not a time for jokes; this was grown-up serious time, so I bit my lower lip and closed my mouth.

"Ms. Sweet…"

"Just call me Laney John, you know better than that, come on." She waved her left hand downward in my direction while holding tea in her right hand and made a silly face, one indicating she thought I was going to bullshit her…which I was about to do.

"Okay, I know Nathan likes my help. In this case, I am only glad to help. I am not doing anything with my summer so far and until I get a job it gives me something to do."

"That is a poor reason to work off someone else's debt."

"Maybe, but he is my friend and I guess I do feel obligated to work on his projects. Maybe we can take it week-by-week and see how it goes?" This last statement sounded stupid, like I was giving up or resigned to failure, so I braced myself for another micro lecture. She just stared in my direction.

"I am sure he would do the same for me." As the words came out of my mouth Laney was shaking her head. We both laughed.

"No he wouldn't."

"I know."

"Take this stuff - it is yours," I accepted the rumpled pages and placed them safely in my backpack. It was time to stop carting them around the city like the Holy Grail. "Do you want more tea?"

"No thanks, I'm doin' fine. Hey, may I use the bathroom?"

After gathering my backpack and preparing to leave Laney said, "Come here you." She gave me a hug in the entryway and patted me on the back. Her muscular arms and back felt comforting and her soft front excited me. All I could muster was, "See you soon," as I walked along Gulliver's trail and headed north to find another bus.

While waiting next to the broken down transit shelter, covered with Plexiglas and framed by aluminum pillars, painted brown by some idiot years before, I felt a projectile hit my ass. Snickering behind me led to an obvious conclusion: Chuck. Without turning around I pretended to pick up a rock, turned quickly and faked a throw in his direction. He and two friends scattered behind some bushes near an adjacent house.

"Hit that punk in the face!" The voice of an older boy indicated I was in trouble.

I whirled around in a crouch and maneuvered to the other side of the Plexiglas, ready for an onslaught. The elderly woman sitting on the bench to my left looked at me like I was insane. Her white hair framed horn-rimmed glasses curving skyward on the edges, the opposite direction of the corners of her mouth, which drooped in a show of frustration. She held her purse tightly between her legs; her freshly pressed white dress adorned with blue flowers was spotless. As I reached down to form some dirt clods and store up ammo, tons of small rocks and pebbles landed on the Plexiglas and alongside the shelter. "Ping, ping, ping…" background laughter from three or four perpetrators added to the chaos. The sound of cracking plastic followed.

"Stand up sucker," yelled the oldest of the group again. "Time to take your beating."

While combing the damp ground for rocks since it was becoming clear dirt would not terminate the advance, I heard a heavy object pounded into the shield on my side of the shelter.

"Hey there! Hey there! You little turds want some of this? The onslaught ceased.

"Whoa, let's go!" Little feet slapped pavement in the distance.

"Find someone else to bother…you…you little shitheads!"

I dropped my dirt and looked over at grandma. She was pounding the butt of a silver .357 revolver into the plexi and pointing at her weapon of choice for the boys to see. I stood up, dropped my weaponry, and silently waited for the bus. We made eye contact and did not speak. She put her gun back in her purse, straightened her dress and sat back down on the bench.

DELEGATING

Isat on the other side of the bus from grandma the pistol packer and briefly fell asleep on the way home. A bumpy road redirected tired eyelids. Warm air venting through cracked windows added summer tint to a dreary day of errands. As the driver crossed Yesler, Seattle's dry hills offered views of distant mountaintops and glimpses of Puget Sound through downtown buildings. Travels on First Avenue South past stadiums and railroad tracks were less stimulating. I was long gone before we crossed the Duwamish River and only the jolting sensation of the bus stopping in Delridge shook my brain awake.

Longing for a sandwich at the Vietnamese Deli on the corner I noticed some fresh graffiti. Under a cute sign for the local daycare, "Know and Grow" someone finished the passage with the touching, "Ya dumb hoe." Constant giggling followed me the rest of the way home. Spying new messages on benches, buildings and street signs kept me occupied as I trudged home with a hungry stomach. Only two blocks from my destination, the mysterious two-some from the skating rink appeared in a decrepit two-door Honda zipping through a stop sign. When I stared they stopped…and it was not a run-of-the-mill slow down. Tall boy hammered the brakes and screeched to the curb.

"John, what's going on? You seen Nathan lately?" Mr. beefy was doing the talking.

"Nah." By this time I had veered right and walked to their car.

"You need a ride?"

Tall boy just smoked and looked over at me while I kneeled down to speak with both of them. He looked like he had been practicing James Dean expressions in the mirror. He wore a Fila headband and some really nice clothing; a fancy cashmere sweater, with a dress shirt and collar underneath. He looked like someone trying to sneak into a country club by parking his crappy car in the back lot. Even his partner had fresh jeans on and a clean shirt this time. As the driver drew down his pouty lips his friend was serious and amped – full of life, looking as crazed as ever.

"Thanks for the offer but I just live a couple of blocks away. Last night was interesting. Do you guys invade houses often?"

"Actually, we do like to have fun man." An unbelievable pause made me think they were both on something. Beady eyes scanned my face, seeking interpretation. I just stared back. Mr. stocky continued. "We like to do…we like to do a lotta things." Not wanting to offend, I led into conversation that might casually clue me in as to why I should know them.

"Have you guys seen Nathan lately?"

"Last Friday," said the nimble-tongued boy driving, finally showing a different persona. We'll be connecting with him again tomorrow. He's been pretty busy chasing that gorgeous kitten around town." I could only muster a fake laugh, blink both eyes and refocus with clenched teeth.

"She is fucking hot man. I wish I saw more of her than Nate." As he spoke of Torrie passenger side boy became even more animated. He started moving his hands up and down and moving his ass around in the seat.

"You should join us this week. I know you don't like to get your hands dirty but I saw the look in your eyes last night. You looked like you were ready to throw down if necessary. We've got a gig on Wednesday that might interest you – talk to Nathan and see what he thinks."

"Heh-heh. Yea, well you guys were impressive. What happened to your friends?" I wondered why these guys knew so much about me.

"I dunno. Those guys probably had to clean out their underwear when the cops came." Tall boy just kept smoking and staring in front of the car while habitually checking the rear view mirror. I laughed at his joke to keep up the awkward camaraderie. The conversation was likely to end well or painfully.

"Okay, I am going to talk to Nathan and make sure I am ready for Wednesday…or at least find out if there is something I can do." I had no idea what I was talking about. After clasping hands with stocky man, who was now bouncing his knees up and down and rocking forward in his seat, they burned rubber and speed off to cause more mayhem and baffle more strangers. I practically ran into the house seeking peace and safety.

Quiet time lasted for nine minutes – Mom's shattered my program by invading the living room and talking endlessly about Pop and his new job in Pennsylvania. She drives me crazy with this stuff. I was again sitting by the green table – on the floor no less - folding laundry and eating half a leftover baloney sandwich when persistent sobbing overcame my senses.

"John, I called your father and he had no interest in even speaking with me about his plans. He treated me like an old fish wife asking for money. Do you think he is with somebody else? Huh-uh-uh-uh." Her breathing was fast and wild.

"No…no..no. What did he say that led you to this conclusion?"

"First he acted like he didn't know who I was, and then he told me to call back in a couple of hours. After leaving me all alone. Can you imagine? He is so cruel to me."

"Did you wake him?"

"Probably."

"What do you mean?"

"Well yes, he mentioned something about napping." "Come on, you know Dad, he can fall asleep on the toilet, and if he is tired, stirring him is a twenty-minute process."

She wore the same clothes as the day before and her hair appeared shorter. I suspected she had been cutting it behind closed doors in her bedroom. Everything was lopsided as if someone had created a step system going from left to right. Her eyes were red and bloodshot.

"Did he ask you to call him back?"

"Yes."

"When?"

"In a couple of hours."

"What time did you speak with him?"

"About forty-five minutes ago…" she trailed off amidst intermittent sobbing. I rose and grabbed some tissues in the bathroom. When I returned my mother was no longer standing, she had migrated to the couch and was spying the remnants of my sandwich.

While handing her tissues I gently inquired, "Have you eaten anything today?"

She nodded which meant "nothing of substance" if I know my mother. As I prepared a grilled cheese I chatted relentlessly in an effort to calm her nerves, which generate righteous electricity when communication is limited. This is the strange aspect of my mom's personality because she is always operating on a private schedule – never changing anything for anybody. She does not nag or bother, her loved ones live independent lives. But they must be communicative or emotional stress rises like Seattle fog. Wendy Kennely lives to worry and when I said earlier that she gets on my ass – what I really mean is that the world becomes rife with danger, crises and impending doom when people near her heart alter things. Mom's has always viewed life as a series of small problems. Dad views his day as an orchestra of challenges, each requiring effort and decisive action. Their combined viewpoint results in inaction and separation. Mother worries about events and people she cannot control and Pop's always ignores everything that he might not impact. He only targets sure things. In practice the system works like this:

When the Road Pig places a rotting dog on his fence my mother will stew, call neighbors and debate whether she should call the police and complain about what she perceives as a public health hazard. She has probably already called. Pop takes a different approach. He will ignore the smell and ugly image – in fact he might appreciate the protest art. He minds his own business. Bad example? Perhaps. Years ago, Mom's was concerned because we were slated to visit some friends in Spokane during the winter and Snoqualmie pass, the easiest route over the mountains, kept closing. News people and the state patrol were all freaking out about impending danger.

"Somebody is trying to get some overtime this weekend," said Pop as we barreled east in a rickety Plymouth with bald tires. He is always suspicious of snow plow drivers who work for the Department of Transportation. He knows some of those guys and how they work. To prepare for impending doom my father had a better spare than any of his actual running tires in the trunk and every possible tire changing apparatus available on the common market. We could have helped a semi operator in a pinch. When he reached the checkpoint he calmly told the officer that the car was four-wheel drive. The dude must have been sniffing glue. Any jackass could tell that piece of junk was not suited for bad weather. Nothing about this scenario bothered my mother. She just left everything in the hands of the experts.

She did get pissed when she realized the calendar we were bringing the Rubin family had been left behind. "What on earth were you doing in the driveway?"

"I asked you if everything was in the car."

"Everything was in the living room."

"Then everything should be in the car."

"I have never been so embarrassed." Ten minutes later she was still embarrassed and thirty minutes later as we skidded off the road trying to locate a gas station Mom's was still fuming about the calendar. As my father slowly slid down a small hill into darkness in a deathtrap of a vehicle her concern was how to mail the stupid calendar. She finally showed some concern when another family "looked cold in their car."

She should have asked our robotic chauffer to go fetch the item before we left because he will follow any path as long as there is a destination in mind. The key is direct communication, or at least that is my perspective. Father is never persuasive – he just reacts. Mother wills participation and subtle changes of plans. Her preference is to do so silently, which is a terrible method. Have you ever seen one of those people waving signs for a store or a burger shop on the side of the road? Usually some nut case is paying them to serve as human billboards. That is my Mom; she is the person holding the sign, but she never dances around like some of those goofballs. She passes along information and expects people to react.

During the trip we stopped at a Kentucky Fried Chicken in Moses Lake. Richard ordered generously – eight pieces of chicken, mashed potatoes, corn and biscuits. After we merged onto the unplowed Interstate-90 my mother began dispensing the goods. "Please pass the butter Me- maw. Mmmm, I should have ordered more biscuits. They aren't homemade but they good."

"Richard they forgot the butter and the utensils."

"What! Damnit. That kid was too busy lookin' out the window. Damn. Okay. Shit!"

"Take it easy and please watch the road."

After a few more seconds of head shaking and muttering: "Well screw it we need to make time. Can't go back now. Yer gonna have to eat with your fingers boy. Did plenty of that growing up…the only difference was that our biscuits were better…he-he-he."

As Mom placed the greasy chicken on napkins and small plates Pop suddenly turned gravely serious, an inquisitive look came over his face.

"Did they provide any honey for the biscuits?"

After a quick glance in both sacks the answer was a confirmed, "No."

With one crazy turn to the right onto an icy off ramp just outside of town, Richard Ramos began his trek backwards toward the sacred honey dispenser. I was laughing so hard I almost fell into the space between the front and back seats.

"Richard, be careful."

"You can't eat biscuits without honey Goddamnit!"

When we returned the drive-up line was lengthy, so my father told me to run inside. All sorts of idiots were sitting in the line because the weather was crappy, really cold outside. I was the only person inside besides employees so it took a while for anybody to realize that I was standing by the cash registers. A worker festooned with a headset looked shocked as I explained our grievances. The short Latino woman seemed to understand my plight but I got nervous when she starting speaking with her stiff, blue-shirted manager, who looked like he had been up all night, rubbing grease on his shirt and scratching his balls. His lips remained sealed as she talked and he frowned and shook his head. After he pointed to something in the corner of the kitchen I lost track of the girl and he returned to his office to do whatever he did. A full sack of butter, salt 'n pepper, utensils, napkins, small plates (I didn't even know they had such stuff) and enough honey for a zip code in Spokane was provided after a couple of minutes of fumbling around. The girl's large round brown eyes were alert, she was focused on helping me with   my condiment problem. All of the Mexican-American workers in the place were about five-feet-tall – a cute little army of helpers; and very competent compared to the locals stumbling around the place, shaking like they were coming down from a session at the methadone clinic. We had so much stuff, we stopped for more biscuits later on the trip and my father suggested we give out honey instead of calendars. "Only dumbshits sit around and look at that crap," he reasoned.

While waiting for my bounty I could see my mother staring out the passenger window aimlessly while my father made wild gestures with his hands, sideways, forward, up in the air. Pointing toward the restaurant finished every small rant. I imagined his head exploding and his body continuing to drive us to our destination while jamming biscuits and unopened packets of honey down the hole at base of his neck. Fortunately, mom prepared his meal so we did not rove across two lanes when the serious eating began. No doubt the steering wheel, slick in places (grease and sweat), was safer in the weather with its sticky new honey base.

After we arrived safely and spent a boring morning with my parent's friends we carpooled over to Riverfront Park and started walking the grounds, foreboding in December but full of sun on this day. The hum of the Spokane River cast a spell over me as I strode along the pathway. Serenity was my goal after riding to the park with the Rubin's and their cute five-year-old son Meyer, half my age. I pretended not to watch the kid pick his nose; which he did with desire. I thought he might hurt himself. "There, there, there, there!" he yelled when he saw the grounds. "Dad, do you think we will see some bums in the park?" The question made me chuckle. There was no reply from the front seat. I kept hoping Meyer would run into traffic or something so his parents would pay attention to him. His father, Wyman, seemed stoned out of his mind and only listened to jazz and blues in the car, a yellow Buick that smelled like diapers from 1974. Mr. Rubin just stroked his beard, a beatnik classic, all day long. Mrs. Rubin wore glasses that tint in the sun. She looked like she was heading to the beach when piling out of the car…and boy could she pile. She practically jumped out of the Buick and then stabilized with a torrent of steps, like a runaway locomotive. You can tell she was once an elegant woman, maybe a dancer or something. She probably started going to Hell when her hubby wooed her with hip jazz and moody poetry. Now she weighs about four hundred pounds and her feet are the same size. Her moves around the parking lot reminded me of the elephants in "Fantasia." When she started to topple one time pops started giggling and my mother glared at him till he got it together. "She probably would've eaten the calendar," he whispered.

The Rubin's do not believe in smiling and they walk as far away from each other as possible. They act like their son is cute and stupid, a combination they loathe. The retired dancer and amateur jazz artist still harbored plans of travel and grand performances during this visit. As dew turned to steam and plants rose, basking in the sunlight, the six of us meandered along a landscaped path. Meyer sprinted out in front, yelling, "Wow, wow, wow, wow," Mrs. Rubin shuffled along behind, creating enough friction to run a power plant. Her husband was so far back he was probably trying to ditch us.

After navigating a sharp corner a stately couple came into our view. Their walking sticks moved from side-to-side as they walked in unison with a seeing- eye dog following behind. Smiles were permanent and sun warmed both faces. Holding each other tight while wearing ragged clothes and shuffling along, they were the most content couple in Spokane, at that moment the happiest pairing on earth. The man was tall and proud. He wore a hat and his face showed off a majestic grin. He was with the woman he loved and he required no gimmick or stimulus. His right hand gently rubbed his mate's cheekbone as she twirled tied knots at the end of the sleeves at the end of her green dress. I looked to my right as we passed them and tears were streaming down my father's face. Emotional outpourings are his specialty. He is unable to handle handicaps or sadness that he does not experience himself.

"Look at the statue," said my mother while my father cried. "Is that supposed to be an Indian?" Their minds are always on different wavelengths.

My daydream ended. "I do remember something about being on call twenty-four hours a day in the telegram." Silence indicated my father made this point clear. The information was probably dispensed in a brusque manner. I imagined him standing in his underwear in a dingy room yelling, "I am on call every day and every hour, this is no joke. I work for you and your lazy son. Call me when something important goes down!" After the receiver made violent contact with the phone casing I am certain ten consecutive phrases beginning with "Jesus Christ woman," were muttered as he fell back into a deep sleep.

Cheese sandwiches stemmed the emotional avalanche for a few minutes. Spirited chewing and a persistent frown proved mom was working through the impending call in her mind. When the time arrived she softly asked my father when he would return and how much he was making. Halting speech barked from the receiver from the other end. Impatience and loose energy pushed me toward the picture window, where I glanced outside at the rotting carcass. My night was being ruined by parental nonsense.

"Wow, he really is making good money out there."

Mother's smile and affable demeanor drained my head of pressure. I was ecstatic. Her cost benefit analysis had turned up no major flaws in the Pennsylvania work plan and this development guaranteed a few days of peace. Now general Freehold family crap was the only thing top of mind.

Reading and napping followed. I feel like bum in these situations – when I sit around the house with no major chores or job to do. Since it was a Monday I felt particularly stupid with no work in sight. Pop pushes me and I hear his voice all the time. Wading through job openings in the newspaper turned up little. Nathan periodically asks whether I want to work at Big 5 but I spend enough time with him already and watching him smile and coo at Torrie during and after work would make me puke. My gift for bullshit makes me a candidate for something besides retail. I fell asleep while dreaming of running my own dog grooming business, being a farmer or working as a landscaper – the funniest one of the lot since I hate yard chores.

Powerful thrusts with a plunger in our home's lone bathroom awakened me. I don't know what my mother does in there. I was drooling on the jobs section of the paper and the stains were not blazing a trail to fascinating ads. Number one on my list was a security guard position at the University of Washington and the only other job that matched my limited qualifications was selling skateboards and snowboards to hippie kids near downtown. Both required applying in person so I made plans to take the bus south the following morning. A plan to me means one that I do not share with anybody else. I hate it when my mother gets on my shit about meeting new people or impressing a potential boss. Nathan's call at 10:00 pulled me away from some television mystery I was pretending to watch while sitting with moms.

"Hey, what's up."

"Not much. I met a few associates of yours the other night and then again today in Delridge."

"That's what I hear. Those guys are a trip."

"They mentioned something about helping them out on Wednesday." Nathan's long pause was what I expected.

"K. If you want. Do you know what they are talking about?"

"No, but they think I do."

"Shit. I knew those guys talked too much. Can you stop by the 5 tomorrow before or after work?"

"Sure I need to apply for a few jobs first…what time do you need me over there?"

"Let's see, I start at 11:00 but I am always running tight in the morning. How about after 5:00? I will just be hanging out in the video store. Stop by anytime."

Torrie giggled in the background. She sounded like she was also on the phone with the TV on in the background. Her mannerisms were part of my brain's recall system after witnessing her in class for years. Hair flips, wiggling toes in sandals, sauntering down the hall, while talking to friends, all of these images are vivid in my mind. I wonder if her parents are ever around or if she just has her own wing of the house from which to entertain Nathan.

"You there?"

"Yeah, I will see you tomorrow."

"Can we just meet at Shartel's?" I knew he would change his mind eventually.

"Okay, I will be there."

"Night."

I think I said "yep" as we simultaneously hung up. I knew Nathan wanted to have a heavy conversation because Shartel's is a restaurant and he probably wanted to sit down for a while – his idea of a business meeting. My mind wandered to Torrie again. After pacing for a while I considered catching a bus to the Central District to spy on them. The concept sounded ludicrous and a waste of time but all other options were weaker. Reading the paper, watching replays of "George Michael's Sports Machine" with my sleep deprived mother or walking back to the skating rink or the bowling alley sounded awful. Nobody was across the street to monitor. Earlier in the day the Road Pig's friends, all bikers wearing leather and jackets, bandanas and heavy leather pants or jeans, held a formal ceremony for the fly-drawing bones and flesh stuck to the fence. As the Road Pig sobbed two acquaintances scrubbed the fence with wire brushes and a hose. The Pig eventually went inside with the other two before they finished – he was a wreck. These boys were menacing. I doubt the smallest of the group weighs less than 250 pounds after breakfast. Their grunts and solemn, deep-voiced commentary included bibles. When everybody convened a second time in the yard, the group of five drank beer and ate hot dogs, keeping a massive red cooler with wheels nearby. Smoke from a backyard grill filled the air and I watched the Road Pig wipe away tears. The Olson's were not in my line of sight – they were not even peering out the window.

My curiosity peaked before my nap when I heard shovels and a pick removing debris and slicing through soil. I figured something new was happening. The Pig is not a gardener, and the body of the dog was laying on the yard when I returned home so I guessed accurately. All five men took turns upturning dirt and placing it in small individual piles. Their tight circle provided just enough space for the swing of the shovel. As they worked there was silence, as the former yard patroller's bones lay carefully wrapped in a red blanket. I was fascinated that the proclamation of death earlier was followed by a social ceremony. When the hole was deemed ready for her prey, the Road Pig gently cradled his furry friend, both arms underneath the blanket, carefully spread so the outer points of the animal were hoisted by meaty hands. He wore a serene expression as he awkwardly bent over and dropped to his knees. His upper torso disappeared into the hole as his ass rose higher and two of the men positioned themselves to catch him in case he could not contain his girth and an embarrassing tumble followed. After saluting his comrade, the Pig sat down and hoisted a beer from the cooler, an old Olympia he had saved for special occasions. Tears followed, streaming under rectangular goggle-like sunglasses. His face glistened in the sunlight and he wiped away moisture every fifteen or twenty seconds. He looked peaceful with his friends. Clearly, he did not want the day to end. No replacement puppy was in sight, sadness ruled the hour.

As a partial sun, shrouded by Seattle gray, bronzed and slung low on the horizon; struggled to overwhelm lingering clouds, hot dogs and hamburgers came off the grill. S'mores with melting marshmallows blackened with long steel rods, fastened together by a welder or someone who makes things that last, followed. Nobody cleaned their instrument; they just burned the excess and kept placing virgin marshmallows. One lone guy in the corner wearing a Dallas Cowboys sweatshirt chewed tobacco and made jokes about the perished dog's gas. I suspect he suffers from a similar condition since everybody kept their distance. I listened to their banter, placing my ear next to the glass, watching from the picture window. Their episodic journey into night left me dreaming of the Olympic Peninsula and a fishing hole on the Humptulips River my father cherishes. My day wasn't as sad as the Pig's, but it was bad. Boredom and daydreams about spending time with someone fun occupied all thoughts.

I never sleep on the dusty couch in our living room – it creeps me out imagining my mother staring at me as I stir. When I awakened at 4:45 in the morning I promised myself that I would get out to the county soon, even if the journey required hitchhiking. After rummaging around for change in the bottom of my drawers and backpack I had enough for the bus. I showered and cleaned up for my big day of job hunting. The early bus took me downtown, near the waterfront, where I entered the ferry terminal and scoured want ads in abandoned newspapers. Retailers were the primary targets so walking around in the rain was necessary to view help wanted signs. My best lead was in a shoe store near Pioneer Square. I lied and pretended that Nathan's experience was my own. I even used him as a reference for my fine work at Big-5. He can pull it off if someone calls him directly and asks if I am a model employee. I gambled that nobody would follow-up before I met Nathan in the afternoon and I didn't really care anyway.

The dude who asked me all the questions was particularly focused on whether I owned blue or tan slacks – the required uniform at Jimmy's Shoes. His big focus was running shoes so I fed him bullshit about me being a member of the cross-country squad at school, an organization I joined for four days. I am no runner but he spent his time sitting in a corner combing his hair and preening in the full-length mirrors all over the store. I figured he was not even paying attention – which gave me even more confidence to keep bullshitting. He kept asking me questions as he walked around the store placing shoeboxes and t-shirts. He was incredibly fascinated with his own ass – always looking backward to check himself out as he turned in front of any reflection device, a little sunglass display with small mirrors, a blackened office window or an empty coffee pot. His name is Brian Lamb and his pants are about two sizes too small. I don't know how he walks at all. His long black hair is shiny and parted in the middle and he wears referee tops with sleeves turned up to show off his arms at work – what a nipple. Lamb is shorter than me and he contorted his body at an angle when glancing in my direction; like a giant lizard. His diagonal looks were really weird. But he seemed interested and said the store had 30-35 hours a week available. In a strange fit of confidence I announced, "Well I am your man," shook his hand and bounded outside to search for another sign, bus or free paper.

Before heading toward the meeting site in White Center I walked along First Avenue South, poking around warehouses - places where real work was taking place - the type of stuff that would make my father proud: forklifts, lumber and backbreaking work for young men. Unfortunately, fat middle-aged dudes were the real employees in these districts, even during summer time; probably union work. I randomly walked into four places inquiring about opportunities and nobody was hiring. One guy even asked me if I mowed lawns and I was interested until I discovered he lived north of the city in Mountlake Terrace. People must be making good money moving parts around a warehouse if they are paying losers like me to mow their lawns.

When the gray outline of the fading neon Shartel's sign came into view Torrie's car was parked beneath. Nathan is never early and I was fifteen minutes ahead of schedule. I prayed that Torrie was not inside. My body odor was appalling and I smelled like an old bus. More precisely, an old sock in a dust-filled corner beneath one of the bus seats. When I pulled the large fake bronze rectangular handle on the front door of the restaurant I noticed a fidgety Nathan sitting in the corner glancing out the window. I ignored the hostess chatting with her co- worker and skipped over to the table, pleased as hell that Torrie was not in attendance. My smile gave me away.

"What are you so pumped up about?"

"Just excited to be off the bus."

Nathan wore a white polo shirt and tan slacks. I imagined Torrie ironing his clothes and removing stains by hand – working her hands to the bone so Mr. Smooth could look like a tennis pro. My bitter observations subsided as Nathan's long face indicated fear – an emotion he never portrays. He leaned forward and almost whispered.

"Ramos, those guys you met the other day are part of an operation I set up that I am not proud of…but it has provided me with some serious cash." There was little color in his face and his stare bore into my eyes. I wondered why he didn't pay off Foster and then it dawned on me that he would have to explain to his mother why he was handling so much cash.

"What can I get you two?"

"I think I need a minute."

"Can I have another iced tea?"

"Sure, I will check in with you shortly."

"Order up Ramos, I have some cash. In fact, we can pay Foster back as well…I just don't know how to do that without making my mother suspicious." I almost fell out of the booth. Nathan never pays for things. In fact, he owes me so much pocket change from past borrowings that I could probably pay for a year of college if he ever gave me the money back. For the past two summers I worked for this funny little guy named Timmy Nelson, picking up pallets all over the city and recycling them – or at least selling the used and discarded versions. Actually, I picked them up and brought them to Nelson, who did the rest. It was good money and I had my own beat-up truck to drive. I even think my father was impressed. Unfortunately, Nelson lost his primary customer, some Boeing division, so he is out of the pallet business this year.

"Let's move forward with our current plan for your mom. I agree, there is no need to freak her out and she would never believe that either of us picked up quick cash."

I paused and combed through menu items while waiting for Nathan to continue. He took forever so I picked up the conversation again. "Plus, I kind of think that Foster dude likes me, not like I am the son he never had or something, but he seems to like the fact that I, or I mean we, had the balls to come down and see him in person." Nathan wore a confident smirk, his mouth tilted to the left and he ever so slightly moved his head in that direction. "Our plan was so weak and silly I am sure we appeared more professional than we really are." I was pleased my running commentary finally triggered activity on the other side of the table and I wondered if he was parroting his mother's thoughts.

"So, those guys are close with Leo Romar and his brother, Erik, who both work security at Nordstrom's." He leaned forward, talking softly.

"Yeah, I don't follow."

"Those guys sit in a little box downtown and watch security cameras. They have been there for a few years and each camera covers certain parts of the store. If they see something, they walkie-talkie down to the guys on the ground, just like that crap you see in the movies when they show security in Las Vegas or Washington D.C."

"Have you two decided yet?"

"Ah…yeah, I would like that turkey melt you have on the menu. Ramos?" Nathan raised his eyebrows and unleashed a big smile in the direction of the waitress, who, like most service industry veterans, paid no attention to his warm gesture.

"Just two eggs over easy is perfect for me."

"Any meat?"

"Ham please."

She had hardly moved out of earshot when Nathan continued his dialogue, more comfortable with his presentation by the minute.

"Anyway, these guys act as drivers for a couple of women I found who go into the store and take clothes."

"Which guys?"

"The guys you just met." I was getting a little confused, but I shut up and listened.

"When the Romar's tip them off about when they will be working and which one of their co-workers has a break or lunch hour, or if they work together on the same shift they tell Tony and Zip."

He took a long pause and gulped down some ice water. "The clothes go out, nobody is alerted and they return them at other stores, unused, a week or two later. Nordstrom is very focused on letting customers get their way."

"I hope you guys have some older people returning the clothes; folks that don't look suspicious."

"Ahh…that is a good idea, we do need to work on that part of the plan."

"Zip?"

"Yeah, he is the shorter, beefy dude."

"That cannot be his real name."

"Probably not…but I don't really want to know his real name. These guys do not talk and I like it that way. They were impressed with the way you kept your mouth shut the other night, and since you are a friend of mine they hatched a plan for you to help us if you are interested."

"Weird. I still do not know how those guys even know who I am."

"They do go to Sealth Ramos." Nathan's broad grin broke into a prolonged chuckle as our food arrived. As he asked for a pepper shaker I sat back and wondered what on earth I was doing with my life. Hanging out with shoplifters sounded like a bad idea.

"Jesus, I don't remember seeing those guys at all…at school, I mean."

"You probably didn't see them." He was chewing quickly now, like a hungry wolf. "They probably were getting baked in the back of the school most of the time."

"Anyway, if you are into it, we need a person to shop near the girls and be a distraction for the workers on the floor – you know - ask questions and pull them away from their little areas." Since I have played a similar role for Nathan for years, I instantly knew this was *his plan* and had nothing to do with his two henchmen. He had probably outlined how I could assist on several occasions. Suddenly, I was concerned about *his* big mouth.

"Who else knows about this stuff?"

"Only the people involved."

"Any of our friends?"

"Nope."

"Torrie?"

"Are you crazy man? I am not that stupid. People talk."

I gave him a really serious look, trying to study his expressions as he took another bite of his food. I have no idea if he is telling the truth most of the time. "How well do know these guys?"

"They know what would come down if they screwed up. Plus, I am not really doing anything…or at least I am not directly implicated, or doing the deed."

Nathan paused because he knew that even though he was the mastermind, chief strategist and moneyman, I would figure out that my neck was more on the line than his. For the first time I was impressed with his maturity. He had finally realized he could no longer talk his way out of everything as he wormed into adult world. It dawned on me that he felt, as he proved with Foster and his eviction crisis, that I was better equipped to bullshit authority figures. Or at least I persuaded myself that this was the case so I would not be upset about serving as the gullible helper. Laney's comments helped as well. Maybe Nathan picked up his persuasion skills from her.

"We could really use your help. With you we would have all the elements in place, no more hoping that everybody clears out at the same time."

"How many times has your operation been in play?"

"Thirteen."

"Jesus."

"About twenty-eight thousand dollars. With you, profit will be higher. We, or they, are not grabbing the right stuff." I wondered who was doing the grabbing. He hushed up as the food arrived and remained serious as I worked through my eggs. I could tell he wanted to talk some more so I ate quickly. Nathan leaned down with clasped hands on the table, his sandwich unfinished, staring. I was almost done, nervously eating, anxiety flowing through my fingertips with a stiff posture like I used in typing class.

"Do you have any benefit plans?"

"No, but you can make more money, or at least as much as a great part-time job, without all the hours."

"Fuck it, let's do it." I took another bite of my eggs. Nathan picked up a lingering french fry with a big smile on his face.

When the waitress stopped by to fill water cups, I tried to be nonchalant and say thank you very seriously. No change in her expression, nothing, just a bored look and no response.

"Thank you," Nathan imitated my deep-voice serious tone and I giggled. "Are you running for mayor or something?"

"No, I just got a job in security."

We both laughed and began discussing Major League Baseball and Nathan's favorite recent customers at Big Five, including some guy who came in to ask for spray paint and shoe polish in his clown outfit. Apparently, he wanted to spruce up his red shoes before a kids party. They didn't have any spray paint and whenever the clown bent over Nathan pretended to dry hump him, which amused his co-workers.

"He looked like a giant yellow banana. Man can you imagine wearing make-up and acting like a clown all day?"

"It's a job."

"A shitty one."

"At least you can work for yourself."

Nathan rubbed his right hand over his face and then unmasked himself with another relaxed smile, his sandwich conquered. "Man that would be a trip." As our conversation waned, a plan was hatched for the following morning that included me riding with my Skate World buddies and being dropped off a few blocks away from the mall. I was expected to walk in like a character from the movie Jackie Brown and serve as an innocent bystander when my co-conspirators reached their destination. My only silent request was that the girls were cute so my job would provide enough intrigue that I could get my mind off Torrie for a few minutes during my "shopping" sessions. Nathan was confirming everything over the phone when I left the restaurant and started home. We agreed less group communication was best for this task.

10

Underwear

At 9:45 the next morning Zip and Tony, or Tony and Zip as they like to be called, picked me up at a gas station on Delridge. "We're heading over to Bellevue. Did you talk to Nathan? Everything okay?" Zip was doing all the talking.

"Oh yeah." I instinctively leaned forward and sat in the middle of the back seat framing my navigators visually. Trying to look confident and undeterred by the mission, I casually leaned back in the sun-damaged backseat and spread my arms across a worn blue cover smelling of fresh and ancient cigarettes. The stench induced a cough. I am a real wimp considering I'm a smoker myself.

Then to add some intensity I busted out, "This will happen."

"Rockin! That is what we need to hear." Zip wore sunglasses and a little flat gangster hat. A red bandana tied fat in the back was under his dome cover and he nodded to rap music with some heavy bass. Anthony just looked serious as usual. He wasn't wearing any caps or headbands, just some old-school sunglass, fake brass sides with mirrored lenses.

"Let's do *this* motherfuckers! Whooo. Ain't no stopping us now." Zip turned to me and raised his bushy brown eyebrows. "I like that cash." He looked insane but I had total confidence in him for this operation.

After making our way across Lake Washington we pulled into the driveway of a 1950s ranch home with a big yard on 95th street, close to Bellevue Square Mall. "Bitch has a sweet pad," proclaimed Zip. "Or her parents do," muttered Anthony. I wasn't that impressed, but I guess if you get excited when you live five blocks from the mall – it would be a great place to be. Malls bother me because once I get inside, they feel like prisons. I have to walk past a bunch of bullshit that I don't want to see or buy. The garage door was open; the pungent smell of weed filled the air as we exited our thief caddy. Smoke rose around old wooden furniture, the garage was used for storage rather than cars; three silhouettes were smoking and chatting. Two of the forms were skinny with weak stick-like bodies, like shadows in some comic- book drawing. The middle one, flanked by the weightless wonders, stood upright and sturdy, her curves showing in the light.

"Nobody better grab any underwear, that ain't worth shit."

I knew the voice, it was Jen and I was speechless. That shithead Nathan knew all along Torrie knew and now I looked like a big loser to T and her mouthy best friend… in fact it was worse, I was the little clean-up guy, Jen was the big bad expert, and Nate was the Kingmaker. Even Zip and Tony were operational guys – drivers. I calmed down by telling myself that I was the best of the bunch at speaking to adults and sounding believable, but I was still pissed off.

"Perhaps you can shove some stuff down your shirt."

As Tony laughed at his joke Jen slapped his left arm. "Hey," she said, making eye contact with me. No smile, just a flat line.

I moved my right hand at an angle and sent a small   wave her way while forcing a pained expression meant to be a smile. Blood rushed to my face and the dusty exterior was a welcome venue. I prayed the poor lighting and shadows would mask the blush taking over my cheeks. My lips were narrow and parsed as I tried deep breathing to calm down.

"Grab light dresses that you can stuff in here and pretend to forget," she said as she opened a large purse with an inside compartment. After five minutes of discussion and ten minutes of criticism, analysis and questions, we moved toward our cars with explicit instructions to only contact each other in an emergency. It was reiterated to all of us by Jen, Zip and Tony that there was to be no discussion about any of this to strangers and then they talked about the importance of showing up in incremental waves of time, instead of all at once. We had too many leaders and not enough soldiers, but all business seems to work that way. I rode with the boys, who were instructed to drop me off a few blocks from the target near the entrance of the Boys and Girls Club. They were then expected to maneuver into their getaway position at an outdoor corner in the far northwest parking lot at Bellevue Square, the mall housing our special "store."

My task was to walk as conspicuously as possible into the mall, then Nordstrom's and reach the designated shopping zone in precisely thirty minutes. The job was not complicated but everybody was predictably nervous about my first foray into the program. "How ya doin' brother?" Even Anthony was trying to prop me up in   his raspy voice. "We really need your help. We *really* need your help. Standing out is *key* in this line of work." Both boys looked me over up and down from the front seat. My head was spinning and they were even weirder looking than normal…I kept imaging their voices getting higher and the shapes of their heads changing. As that phrase hit me, "line of work," I realized these guys took this "operation" more seriously than anything else they did in life. "We had a few co-shoppers before but they always pussed out," said Zip.

"We'll be okay." I felt cocky.

As I slowly lifted out of the car a calm pall came over me. It was a weird feeling, a personal moment of truth. Thieving is not my thing but being the getaway watcher –

man I have been doing that for years. Hidden talents rose to the surface of my personality. Even stupid professions require specialization. The faces of my associates in the car flashed in my mind. A distant horn finally woke me from my daytime glaze and I picked up my pace and ceased strutting and sauntering. Heartbeats thumped louder. As I fired up a cigarette and crossed traffic-less 100th NE Street wearing white slacks, dark brown work shoes and a blue sweater – I transformed into a dude with a light-hearted, don't-give-a-shit attitude. You have to think that way when you are involved in something stupid. A white dress shirt, three-years-old, a little frayed at the edges, poked through the sunken blue collar. I forced myself not to itch and pat my skin because it felt like heavy starch laundry was spreading some disease taking over my body. I have only worn a tie once in my life – to a funeral for our neighbor, Mrs. Nester, and I still remember how much that sucked. Sweating and tugging at my shirt while every family member talked about ol' Nester, who was a nice woman, I felt like I was melting. At least the mall had air conditioning so a big wet patch wouldn't spread across my back. I could feel the top of my dress shirt darkening with moisture. I am pretty good at being conspicuous, but it is embarrassing when you are noticed because you are a slob.

After conducting my normal routine of walking through bushes and jumping over little fake brick walls around the premises I caught myself, slipped back into task mode and backed out to the sidewalk. Hands dropped to pockets, I nervously patted my hair down, glanced at my brown loafers and slacks, and took a deep breath. Muttering to myself was comforting. "You are not the key here, just do your job…you are only a distraction, do not make it more than it is. Hang in there baby."

Instead of trying to blend in, I nervously glanced down hallways as people strolled out of the mall entrance between high glass doors, centered with metal handles, overwhelmed by a white facade surrounding the structure. After walking the equivalent of a few blocks I settled into a confident rhythm – for the first time in my life I felt like a shopper, someone with a purposeful understanding of malls. Of course, this was a role anyone could play.   As the hallway curved left the stately Nordstrom sign at the end of the massive corridor shone above. The store filled three levels, my destination was the bottom floor. I weaved across waves of hapless teens pretending to shop and bounced onto the escalator, still confident and now preening in a window showing curves and contours on my reflection, making me look older in my grown- up attire. A smile came across my face when I realized that my dress-up for the mall mission was better planned than my pursuit of employment. That is always my way – intrigue and excitement trumps priorities.

The opening for Nordstrom's bottom floor is a massive cut-out with angled wood on the sides at the top of the walkway, an attractive, symmetrical view. Coffee stand denizens and small café tables, covered in dark green tablecloths and white decorations, dominate the right corridor. Female suits, in dark blue, white and yellow carefully placed in round, silver and gold clothing racks – a group of woman sailors could invade after taking their morning coffee. Whistling and avoiding eye contact, I continued setting a brisk pace while heading to the men's section to waste time. After spotting my ultimate destination I zipped back into the hallway and located a teen store with video screens blaring music out of speakers under a giant pink digital clock. I had fifteen more minutes to kill and everybody in Nordstrom's was serious-looking, a bunch of old women really checking things out. It made me think people looking for clothes would tattle on us.

In the teen shop a bunch of Disney dance girls, smoke machines and thumping music dominated the screens. Looking at silly videos reduced pressure in my head. My throat was dry and I kept rubbing my neck with a stupid, pained expression on my face, Al Bundy style. The people working in the store wore black- and red- hooded sweatshirts and colored their hair. A bunch of Eastside princesses trying to look tough.

As the clock showed six minutes to go I sauntered toward the escalator bed, slowly walking - pushing my chin up – confident, yet slow and stupid looking, in a trance. If someone was watching me and knew what I was up to, they would think I am a shitty actor. After reaching the second floor, which houses men's dress clothes and women's special items, whatever the hell that means, more time was wasted walking in a circle around a few displays. Finally, the escalator pulled me up to the key floor. No security guards or random employees were in my sightline. Only workers attending to cash registers or moving and folding clothes in little corners were visible. The entire area was pretty vacant, and everybody moved at the same speed, even old ladies trying on dresses and blouses with their eyes were in rhythm, moving to a specific tune. Dainty piano music drifted up open corridors from the first floor – a Nordstrom delicacy – live piano during shopping timeslots so the old bags can feel like it is 1947 all over again.

Members of my posse flashed in the corner of my eye, two girls making lots of noise and giggling about clothes that looked terrible when held up to their figures. I purposely turned the other way. They were impressive, these young thieves. They sounded like festive girls having fun. Directly ahead of me was the closest worker on site so I made a beeline toward her station, where she was reviewing something on a screen.

"Can I help you find something?" she asked without making eye contact. This talent freaked me out because of the floor show taking place down a few aisles.

"Ahh, yes, this is kind of embarrassing…but I need to buy some underwear for a relative that is visiting – my mother sent me over with some money. I have her, actually it is my grandmother, size written down here." I pretended to look at a piece of paper and then just gave her my mother's size, large, since that is what I notice when I see her tags in the laundry at home.

A big smile and movement around the counter followed.

"I can get you set up, just follow me."

Which I did, watching for head tilts or any other indicators that this attractive middle-aged woman with dark bouncy hair and high cheekbones was paying attention to nearby customers. Before she left me alone questions about price, color options and return policies were asked to waste time. Amused more than exasperated, she finally just grabbed some items and put them in a stack for me.

"These should do fine."

I followed like a puppy back to her station and watched her fold and carefully place tissue paper between the red and tan pairs of panties for my fake grandmother. I was only able to afford four pairs and when facing the escalator there was no sign of the noisy ghouls from the garage. No timeframe was given, a Bellevue bus was my ticket back to the other side of Lake Washington and absolutely no contact with my fellow conspirators occurred so I milled about the mall carrying a bag of women's underwear.

A trip to Orange Julius and loitering in the bookstore, where they took my application for employment and showed no interest in me whatsoever, followed. The red-haired manager grabbed my paper with his pointer finger and left thumb and reacted like the form was covered in plutonium waste. To pay him back I spent more time in the magazine section reading everything and buying nothing. Then I walked around the mall playing a game I call 'find the biggest ass.' It was competitive. At least three vied for the title until on the second floor a woman with long black hair and a delightful chuckle shut down the other contenders. She walked between two friends and clapped, laughed and jiggled every time one of them mumbled something. I realize this is a mean game and probably unfit for someone over the age of eleven…but what else should one do in a mall?

By the time I reached the bus depot on the other side of downtown Bellevue the great strategist was calling. "Did things work out?"

"Everything was smooth on my end. Did anything go wrong?"

"Nah, I think everything went very much right – great job J. Pay day is in a week or two but everybody is asking if you can do this again?"

"Sure, I have nothing better to do." My comment derived a chuckle.

"Well, you are perfect for the job so we'll keep feeding you opportunities and keep our fingers crossed." He sounded like a camp counselor trying to boost my ego.

As usual, I felt like Nathan was somehow directing and planning my life. Even though he is younger than me, he feels like a dumb, yet clever, older brother sometimes. We finished our banter with some basic commentary about sports and mall girls – Nathan was pleased with the reports from my ass contest – and I jumped on the 71 bus and headed back to base, feeling like something was accomplished that day.

Twenty minutes later as the big rig merged onto Interstate-90, a knot in my stomach, forlorn gazing out the window and women's underwear in my hands incited soul-searching. Why did stealing provide such a high. "Going nowhere," I mouthed out the window to nobody in particular, a message designed for me. Seattle rain sprinkled through blades of sunlight, succumbing to a changing skyline, adding context to sad thoughts.

Fifteen minutes later the sun woke me as the bus turned toward the Seattle Tunnel. The bag with the underwear was wet, soaked by my drool while serving a dual purpose as a germ brace from the window and a pillow. I matted down my hair again with both hands and bounded for the aisle seeking shelter on another bus.

11

THE FOSTER'S

Thursday brought horrible weather, dark skies and wind; the later a rare occurrence during Seattle summers. After four unsuccessful calls to Nathan, I never expected to see him at the Foster ranch, but I persevered, keeping our deal intact. "Shit," I whispered when the designated clean up zone fell into my sights. The landlord's home sat on a sloping hill with tons of foliage, and a killer view of Lake Washington. The old three-story monster in the Madrona district was old and elegant and you knew the cheap bastard had never paid a gardener or a helper of any kind to do any work. I imagined years of favors playing out in the backyard. Everything was so overgrown that the neighbors were hidden from view.

Foster was probably in the can or something when I arrived because his wife answered the door with a big fake smile. Her teeth glistened and her frosted blonde hair made her look like she was trying to be seventeen again. Her short attractive figure was a compliment to the lumbering fellow with the big red nose she shared a bed with. Grunting from some far away nook was audible, "Cybil, have you seen the paper?"

"One moment please. It's on the kitchen table." I was certain that if a guest was not in the house she would have yelled at him to get his own paper. She had that look about her – a sharp tone when answering his yell. "Now then, are you Nathan?"

"No, actually, I am John Ramos, a friend of the family."

"Right, you are the young man who met with Jim, correct?" She spoke quickly, unlike most Seattleites, but she favored the flat elongated vowel patterns of the Northwest.

"Yes, ma'am." My response surprised me. I sounded like a servant. Upon reflection, I realized I was performing for two masters, Nathan and Foster the landlord. While contemplating my predicament and staring out the window Mrs. Foster claimed my attention.

"Follow me John," she said while walking toward another part of the house.

This was an easy task as the bubbly Cybil led me through an entryway glistening with polished wood flooring and high ceilings. A large sweeping banister leading to narrow stairs, a design from another era, on the left, the living room, which appeared unused since about 1987, sat in perfect order, last week's vacuum lines circling over the top of the previous week's design. Mrs. Foster swished back-and-forth and swung her arms as we headed toward a heavy door leading into the family meeting zone, the kitchen. Mr. Foster sat reading the sports page, wearing an ugly gray sweatshirt and paint-stained green slacks. The white marks looked like someone tried to emulate the camouflaged markings you see on fatigues. The interior of the house was clearly Lady Foster's domain. Her husband's oversight of the outdoors fell far below her standards.

"Hey there, would you like some coffee?"

Mr. Foster rose to his feet as he asked the question, overturning a fork on a plate full of muffin crumbs. After picking up the object and pretending to pick up some debris on the kitchen floor in front of his frowning wife, he was upright again.

"No thanks, once I get my blood flowing, I usually can stay awake."

"Ah youth, I wish I had some today. Well mommy, ahhh, let's see…we are going to go in the back."

"You mean John."

"Yes, John is going to join me in the backyard, in fact, we'll pick up some gloves in the garage and then we will get started. Is anybody from the unit showing up?"

"Yes sir."

"Well I hope so. You should not be on the hook for all of their promises."

Mrs. Foster was already cleaning up her husband's microscopic mess, a small brush in one hand and a little dust pan in the other. Her floral yellow patterned dress eased into place around her bending form, like an image from one of those mothers on *Leave it to Beaver*.

"I will bring out some snacks a little later." Mrs. Foster spoke without looking up.

"Marvelous." Foster's return volley was spoken while turned in the other direction.

I instinctively followed big F toward a hallway leading to the garage, which sat on the other side of the house along a side driveway, perhaps once a carriage house for real servants. White, dirtied, gloves were selected by Foster for his big, fat hands and he opened a new pair for me. He seemed proud of himself for finding this item in the bowels of his workbench. He is the type of guy that doesn't swear when he can't locate something, but he grunts a lot so you know he is getting the red-ass.

By the time we made our way outside Foster looked like he needed a breather. He leaned against his big wooden house and contemplated what to do next. "Ah-hmm, yeah." Eventually, he settled on weeding near some rocks at the crest of the hill in his backyard. I guess he decided it was time to actually *see* the view of Lake Washington. He asked me if I minded using a machete or some clippers to slice up some brush. I answered "yes," quickly before his wife got wind of the operation in back and starting worrying about liability or some other bullshit. The worst thing about helping slow moving people with their tasks is being forced to work at their pace or having to wait for them to putter around while you want to get moving. I confidently grabbed a machete and started hacking some blackberry bushes that were swallowing the yard, a little walkway and a bunch of rocks and old bark dust. Swift, controlled swings released aggression and eased my mind. Frustration with Nathan for blowing off the work event subsided as I focused on the task.

After picking up fallow limbs, sticks and dead green stuff, I placed the materials in a compost pile near the base of a deck off the kitchen covered by muck and mud at its concrete feet. I smiled when imagining what my father would say about a compost pile. "You mean some dumb motherfucker is piling up stuff so it rots and worms eat it? I'll show him a place where he can play with some compost…" I jammed the rest of the debris into some garbage bags. As I began loading my fifth bag I looked up to a horrific site: Foster bending over and showing so much butt-crack that a small child could get lost in there; a surprising sight because his jeans appeared to fit. Bending over rendered his belt useless or the moisture pulled his faded jeans to their breaking point.

I could not stop chuckling but a ruckus on the deck diverted my gaze. "Hi John."

"Hi."

Nathan's mother had arrived to lend support and I picked up that she was charming Mrs. Foster with tales of raising two boys. Mrs. F is one of those people who appear really surprised when you tell her something obvious. Her face moves all over the place so you do not know if she just finds you amusing or actually gives a damn about what you are talking about. Laney was nursing a cup of tea so I knew they had bonded. She wore jeans, a red sweatshirt and a blue and white bandana. She was either ready to do some hard labor or pose for an Uncle Sam poster.

"John, where is my son?" Laney's furrowed brow conveyed frustration.

"He-he-he, I'm not sure." I smiled and continued working – like a good boy. Nervous laughter indicated this was not a subject I wanted to tackle.

By this time even Butt-Crack awakened from his slumber, tripped over a limb yelled, "Ahhh," and said, "Well hello," as he wobbled to a set position. "Are you here to give us a hand?"

"Yes, and I really appreciate you allowing us to work for you."

"Quite alright. As you can see, this property needs all the help it can get."

"I am going to begin putting together some lunch Jim. Were you thinking sandwiches?"

"That sounds great Mommy. A pickle please."

When the door shut work beckoned. Fortunately, Laney was directed to work in my territory so we kibitzed while whacking down brush and pulling weeds. Foster continued to give his crack some air and the glow of an actual orb surfaced in the distant sky, filtering tiny droplets and moisture still hanging in the dense, heavy air. Steam from our breath dissipated and warm air erased morning chill. Drying plants and trees shrouded the area in a mystical state like a trail with no end in sight. This metaphor dominated daydreams as I moved like a robot cutting, pushing down, gathering, grabbing and placing. Little piles reminiscent of field mines scattered about, evidence of work, or at least progress, in all directions. After a while Nathan's mother rescued me by picking up the muck and forcing me to move away from my secure semi-circle.

"I hope you are working up an appetite, cause this woman doesn't cook. I think our lunch is being catered."

"What?"

"They are ordering lunch for us, even as we work off a debt." Each word was lower in volume as Ms. Sweet kept our conversation confidential. Sound was emanating from the corner of her mouth and she only glanced my way during pauses in the sweeping motion of her heavy rake. Forearm muscles bulged, and when Laney pulled her shirtsleeves up to elbow level her limbs were larger than anything on her fat-free body, like a Popeye cartoon.

"What is Chester up to today?"

"He is spending time with Senal today. He likes to run around their yard, chase their dog and jump on their trampoline." After a long pause, "Kind of sounds fun doesn't it?"

"More fun then this?" It was my turn to whisper.

Distant chatter drew Laney's head skyward, away from the rake. She sidled up to the side of the house and peeked around the edge of the deck's basin toward the front of the home, along one edge of the primary driveway. The castle's slope and hillside provided a perfect vista for peering between branches and spying on a mailman or hidden lovers. If Foster wasn't so cheap and he hired a gardener the spot would be even better for spying because overgrown bushes blocked other portions of the property. Windows in the kitchen and master bedroom peeked out in the other direction. Foster was off on another side of the house, stumbling around, making enough noise to raise the dead, so Laney knew we could take a break. When she made eye contact with me she was shaking her head, furrowing her brow and a 'Are you kidding me?' expression came across her face. Her right pointer finger beckoned me to join her. As she turned again toward the driveway I focused on personal hygiene, checking my pits and wiping at the cold, caked sweat on my face. Lifting my shirt kicked off the dust and dirt and a little shake left stains but removed loose particles.

As I peered over Ms. Sweet's left shoulder she smiled the most sarcastic of smiles and motioned with her left hand like she was presenting somebody from afar. I viewed Nathan, poorly dressed for yard work, in a white oxford shirt. He looked like a fan attending a high school chess tournament. Grey slacks and shiny black shoes completed his outfit. I knew instantly that he dressed this way on purpose to get out of work. Potential excuses filled my mind. He was chatting up Foster's daughter, who was washing a car and smiling and laughing at Nathan's banter...she was watering the driveway while listening to the young prince. Turning to my left and noticing Laney's facial combination of frustration and embarrassment made me wonder how silent and observant she has been over the years. Fooling her is impossible, yet she is not demonstrative. Long talks and philosophical questions are her ideas of a lecture or lesson so you never really know what is going in inside her head. And she would never embarrass her son in public.

Memories of past Nathan antics filled my mind. The time he was wasted, fueled by vodka running around our high school field half naked, trying to tackle homophobic Randy Adkins. Or a ninth grade dance that began with Wanda Linette on his arm and ended with him making out with vivacious Simone Fatima. My personal favorite is the Food and Culture class he disrupted with Ex-lax in a batch of brownies baked by some geeks in the corner. Mrs. Rubens is still searching for the culprit.

Instead of watching their daughter in action, the Foster's grooved to their own beat. When the catering truck pulled up, Cybil opened the kitchen window and her little radio played, "Brandy, you're a fine girl," by the *Looking Glass*. "Turn it up babe," bellowed Jim on the other side of the house. Sheer intrigue drew me around the pillars and   to the other edge of the deck where Foster's butt was shimmying to the music. He twisted side to side, elbows out, knees bent. Lyrics flowed as his left cheek spastically moved upward, followed by a short burst from the right. A nearby branch served as a microphone. Smooth guy this Foster. *"He came on a summer's day, bringin' gifts from far away, but he made it clear that he couldn't stay, no harbor was his home."* Foster took a deep breath as he geared up for the chorus. *"The sailors say, "Brandy, you're a fine girl, what a good wife you would be… Yeah your eyes could steal a sailor from the sea."* Man, I wanted a video camera so bad at that moment.

The beguiling butt cheeks were drawing me in, I started laughing and moving a little myself, at hip level. "Oh lord," said Laney as she stepped around and peaked at the sweat-infested Foster dreaming of stage and stardom. "Jim, lunch is here." Us groupies scrambled back to our posts as the concert ended. Foster pulled up his pants with both hands, slowly turning toward the garage and the secure confines of a bathroom. He probably sang to himself in the mirror. Since he was acting like we did not exist we kept working until the Mrs. came out and started hollering again, telling us we could use the bathroom in the garage to wash up. "Just in time for lunch," Laney said with a smirk when we reached the beginning of the stone pathway and Nathan and Lacey came toward us on the north side of the house.

Nathan flashed a smile and laughed softly, Lacey Foster, tall and cheerful, followed behind as if Nate lived in the house and she was the guest. Laney moved quickly to introduce herself to her landlord's daughter. "Hello, I am Laney Sweet, Nathan's mother."

"Pleased to meet you Mrs. Sweet," responded Lacey, her confident demeanor indicated proper grooming and habits picked up from her maternal side – she did not suffer from the unfortunate habit of grunting that dominated conversation with her father. Laney did not correct her and say "Ms.", like she would with most people. There was no need to hear, "I am so sorry," or "I apologize." Young Foster was trying to make an impression and she was way ahead of most young women anyway. She required no assistance with manners. Long golden brown hair was brushed back by her left hand as she extended her right hand for shaking. Long legs supported a jean- skirt, high socks, matching sneakers and a glistening white top covered by a charcoal preppy sweater. Nathan was surprisingly close to his new friend - what a vulture that guy is sometimes.

Laney was courteous and introduced me as well, the preppy even smiled. Her face was really shiny. It was obvious she slept deep into the morning, groomed for a while, brushed her hair and took a shower, the normal routine for a young princess. Her telling glances and body language near Nathan made it clear her next move would be to make her parents uncomfortable by fawning over the cute young visitor pretending to work at their house. On the pathway Nate gave me a little shoulder squeeze and a wink. "Man, I really appreciate everything you are doing for my family J."

"No problem. We were concerned you might not show up."

"Yeah, sorry about that, I will explain later. Hey, what are you doing next Thursday?" The question indicated there was more work on the horizon. I was certain it was related to my strong performance at Bellevue Square.

"No plans currently."

"If you can help me out during the middle of the day I would really appreciate it."

"Let's work it up later."

As we filed in to 'wash up' for lunch Laney remained aloof and Nathan ignored me to ask questions about items in the garage. The joint was lined with multicolored bicycles as though Foster were a trainer for the Tour De France or something. The wind picked up outside, debris pooled in the air. Laney, who was first out of the washroom, made sure our piles were intact. Rather than follow her outside and lay rakes on the dead foliage I opted to mosey inside.

Like all fancy houses that pretend to serve food with great aplomb, special procedures followed. Everybody had to wait until every chair was taken and the food was placed. Then we waited for a few seconds to make sure Mrs. Foster was seated and ready to go. It was like being at a big table with a bunch of stiff people at a restaurant. Big F started us off by grabbing two sandwiches and sending the rest around the table. Roast beef, turkey, even a vegetarian option was available, enough food for an army. Potato salad, regular green salad, macaroni salad and pasta salad. I almost made a joke and said I was disappointed that no Jell-O salad was on hand but I realized my joke sucked.

"So Nathan do you and John attend the same school?" Mrs. Foster was beginning to laser in on the boy making her daughter giggle.

"Yeah, but I am heading into my senior year and J already graduated. Or at least that is what he tells me." His voice was plain, strong and delivered with more volume than the question. Everybody laughed.

"I hope I graduated. The summer school police have not tracked me down yet." My joke drew no laughter. Then Laney tried to come to my rescue and made me feel even more awkward. "I am not sure what kind of a student John has been, but he is one of the brightest and engaging young men I have met." Her smile was returned but I was embarrassed to be protected in front of the group, who all stared like I was the boy who lost his lunch money. Since nobody reacted she continued. "Some of Nathan's friends are practically incapable of speaking in front of adults." This comment drew laughter and nods from heads busy chewing and my time in the spotlight was over. Nobody asked me the seminal question that pierces people my age: what are you going to do now?

"How about you Nathan? Are you considering options for next year, applying for school and so forth? Lacey is just starting to get serious about such matters herself." Mrs. Foster's face was both stern and smiley. I could tell she takes planning for the future very seriously. Nathan paused and finished methodically chewing a wad of potato salad. His eyes darted forward to Mrs. Foster and back to the table, entertaining deep thoughts about his future. He suddenly sounded serious. "I have some scholarship offers for football, mostly Pac-10 programs and a few other schools."

"Really, which ones?" Big F suddenly awakened, moved from his lull by a football discussion.

"Washington State, Oregon State, Idaho, Utah…Central Washington."

"Have you thought about the Huskies?" Lacey was on the future Nathan bandwagon and sitting across from him, just to the left of her father, who manned the head of the long dark cherry wood table.

"They want me to walk on, but they have a lot of receivers…
so they may never offer a scholarship."

"They have a lot of quick midgets over there but you have
good size, how tall are you?"

"Six foot three."

"What does it mean to walk on?" Lacey is really cute when
she scrunches up her nose and asks questions, like a little
doll. She is one of those girls who never has zits on her face
and talks about visiting Hawaii with her friends all the time.
Her father was suddenly coming alive and her mother got
up to get some more coffee. "It means to walk on the team
honey…football programs encourage players with talent to
do so with the idea that they might offer them a scholarship
in the future."

"What a rip-off. So they just want you to come and trust
them!" A wide open mouth and wide eyes indicated Lacey
was shocked by this sneaky motivational trick." I glanced
at Laney who was amused by the reactions around the room.
She hates big time football programs and enjoys it when people
with plenty are hit with small doses of reality.

"Yes, but sometimes it is a good move." Foster held his
hands out and showed open palms demonstrating the
consideration such an option required with a hand gesture.
He had pieces of bread stuck to the corners of his mouth,
and without speaking, his wife got up during the discussion
after pouring some coffee and placed two napkins on top of
the edge of his plate. Her messages are not subtle. "If you
think you can get a better education at the school using this
soft recruiting method and you think you might be an asset
on the team, which of course would lead to a scholarship, it
makes sense."

Everything on Foster's body shifted into his natural laconic
state, like his private power supply had been turned down; he

instinctively grabbed one of the napkins and went to work on his face. "Well does one of the schools sound better than the others?" Mrs. Foster's pragmatic question shifted discussion away from the philosophical side of the table. Nathan remained expressionless and he started nodding in little quick bursts. "I am just going to go wherever they want me the most and let everything fall into place."

"Wouldn't you take the school that offered a scholarship… or at least the best school that provided free tuition." Cybil's follow-up question was earnest and serious – she was the only one moving forward with a plan of attack. "Can you pick up some sort of financial aid without a scholarship?

"Cybil, the boy is confident, he wants to leave it on the field. It's admirable, compete to win, strive to compete, let the chips fall where they may. You are the sovereign baby, the one nobody can touch. Just think good thoughts when life is getting you down." Foster was pleased with himself. He sat back smiling and looked like he wanted to high-five somebody and rip off a couple of big yells. His wife shook her head and frowned. Nathan looked content and smiled.

Laney's jaw dropped and she stopped moving. I glanced her way as she gasped in little bursts. She could not decide whether to say something or leave it be.

"Were you in SDS?" she finally blurted out. Laney was wide-eyed and leaned forward in her chair brimming with curiosity.

"Yeah, I used to march, and protest and raise hell." There were great pauses between his phrasing, as if Foster were reflecting and being interviewed simultaneously. A proud smile came over this face – he was exhilarated to reveal another facet of his personal history. Foster leaned back in his chair and puffed out his chest a little bit… while grasping the table with both arms like a speaker stabilizing a lectern.

"Dad was a hippie," giggled Lacey.

"Only for a year or two honey," interjected frowning Cybil, obviously embarrassed by this lapse in judgment years ago.

"Cool," said Nathan.

"Why did you ask him about SDS?"

My question initiated group silence. Everyone turned and looked at Laney. "What is SDS?" added Lacey. I was pleased preppy girl had the guts to ask the question. I was trying to play cool like I knew what was going on.

"Students for a Democratic Society," answered Laney quietly. "It was an organization that grew out of campus protests and sit-ins during the 1960s. A number of the participants were against America's involvement in Vietnam, some were calling for broader civil rights and some people truly wanted a new revolutionary form of government." Laney must have realized the rest of us are members of a less serious generation because she smiled and said, "Well then, I guess that sounds a little weird to people in school today."

"No, no, you told the tale well. We wanted to change the world and we thought that non-violent protest was the way to do it. Those were the methods they had used in the South and we were all inspired by the changes taking place across the country. We never thought it would end. We thought we were the new forceful generation."

"What happened?" Cybil was now laughing off the subject, she was ready for desert.

"Well," Foster paused while he scratched the back of his neck. "We screwed up! Didn't get much done in later years… people got a little too greedy, or power hungry, or something. But I do think our generation has shaped the country in a lot of ways if you consider everything together. I mean, who would have thought Earth Day was going to be like a national holiday back then?"

Laney smiled and glanced at Cybil, and then she looked at big Foster with an intense gaze. I knew what she was thinking, "How did this slumlord, property owner change so much over the years?" The entire conversation answered questions for me. I already thought Foster was a pretty good guy considering he could have been a jerk when I started asking him to let us pay off the rent debt with labor. He sounded like a guy with a big heart in addition to a big crack.

"You are not old enough to be a part of that stuff. What was your role Laney?"

"My parents were very active in a number of protest movements, so I was taken along at a young age." She was trying to downplay her childhood but Nathan spilled the beans. "Her parents were Black Panthers, so she spent time with all the freaks and scary dudes growing up." Nathan sat up in his chair, proud of himself. I expected he and Foster to start slapping hands.

"Oh my, oh my," said the great capitalist. Young Lacey looked confused and frankly so was I. Nothing frustrates me more than slow-answering adults who describe events in little bursts like they are unraveling a mystery. Just because they are old and screwed up does not mean every young person is ignorant. Just as I was getting fired up about this stuff I looked across the table and Nathan was staring at his fingernails on this right hand like he just got a manicure or some goddamned thing and Lacey sat with an open-mouthed stare so stupid-looking that aliens were probably controlling her little brain.

"So yes, I spent much of my childhood traveling up and down the West Coast while my parents lived in communal housing and sold baked goods door-to-door raising awareness and money for sickle cell anemia research. Of course, they were involved in some other stuff as well, but they were not the most radical Panthers."

"Amazing, small world!" Mrs. F cleared her husband's plate and moved along the edges of the table. As I stood to take my dishes to the kitchen she belted out, "Sit down, I will take care of it."

"I heard that statement, 'You are the Sovereign baby' at a rally in the University District. I remember it well because there was this heavyset guy at the march, I think his name was George, who was called by that name. I was really young, but it rings a bell."

"George Rabinowitz. Yes, he was a real powerhouse, liked to speak in large groups and a bunch of people just followed him around all the time, especially girls."

"What did he do?" The word girls drew Nate's attention.

"He was a leader Nathan. People found him inspiring." Foster took on a professorial tone.

"I remember George would not say much until he reached the podium and then it was just pure poetry. He would really let 'em have it. It was a real tragedy when he died."

"How did he die?

"Car wreck. His van rolled down a hillside after a concert out in Redmond I think."

"It sounds like he was a better speaker than driver," said Cybil, rolling her eyes. She was back at the table with more coffee, a pitcher of water and cookies, muffins and donuts for dessert. Her perpetual motion finally ended with one swoop into her chair, a long sigh and a big outward breath – a dramatic entrance. "Have some cookies everybody, these are made at a little bakery over here in Madrona and they are just delightful." I made a move for the chocolate chip.

"That is so tragic…so many of those protest leaders flamed out at an early age." Laney was still interested in the subject and ignored her cynical host.

"It was strange circumstances though. He was in the company of a bunch of real thugs, a union boss's kid and some members of the Hell's Angels and he was the only one who died."

"Mmm-hmm," a knowing hum from Laney. She is really into mysteries and conspiracies.

"Those were crazy times back then." Foster looked skyward and gazed at the ceiling with both hands behind his head. It was not a pretty sight. Sweat marks in the armpit pockets of his white undershirt were displayed for everybody to see. The big man had removed his dark Gore-Tex coat on his way in for lunch. What a slob.

"This is all perfectly gloomy stuff Jim. I am sure these kids do not want to hear about the good old days." It was just like a disinterested adult to interfere on our behalf. But I concede that only our side of the table was fascinated by the oral history lesson.

"Where do you go to school Lacey?" Laney finally helped Mrs. Foster change the subject.

"Holy Names."

"Over here on 21st?"

"I guess so." Lacey smiled and giggled. I could see in Nathan's face he was smitten, which really galled me because he is with Torrie.

"Don't you know where your own school is located?" Big F had returned from the ceiling.

"Yes, Dad, but I don't read every street sign on the way there. And I am not driving off of any cliffs either."

"It is a good school, very challenging I think," interrupted Cybil. "I am impressed with the teachers they have added over the past few years." You can tell the Mrs. was the driving force in the school selection process.

"Yeah, it was time for some new blood over there," added Jim.

"Do you have a particular college in mind?" I do not recall the rest of the conversation because it was so damn boring. A bunch of small private schools with shitty football teams were mentioned and Nathan was probably grabbing himself under the table as he dreamed of attending some stupid school and being a football star. When the ordeal ended I helped Mrs. Foster clear the table while the rest of the gabbers kept talking about Lacey's future. I could tell Nathan's mother was bored as well but she is very polite.

Back outside we started hacking away at the overgrown bushes in the yard. Naturally, Nate moved into an easier task, weeding around some big rocks. After ten minutes Lacey joined him with some work gloves on and a delightful outfit. I had trouble concentrating. Her hair was drawn back in some kind of girly ponytail but some of the strands hung down in front and her straight white teeth and soft skin topped a yellow school sweater and black spandex tights that she filled out well. I viewed her bending over in the waning daylight while glancing from my foliage post near Laney. In fact, I could not keep my eyes off of her so my criticism of Nathan is a bit hypocritical. Those two kept talking and laughing for another hour before Nathan left early to supposedly head to work. They exchanged some notes before he left - I am sure he got her phone number. When he finally left the property in Torrie's car he gave the biggest smile and cutest little wave possible to Lacey and her father gave him a hug and a handshake. He probably spent more time eating lunch than actually working and I secretly vowed to not show up during the next rent-reduction work session…but I know I will.

"I really appreciate all your help J," was his parting shot to me, completed with a handclasp.

"You should be grateful to John for doing so much work Nathan," said Laney when he left. "Next time are you going to get here earlier?"

"Absolutely, this was a crazy day and now I need to get back to Big 5." Then he rolled up the window so he could not hear any more bullshit from his mother and was on his way. Again, I felt like a little kid being protected, it really sucked. Lacey lasted about three minutes outside after Nate left so I lost my view and continued to plow ahead until Big F called it quits about forty-five minutes later. After everybody said their false goodbyes and Laney complimented the Fosters on everything in their house and garage we ditched the place.

I got off the bus downtown instead of continuing on to West Seattle because there was about forty minutes of time before the public library closed. I wanted to look into Foster's story about George Rabinowitz.

With the help of a librarian and a computer search I pulled up a couple of articles. Rabinowitz's life story was a big deal in the local papers and the tale around the lunch counter did not encapsulate the story correctly – I know, what a shock?

I had to read quickly before they turned off the lights at the library, but the investigation into his death was pretty detailed and old man Foster's conspiracy theories sound pretty bogus. A bunch of people were hurt badly in the accident so if the intent was to kill off George the Great because he was tipping over the Seattle power structure, the conspirators needed more training. The union boss's son, who was driving, left the scene with a broken collarbone and a fractured arm and everybody else in the Volkswagen van was also smashed up and spent time in the hospital. A guy in the back almost lost his leg and someone else was photographed in a full body cast. Next time I drop by I want to read some of the materials in later years, the impact of old George and what his death meant to his followers. Maybe there is a lesson in there somewhere.

12
TARGET PRACTICE

Money was tight so I began wondering about payment for my work in Bellevue on my way home. I convinced myself to call Jimmy's shoes but I did not remember the name of the guy who interviewed me. Finally, I called and described him and was told he was out on a break and that his name was Lindsey. The apathy on the other end of the phone was so palatable that I decided it was an ideal place for me to work. "I don't know dude, I just try and stay out of Lindsey's way. You know what I mean?" The guy sounded baked on the job.

After a session of serious fingernail biting I got off the bus and waited for a moment at a corner seat at Kentucky Fried Chicken. I was not going to order anything unless I landed the job, but hunger altered my viewpoint and I felt like a weasel for taking up space. As a manager came my way I grabbed the phone and dialed to keep up the rouge. I finally cobbled together enough change for some potato wedges and tap water (free) and protected my precious dollars.

Fortunately, Lindsey remembered me and said he needed to fill 15-20 hours a week. He said I could begin 'training' on Monday morning. I was so excited I picked up chicken for my mother and headed home, feeling confident that I would be able to afford a little food and bus money until other sources paid dividends. "Did you get any mashed potatoes?" That was Ma's reaction when I arrived. She liked the chicken and we spent the rest of the evening sitting on her bed, watching television. After *Saturday Night Live*, which she watches dutifully without laughing, I shut down for the evening. When stepping outside to fire up one last cigarette I resisted my urge to venture out to the bowling alley or any other nutty place and went back to reading in bed. There was no action across the street and low funds left few options. I played a little game where I push the smoke as far into the air as possible.

Dating or meeting a girl was the only goal on my mind since the job thing was temporarily accounted for. With no prospects on the horizon and doomsday feelings I slinked off to bed and teared up. Loneliness is my worst nightmare and I have no solution. When I tutored students in creative writing during the school year, an easy gig during my senior year during second period, I started enjoying the company of one of my fellow tutors. I walked her home a few times and we stumbled through some painful conversations but we always spent time smiling at each other and she never looked at me like I smell or anything. Since I am on a hot streak I might stop by Lisa's house tomorrow and see if she wants to do something. Dates and dances are not my thing but I am pretty good at setting up weird entanglements and some people work better under such circumstances. In fact, I think it might set me apart from other guys if I just act like myself and say exactly what comes to mind rather than put on some lame act and promote a side of me that seems awkward and undeveloped.

Lisa is Japanese and she came to the United States a few years back to live with some relatives when her parents were killed in an auto accident. She told me the story – it sounded really gruesome. They were driving a Mercedes SUV, they obviously had some dough, and her father swerved to miss a bicyclist in Kyoto and the vehicle went onto two wheels and then turned over on its side. In a prone position it was smashed by a bus. Everyone died instantly…or at least that is what the police in Japan told her. Lisa lost both parents and her younger sister.

So at age fourteen, unable to speak English, she went to live with her Aunt Miko, who has a house near the school on the border of the Center and West Seattle.

I remember when she showed up for school on the first day of class wearing a bunch of colors and holding a little pink bag with a bunch of earphones and electronics. She looked like she was on the run from Best Buy. Her stuff was cooler than the junk we buy in this country. Everything seemed smaller and more colorful, even the white components were more vivid. I do not know what they do over in Japan, but it seems like they polish their goods before they go on sale…or maybe the consumers keep everything in good condition.

Saji, her last name, sat right behind me in the last row and she had no idea what she was doing at school. After about three days she started tapping my shoulder and passing me little notes. I remember the first one read. 'Book open know?' My favorite was 'Monies for lunch? Necessary.'

"Yes, open your book now and pretend that you are reading the pages Mrs. Sulkowski described." I spoke slowly in a pathetic attempt to be clear. Her little lips made a circle and she hunched down like she was hiding behind me. I pointed at the spot on the page and then that old bag Sulkowski yelled at me for not paying attention. I took the abuse and did not blame my language-challenged neighbor. After that day, Lisa treated me like a king. We only had a few classes together the rest of high school and our lockers were nowhere near each other, but as her English improved she kept speaking louder, like she was shouting all the time, and smiling constantly.

"John…Johnny." I used to hear her yelling in the hall, waving my way. It was a big joke by the time senior year was in full swing. Chirp and other friends of mine imitated Lisa, waving their arms and screeching. Lisa enjoyed the attention.

"Johnny, do you miss me?" she used to ask playfully.

"Yeah, our time in Biology was really special." My interpersonal communication skills need some work.

"She really likes you," Chirp would say. "Do you think you can get in her pants?" My response was to change the subject. Flirting is not my thing and Lisa was just being silly and frisky at school. Final semester, senior year, we shared second period together and I stumbled along providing English lessons to freshman international students and Saji helped upper division classmates having trouble master Japanese. She really blossomed late and her demeanor changed during our final month or two in school. No longer speaking loudly and acting super excited, like her hormones were on fire, Lisa sat in the same corner every day wearing a calm expression, working with her pupils. She often brought a diet soft drink to class and drank it with a washable straw from home, always different colors. Bright yellow, orange and even black when it matched her mood. Once safely hidden in her corner sipping, Lisa brightened the room from her little zone. We used to speak about baseball, other kids at school and how much her aunt annoys her.

The one topic I dreaded was discussing her plans for the future. My absent blueprint, devoid of thought and planning, is embarrassing. Lisa is a walking calendar and she always looks perplexed when she hears that the person sitting across from her has no plan. Her aunt is sending her to the University of Washington next fall and she is disgustingly excited. A broad smile overcomes her little mouth at the thought of migrating to the University District, which is not that exciting if you ask me. She already shops over there at this place called Red Light that sells costumes year round to people that want to look cool. I am sure it is just a bunch of vintage and used clothing, but they have neon signs in the front and strange mood lighting inside and dark little closets to try on clothes. Maybe Saji feels at home in those little corner spots.

Her clothing changed permanently after cruising around town a bit. She usually looked like a cross between Stevie Nicks, the version on my mother's old "Rumors" album, and a cute little poodle. Lisa wore tight dark stretch pants and colorful leg warmers or black jeans. Bright sweaters or big lace shirts draped over her waist and hips. Giant belts with fake rhinestones or shiny black lacquer sat loosely on hips that swooshed when she walked and Saji was not a dainty mover. A little over five feet tall, her tiny feet fell heavy when navigating desks in the classroom. She opened doors with dramatic explosion, putting every ounce of body weight behind the movement. I imagine that if I were a little rodent like Saji I would gear up for the big pulls as well. She was always organized and mature in class though, even when she looked like a pink rabbit. Among the other tutors she was considered the best in our limited field: high school language helpers.

At precisely 1:15 p.m. the following day I knocked on Lisa's door, or at least her aunt's door, with a big smile and a clean shirt – a tan fuzzy thing with little brown stripes, long sleeves and a collar. I fretted over the choice of clothing after breakfast and before showering. I think Saji complimented me on this outfit in second period once. She was probably just being polite. When the screen door opened with timidity I knew it was Miko coming. She always acts frightened when encountering people. "Oh hi," she said with a smile as she stepped outside.

"I thought I would say hi to Lisa if she is around."

"She went to take her driver's test." My interest in Saji was rising by the minute.

"Do you mind if I leave her my phone number? I would like to talk to her…and see how her summer is going."

"Yes, that would be fine. I am sure she would like to catch up with you." The cheerful woman before me was nothing like the ogre Lisa described in second period. She remembered that I used to walk Lisa home and invited me in to leave a proper note on a cute little 'Hello Kitty' notepad. After a couple of cookies and some small talk about the weather I was back on the road to nowhere. Boys are always offered cookies, donuts and brownies. Sometimes I wonder what girls are offered when they stop by a home unannounced. Do people keep little flowers under their cabinets? Are slices of fruit provided; perhaps apples and pears? Maybe the same stuff is trotted out and girls just never actually take the goods because they are too polite and less inclined to gorge themselves in front of strangers. Since I was already heading into West Seattle I kept moving all the way to California Avenue and browsed for used books and records. The cookies provided energy so I walked about two miles in the sun, it was pretty warm, mid-80s, and my armpits were doing the stench dance so I found a couple of trees near a playground at West Seattle Elementary and read a little book I found for ninety-five cents: *Hope of Heaven* by John O'Hara, in the shade. It is amazing what you discover in these little places, great entertainment for under a dollar.

Lisa's phone call awakened me. The book was sprawled across my chest, my right arm trapped behind my head resting on my little backpack in the dirt. "Yo." Not my best line, but I was still groggy.

"Johnny, what's up!"

"I just stopped by to see what you were up to. Your aunt said you were taking a driving test."

"I passed…can you believe it!" She was positively ebullient; this was the hallway Lisa in a recreational summer environment. Relaxed and free flowing, her voice got my blood pumping. Soon the book was on my lap, I was sitting up and we were making plans.

"Listen, I am not surprised you passed. You probably memorized the lesson plan, knowing you."

"Oh you're sweet. But no, I get nervous when driving with other people who focus on my every move. Miko is crazy. She actually brings a notebook and makes little comments about my turns and parking when we are finished. She will probably still do that shit even though I have my license now. Her harassment was not as oppressive when I took the SAT's but she is always watching everything I do. I need a break from that woman."

Sensing my chance, I made a move. "Would you like to take a break and catch a movie or something tonight?"

"Sure, can we go over to the Ten-Plex in the U-District? That's my favorite theater."

"Was there a particular movie you wanted to see?" My voice sounded really formal to me. I sounded unsure and dippy.

"Ahhh, not really. Oh, there is a new one called Pink Roses that looks pretty good. Have you read about it?"

"Nope."

"It is about two immigrant women who begin selling flowers to make money and then realize that the joy they are bringing to breast cancer patients is even more important to their mission. They begin focusing on their community even more than their flower shop. It is supposed to be a really touching story, really inspirational."

The film sounded horrible to me, the most sappy vagina movie ever produced. "That sounds great…do you know what time it plays?"

"I will look it up."

Once Lisa figured out the time of the flick we agreed that the best way to keep her aunt happy was for me to meet her over at Westwood Center. Miko would think she was going to join some friends at a little theater in Burien and Saji knew she would get agitated if she imagined her niece parking in the busy University District her first night with a new license. Auntie "M" hardly leaves West Seattle, and according to her niece, her idea of a big event is to go to Swanson's Nursery and look at the plants on a Sunday afternoon.

The red Toyota showed up on time and I bounded into the car wondering if we were on a date or just hanging out as friends. I sure as hell wasn't going to bring up the topic. Lisa had some retro new wave crap playing on the CD player and her little car sounded new - like it had been receiving tune-ups every 10,000 miles. Aunt Miko must read the manual. Lisa was excited and bobbed her little head around like a freak when "Rock Lobster" by the B-52s came on the radio.

"I love this song."

"It's a classic." My commentary was riveting. Singing in public is not my thing and when Saji started shouting lyrics discomfort overcame my senses, I didn't know what to do. Needing to relax with booze or smokes or something, I felt out of place, like a fringe participant along for the ride – an excuse for Lisa to visit her future neighborhood and scope things out. This is a mistake that I repeat all the time. After my hopes rise and I gear up for a fun encounter everything feels hollow when it becomes clear that my goals are not the same as my social partner.

"Soooo, parking might be tough so help me find something okay?" Lisa's smile was reassuring but I was already freaking out, feeling uncomfortable; trapped. Fingers were twitching and my toes moved uncontrollably in my sneakers. Lisa wore a jean skirt that came above her knees and a black sweater with a beige and brown pattern. A little pink scarf draped around her neck. There was no need for such an item in the warm summer night. She had washed her car before venturing out that night. It glistened and made reflections in dark windows as we zoomed by. Her smell was dainty, sweet and soothing. For comparison, I discreetly sniffed my black heavy cotton coat, frayed at the edges. A faint smoke smell was ever present. I made a mental note to smoke less with my coat on and imagined ways to upgrade my general odor.

"Do you think there will be anything on 12th? The movie theater is on the corner."

"Boy, I hope so." I forced a smile and I defensively moved into normal school conversation. "I thought you knew this neighborhood Saji, you should be a real parking master over here."

"I can walk over here really well, but I never drive." Minutes of silence followed and she became agitated as spots disappeared. Every time we snuck up on a parking space someone else beat us to the punch. Once Lisa even honked her horn, akin to a violent gesture for her. She kept sighing and making funny little noises and turning the radio volume down. Her smile faded into frustration as minutes dragged on.

"I can pay for a lot if we find one."

"They all look full to me." More silence.

Eventually, we found a spot way up north on 56th Street, nearly a mile from our destination. "Does the movie begin at 7:00?" I asked in an apprehensive, gentle tone.

"7:35." Since we had a good forty minutes to kill I was confused. What the hell were we doing showing up so early to a movie that seven lesbians and a few guys looking to meet girls were going to see?

"I love to watch previews…come on, let's go. They are really fabulous on the big screen, like mini-movies." After the parking fiasco Lisa was suddenly full of boundless energy. She was still cute with her big smile, but her sentiment was starting to annoy me. For all I knew we were going shopping for little cuddly bears and pink crap next. Even hanging out with Nathan sounded appealing. I tried to walk slowly and waste time but Saji's tiny legs were motoring along, there was no stopping the siren of the previews. Attempts to initiate conversation were shut down along the way.

"What was the last movie you saw over here?"

"I don't remember."

"Did you ever check out Vanity Plate?"

"No, that looked kind of corny to me."

"I see; then you probably didn't see Manual Planet either." No reaction, just a forced smile and a shake of the head. I was not being labeled an uncultured bastard or a dumb boy. Nope, totally dismissed and ignored. Just a guy on someone else's time. I felt insecure and vulnerable, which is the opposite of what I wanted to feel on a Friday night. This unmitigated disaster continued in total silence until we reached the line at the ticket window, which drew another sigh from the little queen. When I offered to protect our spot while she hung out in the lobby, Lisa snapped out of her funk.

"I am sooo glad to get out in the city tonight. Thanks for coming along." I sounded like an appendage. "It was the least I could do." My line was delivered in a monotone and was summarily ignored.

"Robbie! What's up?" Lisa's hallway voice came alive as she spied some guy towards the front of the line. She left me behind and raced ahead to speak with a young Filipino kid who was balancing himself on a mountain bike, one leg stationary and one dangling over the seat, the bike at an angle. I don't know why I call people my age "kids." It just sounds better when I am sizing them up. I was unable to hear their conversation but after about three minutes they migrated down the line. My value as a spot holder was increasing.

"John (my name was no longer 'Johnny') this is Robbie." He is a member of the ACC over in West Seattle. I invited him to come to the movie with us but he is too cool for our film."

"Oh yeah, what are you planning seeing? Or, I mean planning to see."

"Nails Forever." I was speechless with envy. 'Nails' was the film I secretly preferred – an action flick about a dock worker who starts kicking ass when his son is kidnapped and taken hostage in Mexico.

"What are you two seeing?" Rob, I just can't bring myself to call him or think of him as 'Robbie,' kept rubbing his left hand over his right biceps and vice versa. He could not stop feeling his pipes; in fact he looked like he was touching himself for pleasure. I could not bear to answer the question so I looked over at Saji.

"Pink Roses."

Like a complete jerk Pipes just nodded and mumbled, "Oh yeah, that looks pretty interesting." No laughter, no obvious shock. This dude clearly wants to be the perfect guy in the minds of girls. He looked tan and contemplative with his little green backpack draped over his broad shoulders, long dark shorts and a tight t-shirt. "You look great," yelled Lisa. "Have you been working out?" She looked like she wanted to lick his arms.

"Nah, just riding my bike a lot." 'Right,' I thought, riding your bike to the gym and pimping it every afternoon.

After flipping her hair in the back and stretching, Lisa said, "That Nails Forever looks fun. I already agreed to see Pink Roses, but that would have been a good choice too." I wanted to strangle Saji for acting like I was the culprit. Daydreams of Saji and Robbie running off together and biking around while preening and posing occupied my thoughts.

After more banal discussion about puppy dogs and how the U District 'rocks,' I managed to stay awake as the two exchanged phone numbers. We all bought tickets together and after we entered, Pipes managed to perform one of those big stretches that result in a flex of his arms at the end. I really wanted to kick him in the nuts and run out the door.

I also realized it was my big chance to amend our movie decision. "Do you want to go to the other movie instead?"

"No, that is okay." Now I was really pissed because Lisa was turning out to be a big phony.

"What is the ACC?"

"Oh right, the Asian Community Center." Her answer was delivered after a great pause because her mind was somewhere else, probably on Robbie. "I bet you have never been there." Her laughter was not infectious. While she was laughing I was thinking to myself that if people at the ACC just hang out and whisper to each other in the corner I have no interest in visiting. Hanging out in a little special club is not my program…if I wanted to do that stuff I would go to college and join one of those fraternities that nobody can pronounce and just drink until I pee the couch. But of course I had to keep the conversation going so I acted like I wanted to hear more.

"No, never invited. What is it like?"

"Nothing really, just a place with a rec center where people host big weddings and family events. I have only been there a few times with the troll," another name she uses for her aunt. "She likes to introduce me to other kids because she obviously needs help in such matters. She likes meeting people in the community but she doesn't feel comfortable talking to strangers so she brings me along." Lisa rolled her eyes at the thought and then unleashed a broad smile, laughed, and squeezed my right arm with two small hands. Her improving mood made me feel awful for thinking such terrible things about her, but I was still suspicious because she kept looking back at Pipes and I think she was making herself excited thinking about him while grabbing my arm in mock humor. Girls send so many differing signals that I am always skeptical of their intentions. Yet, I could sense Lisa was uncomfortable, like she wanted to be somewhere else. I let her choose everything, where we sat, the fact that no snacks would be included and what our plan would be after the flick, which was awful. About fifteen minutes into the feature I fell asleep. My crash must have lasted at least forty-five minutes because I left a drool spot on my right shoulder where my mouth was wedged – like I was trying to sniff my own armpit. At least half of the movie was over. It was a long SOB too. After awakening and violently shaking my head to clear my mind, gravity and a warm theater conspired to pull down heavy eyelids. Only invasive pinches with sharp fingernails and little slaps to my face kept me awake. I wish Lisa cared enough to speak to me so I could concentrate on something other than a movie in which all the stars were either dying or crying about their friends croaking. It was enough to drive anybody into hibernation. Saji just pretended like nothing was askew and her relentless eye contact with the movie screen was alarming…as if nobody existed outside her little micro bubble. No amusement, no kidding around about my plight. She was as dead as the movie and I concluded she just did not care – I was simply a vehicle, or reason to persuade her aunt to permit hanging out in the U-District. Used again.

Toward the end of the film I glanced around the theater, taking inventory. The place was full of exchange kids and immigrants in big groups and they were having the time of their life. What is my problem? Why am I such a loner and a loser? Panic tumbled through my body and nervous twitching at the end of fingers followed. Even Lisa shaped her life, got it together and connected with people in just a few years.

"Perhaps you should write a review of this film and submit it to the school paper." She laughed. There was no way I could pretend I had not slept during the movie.

I accepted her shit and just kept walking and smiling on the way to the bathroom. When I returned it was clear by her body language that the evening was officially dead but we both tried to revive our company by mutually deciding a late night snack was in order. "Do you like sushi?"

"Not sure, I have never really tried the stuff."

"Hmmm, that might not be a good idea then. Thoughts?"

"Do you like Dick's?"

"Nah, I am not really in the mood for a burger right now."

"I am sure I can eat something at anyplace you choose."

"Yeah but it sucks to go to a restaurant that you are not familiar with."

I slowed down and cracked a little smile. "Seriously, I can eat any spot you desire."

"What would be your top choice?"

"Probably the Box."

"What?"

"Jack In The Box."

"Are you serious?" Lisa's laughter was sarcastic in tone. She kept guffawing and opening her mouth. "How can you eat that stuff?"

"Some people like grease."

"Yes, but you need to take care of your body."

"You sound like your impressions of your aunt." That was the wrong thing to say. Lisa went silent for about three minutes and just stared at the ground as we shuffled along 45th Street in the University District. I felt like an ass, and the sad thing is that the words just blurted out of my mouth. I was not even trying to make a serious point.

"Hey, I am sorry for saying that about your aunt. I was trying to make a joke and I should not have said such a thing. I...I really didn't mean anything serious by that stupid comment."

"No you are right I have no right to give you advice. That kind of stuff pisses me off."

"But it didn't Lisa, I was just messing around. I was not offended in any way." She continued to look at the ground.

"Let's go to one of each place – one for both of us."

"I really would feel better if you choose. You are misunderstanding me." I stopped and tried to get Lisa to look my way. "It was a throwaway comment – I was just messing around."

"Okay, but how about Dick's?"

"Lisa, there is no way you want to go to Dick's. If anything, Dick's is greasier than the Box."

"You do not know what I feel like right now. I really want to go to Dick's."

"Okay, I am sorry." She wore me down and we walked north to retrieve the car, which probably reminded her of her aunt again because it looked shiny compared to the dusty, unwashed models parked nearby; relics of students who prefer riding the bus or using their vehicles as placeholders in anticipation of long weekends.

We were silent during the ride over to the hamburger joint, which was packed as usual. As Lisa prepared to turn into the lot and aim for an open spot I cringed when I spied Lem's car. He was the only person at Dick's weird-looking and smelly-looking enough to keep everybody away. Saji parked right next to him and he started laughing when he saw me in the passenger seat, next to little Lisa, who was using both hands to navigate the slot next to Lem's giant car. He continued smoking while leaning against his trunk, waiting for me to come hither. The cars lined up so my passenger window looked directly into the driver's side. I only had a moment to set the scene for Lisa.

"Do you know that guy leaning against the car over my right shoulder?"

"No, but he looks familiar…oh yeah, he is that really loud guy who walks around talking to himself all the time at school…right?"

"That sounds like a perfect description to me Lisa. His name is Lem and he is really weird." My commentary was finished because Barnes started making strange noises outside and he could tell we were whispering.

"Ramos, stop masturbating in the car." It was time to bounce out and talk to Lem.

"What's going on?"

"I'm waiting for old turd face."

"Huh? Who is old turd face?"

"Sam Dennon."

"Lem, this is Lisa Saji, she went to Sealth with us."

"Hey, how're ya doin?

"I'm doing well," answered Lisa softly. Lem nodded with a casual smile and said, "Super." He looked stoned and wore a red cap, old jeans and the top of a blue and white track suit.

"Do you want something over here?"

"Nah, you two chicklet's have fun."

"Why did he call you a chicklet?" Her question came while waiting to order, safely out of Lem's range.

"Not sure. That is a new one on me."

"Is he baked?"

"I think so. He works really hard, I mean, he is always busy and I think he does all sorts of things to relax." Every time I looked over at Lem while in line he pointed at me with his right pointer finger and pretended like he was shooting me with an imaginary gun. I kept talking about hamburgers, the weather and Lisa's plans for the future so his distractions would be ignored. I was failing. One time Lisa started laughing at something behind me. I looked over and Barnes was grooving to some headphones that had been sitting on the trunk door. He moved his head from side to side with his sunglasses on, stopping to gaze at his hands in the light above his head. He looked like early man. The good news was that Saji was so focused on Lem that she forgot how much she hated the food at Dick's. She only ordered french fries and a Diet Coke. I bulked up on the double burger and a shake. Barnes turned quiet as we walked back to the car. When we approached he looked at me with a big smile.

"How is it going zit ranger?"

"We ordered very effectively Lem."

"Yeah, but how does it feel?" His booming voice imitated a crazy fan who shows up for Sealth football games and always yells the same question to players doing exciting things on the field. For example, "Hey Freehold, how does it Feeeellllllll?" Then he points at his target. The guy has sat in the front row at home games for years and his weird antics are as legendary as his big shaggy beard. After faking laughter, I jumped in the car, where Lisa was already in place, saying, "Oh my god… what a weirdo!" Warm summer air made the car a sauna without any outside flow so Lisa put the windows down and we started munching our snacks in the car.

"Is it okay to eat in here?"

"Yeah, she will get over it." Lisa had finally mellowed out about her aunt.

"Let me know if you want help cleaning up some crumbs or something." The burger was delicious, but by my third bite Lisa turned silent, her face ashen. Her little mouth quivered as she glanced at the floor looking away from me. She folded up her food in a little clump of aluminum foil. I turned to make eye contact with Lem's fruit bowl about an inch from my face.

"Oh, Jesus Christ. Can you roll up the window? Barnes, keep your meat to yourself." I might have done something more drastic, like poke him, or ring his chime, but I figured Lisa would find my behavior uncivilized. Just knowing Lem looked pretty bad. As the window moved skyward and Lisa looked directly ahead, a little squeaky voice emanated from Barnes as he wiggled his dingle. "Mr. penis here… can I have a french fry please?"

"Oh my god. Does he need some medication?"

"Yes."

"I didn't realize parking here would include a penis show." I depressed the automatic window button so only an inch and a half of space remained at the top.

"Say hi to ol' turd face for us."

Mr. penis climbed back into his cave. Zipper fumbling indicated the little guy would rest until another guest arrived at the Barnes Café.

"You got it."

Lisa backed out cautiously as if we were leaving a madhouse. "These fries are really greasy." She was silent again. 'Perfect,' I thought. Four blocks later, in heavy Friday night traffic, I was still listening to Saji complain about what a sick bastard Lem is and entertaining questions about what disturbing childhood experiences must have led to his behavior. I kept thinking, 'what if she met some of my other friends?' Lem is a sweetheart compared to those guys. He just wants attention, and since nobody ever gives him any, his sense of humor, which is on the weird side, takes over. It is not like his parents beat him or his older brother tried to run him over or something.

"He is lucky someone has not called the police for shit like that."

"I imagine someone will at some point; and he will stop waving his wang around."

"Does he think that turns people on or something?"

"I doubt it." I hoped the conversation would turn. As we crossed over an overpass above Interstate-5 a dark sky bringing summer sprinkles loomed in the distance.

"I could use some tea, how about you?"

"Sure." I did need something.

After we spent another year searching for a parking place and walked six or seven more blocks to reach "The Himalayan Tea House" we sat down next to some of the University District's finest – young kids wearing oversized dark green or black overcoats sipping coffee and tea, discussing saving trees and ending oppression. Silly mustaches and long scraggly hair added to the look. If you closed your eyes and imaged this same group of people one or two years earlier as seniors in high school they probably had short hair and were on the swim team or in the band. Now they were a bunch of meat gazers waiting to see what their new friends would say or do next. I suppose being on some team or following directions from some coach in high school is basically the same thing – but at least you don't have to look bored all the time. Lisa didn't pay any attention to those goofs but, like all girls, she had a secret agenda in mind. Her friend Paola worked at the joint and they were excited to see each other between tea orders. Lisa stood by the counter while I was stuck at a dingy little wood table, full of carvings of ships, monsters and multicolored drawings courtesy of time-wasting students. It took about fifteen minutes of conversation and me listening to the philosophy boys while pretending to read an abandoned newspaper before they both came over and I was introduced as a 'neighbor.'

When greeting me, Paola faked a smile and continued talking to Lisa. The 'hi' she sent my way a simple pause interrupting a monologue. The girls were planning a future vacation to Italy and they both sucked down tea and declined to offer me anything. After a while I wandered around the room searching for more bits of the newspaper. Paola kept bouncing up and down, her little white apron and matching white hat shifting and shimmying.

"Rome is a must," said the little dark haired girl with the white outfit. She is short and Filipino so I figure she is also familiar with pipes. That was probably the topic of the earlier conversation at the front of the shop.

"You also want to visit your namesake right?"

"Yes!" A gargantuan giggle and a shrill scream followed. The gloomy boys shot mean glances their way; their analysis of world politics interrupted. Any one of them would give all the money in their bank accounts to see a vagina but they sensed they were as exciting to these girls as pieces of furniture so they were pissed off that their scene was being disrupted by giggling.

Apparently there is some town in Italy called Paola and that was on the agenda. They yapped on about that area for a while and then somebody knew someone who once went on a trip to the Amalfi Coast. "The pictures of the little towns on cliffs are incredible," said Paola. A tuft of shiny black hair bobbed below her hat, bouncing when she moved her head in a circular motion – which happened every time she said something with authority, followed by a little circle wave with her right pointer finger. She moved like one of those little people who imitate Oprah Winfrey on comedy shows.

Thirsty and frustrated, I moved halfway between my cushioned armchair in the corner and the travel planners; then decided just to get out of there. "I think I am going to take off Lisa, and check out the record store up the way. I will just grab a bus home." I was planning a secondary lie if questions were raised about which store, but there was no need – they did not care.

"Oh, are you sure?"

"Yeah, thank you for driving me to the movie…and I am sorry about Lem."

"Oh my god, we ran into one of John's friends over at Dick's…what a loser. You will not believe this…" I left before the psychoanalysis began.

Classic Seattle drizzle ceased as I left the building, the warm night accented by suddenly clearing sky. I did not want the evening to end so I started walking north along University in a pathetic attempt to find interesting sights. Misshaped buildings and little stucco one-story   jobs mixed with brick two-story storefronts. Newer wood construction formed a wall of ugly service businesses perfectly placed to entice the least inspired members of society to stop in for a drink or snack. Various colors of margaritas and daiquiris were spilled on porch fronts and under little umbrellas on tin tables behind decaying fences, waist or chest high. As I traveled further I was reminded of the book we read in English class last year, *Heart of Darkness.* Ravenna Park's tall trees loomed in the distance, making everything darker and gloomier at the end of the street, a barrier of sadness; the end of the road. I imagined drunks stumbling across the road and passing out in the mist under picnic tables after a long night.

Our literature instructor, Mr. Thomason, kept talking about how the Marlow character felt as he pressed further into the jungle. In the story, the strange surroundings made him lose his cool and calm demeanor. I felt the opposite moving along the dirty old avenue. As the old joints passed before my eyes on alcoholics row, my night became clearer, the University District transformed into the Center before my eyes.

"What are you into this fine evening young fellow?"

My new suitor was a youthfully dressed forty-year- old-looking guy sporting a St. Louis Rams cap on top and a trim little brown beard. He was smoking and slouched forward. His big smile indicated he sought a comrade. His cheeks were bloated and red, signs of a man who likes to have a good time. He had a small stain on his faded white t-shirt that displayed some surfing logo and he wore white guy jeans, the kind that fit well in the thighs and the hips but droop on top and bunch up at the bottom. Everything had been washed about 1,000 times so our wardrobes looked similar.

"Nothing at the moment."

"Would you like a drink?" My new friend was just on the other side of the fence. "Hey Rich, leave the kid alone, he might think you are a fag." The bouncer at the front of the place laughed as a tall gangly guy who looked like he could be Lem's older brother cracked wise.

"Don't listen to those fools…Rich's words were slurred, but his eye contact was laser sharp."

"Okay, are you buying?"

"You drive a hard bargain…but okay…ah ha, ha, ha."

I slipped in the front gate just as the bouncer made his way inside, pretending to ignore me. I am sure when business is slow ID cards go unchecked at outposts at the end of the line on University. A chair was pulled out for me, I felt like a chick. Cold white metal furniture near lattice that had missed the sun that day sloppily sat near wood tables full of random etchings, graffiti and carvings of fake or real lovers. Rich is probably a strong proponent of such art – he is the type of guy that would carry a pocket knife around with him all the time, like an old scoutmaster.

While I warmed the chair Rich drifted inside. Just as I considered leaving he arrived with a vodka and cola that was heavy on the former. "There you go." I hope you like what I drink because that is the only thing I ever order… ha-ha-Ha-HA." His sequential laughter cadence increased in volume until the big hacking finale, which sounded like he was making fun of me as much as laughing at his joke. His slumped shoulders were more pronounced in the light. He looked down, not at the ground, but as if studying a fascinating portrait in the distance on a downward plane. He suddenly rose back up to full height, sat down with authority and blinked his eyes.

"Well my boy, what brings you out on the north side on this fine, fine day? Oh, excuse me, Rich Seabright, glad to meet ya." A shaking, cool, clammy hand reached across to make my acquaintance. Then he sat back in a creaking chair and smiled by puffing out his checks and keeping his mouth closed.

"Just a movie and a girl." The drink was terrible, too much for me.

"That's a good combination. Where's the girl.. ha-Ha-HA."

"I lost her at some tea house on the other side of the U-District."

"I see, well my friend, there are plenty of women on this side of the tracks." Rich was enunciating at a level beyond normal conversation – he kept over mouthing everything, trying to sound really smart and proper. I am pretty sure he was just drunk and trying to act like he was in great shape.

"Well my friend, there are plenty of other leaves on the trees. If I might be so bold, I think one of those leaves might blow into your lap this very evening." As he finished the sentence he set down his drink and pointed his right hand in my direction. He looked like a crazy auctioneer.

"I hope you're right Rich, because I could use a ride home."

"Ha-HA. I think I am going to obtain a mennyou." He swayed back inside; I could hear his crazy laugh in the distance. When he returned, Rich focused on his drink and left the menu on the table so I picked it up after awhile and started looking for a snack. Rich was already on the prowl for new blood.

"Ladies, how are you two doing this fine evening?" The two young women who entered the fence of shame completely ignored my bearded, drunk friend.

"Perhaps I shall go introduce myself pro-per-ly." Rich left again and he walked with a wider gait this time, he was bending at the knees and his neck was giving in to the weight of his cap. As he walked past the bouncer, who was now sitting in a little wood chair near the open front door, he did a little jig with his elbows out. Rich returned with two more drinks. I had barely put a dent in my first.

"This is plenty for me."

"Friend, it is time to relax. Are you a student?"

"No, just, well not at the moment." I eyed the bouncer. Rich turned to look in the same direction and made a dismissive motion with his left hand, the one without the drink in ready position.

"The Seahawks suck!" Rich laughed as he mouthed something else to the bouncer, apparently a hawk fan, who flipped him off and walked back into the bar. "Don't worry about that guy. Age is not an issue here when it is not busy. And that is most of the time my friend...Ha-Ha- HA. I am not reeaaly sure why I come to this shithole. I guess I like their drinks."

"Hello darlin'...whoo-eee, beautiful women walk these streets."

A waitress wearing a black t-shirt, dark pants and a nose ring, with no discernible sense of humor, walked over to our table abruptly.

"Were you going to order something?"

"Yeah, the french fries please."

"You've got to shroom it baby...you've got to."

"He wants fries Rich." The waitress was still not smiling.

"What are you talking about?"

"Fried mushrooms, they are in-deed, the best. In fact, bring me the shrooms baby, got to have them when you're discussin' business." She scribbled something on her little piece of paper and then walked away, head down.

"You know, she has really small feet." I tried to look but our target was already inside.

"I didn't notice."

"Little teeny-weeny jobs. You ever notice how nobody ever makes a big deal out a woman's feet for no reason at all?"

I had nothing to add so I just nodded.

"If a guy has small dogs it is a big deal…you always hear that old expression – small feet – little dick." I smiled and tried to keep it together.

"You never hear small feet – small vagina. Rich was completely serious, stone-faced. "Why not? Why do woman get away with this stuff?" He was certainly more entertaining than the people at the tea house.

"Or girls that …"

By this time a woman about Rich's age sat down about two tables away. She looked serious and attractive, in fact, it would have scared me to death just to speak with her. Dark brown, maybe black hair, and beguiling brown eyes. She was shapely and sat with an air of confidence – her look didn't fit with the grease crowd on the patio.

"Now those are nice sized feet," Rich whispered. "Must mean strong vagina."

"Yeah, but isn't a big vagina supposed to be a problem?"

"I think you mean a loose vagina, there is a difference." Now Rich was loud again. The woman with the dark hair turned to us and smiled, with a perplexed look on her face. "Sorry." The word spilled from my mouth out of sheer concern.

"I have no idea what you guys are talking about, but it sounds weird."

"It is."

"We were trying to figure out…"

"You were trying to figure out," I interjected.

"Yes, if I may, I was ish-uuing commentary on how men are judged, poorly I might add, on the size of their feet and hands and other body parts and woman never receive such scrut-in-y."

She took out a cigarette and popped it on the table once before flaming it quickly with a metallic lighter. She struck quickly before Rich could offer her a light. Her movement was rapid, like a rock star, a bartender, or someone who practices. After a long drag, she made a drop in the round, black-lacquer ash tray. By this time Rich was leaning in her direction, watching with interest, teetering on his chair.

"Do you think it's true?"

"What is true?"

"The feet and the penis thing."

"Nah, because if it was, I would have huge…ha-hA- HA, I digress. Let me tell you something…if God wanted feet to match what is downstairs he would make it un-I- form for everybody."

"Okay, now you have lost me."

"Never mind…I don't know what I am talking about.
Ha-ha. Well my darling, can we buy you a drink."

"No thanks, I don't drink."

"But you smoke."

"Yes, some of us do only one or the other."

"I stand corrected-ded. Well how about a fortune?"

"Excuse me?" Her incredulous expression was accented by high cheekbones and a strong gaze centered on Rich's forehead; thick eyebrows raised.

My new buddy pulled out a bunch of little fortune cookie messages from his back pockets and grabbed two random white slips among several spread out across the table. Then he set them aside and gathered up the rest, dropping some on the ground along the way. He eventually jammed the entire lot into his left front pocket. I made eye contact with the attractive woman during the process and we both laughed. It was the first time I felt comfortable in the presence of a woman all night.

"Now you both ack-nowl-edge that these were selected randomly."

"We do," answered the nameless one for both of us. "My dear, your for-tune is the following: 'Do not seek so much to find the answers as much as to understand the question.'

"I am trying to do just that, right now."

"Ha-HA." Rich's laugh was delayed, he was trying to determine if she was making fun of him. She was. Our visitor was not smiling, her face was pensive; she was waiting for the next statement and gauging if she could relax with her cigarette without too many interruptions.

"So what do you do for a living?"

"I am an administrator at a real estate company. Are you going to read his fortune?"

"Oh yeah…let's see, 'domestic conditions demand your attention.'

"You are too young to have domestic conditions." Then she turned to Rich. "Your fortunes suck." I laughed and so did the mystery woman.

"Well, we are all entitled to our own opinions, and I have mine. Maybe, the nu-ances of these for-tunes sound strange but I believe they tell a greater story than we are all prepared to un-der-stand this fine evening. I would like to toast my in-spira-tional fortunes on this fine…"

"What the hell are you talking about?" The woman just stared his way. I laughed but Rich did not, instead he put his head down and grimaced, looking up with a clenched jaw, confirming someone was making fun of him. I stopped giggling and tried to act serious; in fact, I stopped looking over at our conversation guest because I knew just glancing at her would release the floodgates. Rich stood up glared at the table, nodded, raised his right hand and went back into the bar in silence.

"Oh my god, he seemed really pissed. I wasn't trying to hurt his feelings."

"I wouldn't worry about it – he won't remember anything in the morning."

"That's probably true, but I still feel badly." She scrunched up her nose emphasizing her feelings with a pained expression. Then she relaxed into a frown. Sadness subsided when she opened a gossip magazine sitting in her purse and started reading about the week's events. Another cigarette was cracked. When our waitress arrived with the food she looked at me like I was a lost little brother.

"Did you lose your buddy?"

"No, he just went inside."

"I think I insulted him." I was pleased to hear the attractive stranger was still paying attention.

"That's easy to do. He was mad at me last weekend for cutting him off."

"I see, a big drinker eh?"

"He can be, he is not the worst, but Rich really starts pouting when he doesn't get his way."

"That is really funny, he is doing that now." The patio girl sounded relieved to discover that this was normal behavior.

My attention turned to the fried mushrooms. I motored through them in case my benefactor never returned or forgot he ordered them. Just as I was polishing off the final morsel Rich stumbled back into our little area, followed by a tall woman with long blonde, almost white, bleached hair. She carried a drink, red cheeks framed a big round white face.

"My dear, this is an ac-quaint-ance I made this evening." He then hit his forehead with his left, non-drinking, palm. "I am sorry I forgot your name."

"Gina."

"And what was your name again?" Rich pointed at me with his glass, spilling a little along the way. "Whoops," He quickly moved to cease the spillage and naturally moved his left hand under his glass as if he were protecting a rug or something.

"John."

"Yes, yes, and this lovely lady is Georg-ina. Did I say it right? We have been practicing."

"What a pretty name," Gina smiled.

"Georgg-ina." Rich was practicing.

"That's what you get when you cross a British mother with an eccentric American father."

"I propose a toast to both of you lovely ladies."

"Gina doesn't drink, remember."

"She can toast with her cigarette. Hey, I just rea-ell-ized. Gina and Georggg-ina. HA-HA-HA." His head moved back and forth between the two. Rich seemed amazed by his discovery. The conversation was too stupid to emit laughter so I finished the final gulp of my drink and fished for money in my pocket. The two women were also not amused. Then Rich realized he had another fresh drink on the table. He glided over to sit near his prize. Georgina methodically followed and sat between us with her back facing Gina. She was wearing a light coat or windbreaker of some kind even though the night was humid. Her green eyes were wide and comforting, her smile warm. The garment fell down to her knees and a wide belt at the waist cinched it. She sat in stark contrast to the fashionable Gina who wore tight designer jeans tucked neatly into expensive leather boots and a tight fitting button up white shirt with a little red scarf tied   at the top. Her dark coat was an amenity item and hung over the top of a nearby chair.

"Hi." The greeting was strong and it came from a new voice on the other side of our barrier. Gina was waving back and the group of three at our table turned and spied a tall, striking dark-haired gentleman wearing a fancy yellow Italian dress shirt, unbuttoned a few in front, and navy slacks. He was so good looking that I imagined him preening in the mirror for a while and then hanging his sunglasses at the apex of his shirt, on top of his chest hair. Amazingly, he knew Rich.

"Rich, what's up?" The delayed response was comical because it followed a long gaze at the target and an obvious search for recognition.

"Pat, what are you doing at this dump?" When Georgina glared at him he said, "Ooooh, I'm sorry, ssshhhh," and held his pointer finger to his lips like he was telling all of us to be quiet.

Stud boy greeted the random bouncer and made his way in the door and into our little outdoor corral. "Are you still selling ads for the *Independent?*"

"I hope so." Laughter followed as Rich stood and the two shook hands, one looking fit and tan and the other haggard, broken and drunk.

"You two know each other?" Gina was more surprised than anybody.

"Went to high school together. Rich played safety at Roosevelt." The old warrior sat back down, Pat was the only one standing. He swiftly moved to give Gina a kiss and asked her how she was doing.

"That's Pat for ya," whispered Rich, who then summoned all of his powers and introduced everybody to each other. He even remembered people's names and slowly figured out that Pat and Gina were a couple. "So how long have you two been goin' out?"

"A few weeks, she isn't sick of me yet," said the smiling gentleman, with a somber, mellow tone. Gina responded by elbowing him in the arm. Pat sat next to his woman, facing us. Georgina still showed back and shoulder to our two neighbors. She stared off into space and nursed a beer.

"You missed our fortunes," said Gina.

"What the hell are you talking about?"

"Rich read some fortunes for us. Do you have one for Pat or Georgina?"

"No, no, that will have to wait for another night. Now that I un-der-stand that you are a friend, associate…or if I may… dating the great Pat Ver-non, I defer to the future." He raised his glass randomly. "Are you still farming up north? Rich then turned to me because I probably looked puzzled. Vernon grows or-gan-ic vege-tab-les."

"My family operates a farm and a ranch up near Burlington." Pat smiled warmly as he addressed our table.

"I real-ly respect what you guys do Pat. I see the Vernon farms stuff at PCC and some of these other markets…the big V, OH YEAH! It looks like good shit…real fresh and healthy. My aunt had a bout with cancer recently and I think it was some of that crap she eats all the time that caused her so many prob-lems. Just a bunch of chemicals and addii-ttives."

"Pat we need to go." Gina was getting restless and pointing at her watch. As he stood up to head off to a more popular destination, the young scion of Vernon Farms addressed Rich's familial concerns.

"Actually, organic foods have more carcinogenic material than the highly processed stuff you see at the grocery store." We all looked puzzled and Rich furrowed his brow mouth agape, drink held tightly, giving a look like he was being put on. Since nobody was getting it… Vernon continued as Gina tugged at his arm. "Yeah… the pesticide spray used on crops is designed and tested to minimize the use of such matter and the organic crops have to naturally develop their own carcinogens to protect themselves from insects. I think you would find that organic foods actually contain more carcinogens because of their natural production than regular foods. But, they do taste better in my opinion."

"Look at this guy," said Rich pointing. "Mr. plants, ha-Ha-HA!"

"Nice to see you again buddy. Give me a call sometime," Pat said in a very cheerful, but insincere manner. He then waited for Gina, who was really ready to go, to walk out in front of him. "Thanks again for the fortune," was her addition as she left the fence district, I don't think she even made eye contact with any of us. They both gave a cursory wave after tipping or goosing the bouncer – all I heard was giggling and laughing. I'm sure they made fun of us in the car.

"The great Pat graces us with his presence. Of all the assholes that had to come here tonight...." Rich trailed off. "He seemed like an okay guy." My spirited defense was not very persuasive.

"A little pompous," added Georgina. Her assessment didn't make sense to me since all he did was introduce himself and talk about fruit and crops, which is his business. Is somebody supposed to act stupid when subject matter they are familiar with comes up in conversation?

"Pat is a good guy, he is just disgusting. He's had all the breaks." Rich lowered his head and then raised it again, slowly. "He was a good athlete, a pretty strong student and he always dates interesting, attractive women. But there is nothing really horrible about the guy." At that moment my heart stopped beating momentarily, and even though I am not much of a drinker, I saw myself in Rich. My obsession and frustration with Nathan is getting ridiculous and I realize I cannot bear to be a frustrated wanna-be in the future. I needed another drink so I shuffled around in my pocket for the last of my money and asked Rich for some help. He was too fascinated with the little markings on the table to be of much assistance, but Georgina obliged and took some of my cash for another drink of her own. I was hoping Rich had a tab or something so the mushrooms would be on his shoulders. He just kept looking down and moving his non-drink-hand fingers along lines cut into the table from long ago.

"What are you drawing there?"

"Mexico."

"Okay then." Time passed slowly for Rich as his mind wandered into spaces the rest of us could not enter, but Georgina was friendly when she came back to the table. Mr. fortune cookie wandered back inside, came back when they started playing loud music, and then went back in again…his laps only interrupted when he went outside our little fence zone to smoke and say weird   things to strangers.

Georgina was a drunk as well but either her capacity was greater or she started later in the evening. Her big cheeks kept getting redder and her smile larger and I was being as friendly as possible because I have been around heavy drinkers and when you insult them it is not a pretty sight.

"Oh, I love this song." The tune was "Love Train" by the O'Jays. The juke box was rocking now and the old guard was bringing forth their tunes.

"Do you want to dance?"

"I'm not much of a dancer."

"Neither am I, let's go." She grabbed my right hand and pulled me along the table toward a dark little corner on the patio, near the edge of the fence and under one of two speakers blaring outside. At first I was embarrassed because lone cars would pass randomly but then I realized that nobody would know me in that part of town anyway. I made two fists and started grooving my hips   and ass, hands in front of my sternum – trying to smile   and look silly the entire time so Georgina would not think   I was taking myself seriously. Thinking about dancing is the worst time to try and dance. But after a few minutes I began shuffling my feet, moving with some grace and impressing her slowly – winning trust. She kept making little noises like, "Hmmm," and saying, "Wow," as she turned her butt outward, brought her arms in toward her body and moved closer to me.

When a slow song came on, some crap by Spandau Ballet or some other weird group, Georgina moved closer to me and gently pulled my hands to her waist. Once   my digits were in place, she moved my fingers along womanly curves, up and down, alcoholic breath blowing in my face. The feeling was stimulating. I loved it because these people were total strangers and a real woman enjoyed touching me. It was the first time I felt wanted all day and it was spectacular to be an object of affection. I stopped looking behind and we just kept gliding against each other in our little dank corner. When "Wild Horses" by the Rolling Stones came on Georgina moved my right hand to the little indention at the base of her lower back and then down, along her ample behind. I moved my pelvis forward so our lower bodies touched, her breasts leaned against my rib cage. She smelled like baby powder, fresh and soothing. As my arms moved up her back and slid back to her waist she shook her hips slightly and rested her big cheeks against my jaw, nuzzling her face and head into my neck. I had no idea what to do. My blood pressure starting rising and I looked to my right but nobody was on my side of the fence. Georgina was using me as a human shield.

Finally, her head steered her lips to my left ear and she whispered, "Thank you for dancing with me." Then she slowly moved her face in front of mine and grazed my lips with hers while looking to her left. I still held her tight; her eyes were glazed over.

"You are really cute."

"Thank you."

"How old are you."

"No comment."

"Younger than twenty-three?" I wondered why this was a magic number.

"Oh yeah."

"Perfect. I mean that sarcastically, or I mean, just my luck."

"I don't follow." I found myself holding her tighter as she batted doleful eyes.

"What I mean is that I wish you were older."

"Why."

"Just stop talking." She put her head on my left shoulder, sighed and then gave me a little squeeze. Nervousness overwhelmed me and I stood with statue-like rigidity as Georgina began petting my hair and rubbing the back of my head with her large cupped right hand. Her big dimples shown as she pulled back and smiled. Then she felt my engorged crotch with her left hand and made another sound, "Mmmm." The next feeling I experienced were spongy plump lips spreading red lipstick on *my* lips, and a left arm in the middle of my back pushing me forward. Georgina felt strong and confident and she kissed with a purpose. Her tongue flowed into my mouth, a force of nature. Her big wet kisses made me more excited than ever before; a weird feeling considering she was less attractive to me than other girls and her assets were nowhere near as striking as Gina or other lookers. Her round face and hefty female form made me want to curl up beside her on a soft mattress.

"Whoa, you two are really goin' at it." The unmistakable voice of Rich entering the patio filled the air.

"What do you expect? He is cute." She gave me another squeeze on the ass before moving out of the corner and heading back to the table, I just stood in place for a moment, confused as to what I should do next. When I turned to follow the sounds Rich had a buddy with him, a scrawny guy with a thin mustache and an oversized dark coat wearing a baseball cap.

My stuff had been cleared from the table, except for a drink one-quarter full. Georgina was already sitting on the other side of the table next to the new guy, who seemed to have just returned from the jungles of Vietnam. His mud stained coat was one of those dark green surplus army jobs. His drink was dark red and he looked like he was going to freak out on somebody. His head was darting back and forth from one side of the patio to the other, like ghosts were among us.

"Hi," I said looking in his direction as I moved back into place to nurture my glass. There was no response so Georgina gave him an elbow and pointed at me. "Hey, he's talking to you."

Mustache boy looked at her like her hand was full of acid and he jumped in his seat. Then he looked around some more. Even Rich snapped out of his stupor and said, "Dude, you alright?" I started giggling and could not stop this time. Then crazy dart head man spoke.

"Could you repeat the question?" Then after a great pause, he said, "Please!" He looked straight ahead until he blurted out 'please' and then he turned suddenly and peered at Georgina, who replied, "You're out of your fucking mind mate." His lips were wide apart, his mouth squeezed into a ridiculous expression, like he was whistling in reverse after making contact with a stun gun. Rich just stared at both of them. Laughter was overtaking me so I got up from the table and headed to the bathroom inside where I expected to find a wide range of other zombies. Instead, healthy looking frat guys were calmly playing pool, probably bored with their on-campus lives. The only freaks in the joint were out on the patio with me. I tried to get into serious mode, giving myself little slaps to the face in the restroom mirror to jar laughter out of my body. Deep breathing and fixing my hair brought new focus and I headed back to my domain, steering clear of the bouncer at the other door.

My first two steps on the patio brought me in clear view of the table of shame, where Rich was staring underneath his chair, Georgina was talking to a new guy on the other side of the fence and mustache was smelling his armpits. He was very stealth; moving his chin down into position and then looking up at the sky and brushing his arm against the side of his head. He jumped up in his seat and looked frightened as I approached. This spurred conversation.

"Do you know how to get to…LYNNWOOD?" Again, his head sprang toward me when the final word released from his lips.

"Would you shut the fuck up please?" Georgina did not like this guy. She decided to go to the store with her new friend. Before leaving she came on my side of the table and said, "Are you going to be here when I get back love?"

"Maybe, I need to figure it out soon. Eventually, I need to get over to White Center." "Where is that?"

"Next to West Seattle."

"Oh my, you live all the way over there? What a shame. Are you going to stop by and see us again sometime?"

"Yes…yes, definitely. In fact, I am not even sure how I am going to get home tonight."

"Well, I am sure you will figure it out. Give me a call next time you're in the area." She passed me a note that said: G, 206-568-3677. Her smile was big and alluring as she floated out the door and turned hard right to hit the street. I watched her the entire time but she never looked back. Her ride across the street was a running car; the guy she had been speaking with, who was nondescript and wore a cap, was sitting in the driver's seat in the shadows. As I prepared to leave Rich suddenly came to life, turned to me and said, "Hi, I am…" "Rich," I said, finishing his sentence. He looked surprised, eyelids raised, then he snapped back into character. "Oh yeah, hey man, I was just kidding. Are you taking off?"

"Yeah, I need to get back to the…ah West Seattle."

"Do you have a…Cccc…Car?" This time my head snapped to Vietnam man.

"No, sorry, takin' the bus."

"Don't you worry about this guy," said Rich, while patting his new friend on the shoulder. We will make sure he puts his Huggies on and makes it home tonight. Boy, look at that clear sky my friends. Mar-vel-ous. Hey, you look like you need another Bloody Mary my friend."

I lit out before another order was taken on my behalf. Waiting for a bus after I got downtown was a bit of a challenge. I was forced to linger alongside the old hounds that sit around bus zones on warm summer evenings. One old guy took a shine to me and came over to chat, but once he discovered I wasn't going to give him any money he bolted to his next target. After our interaction an even older gentleman, sprawled across the only bench in the area, sat up and rubbed his eyes with closed fists.

"Boy, you look like you have been sufferin' tonight."

"Yeah," I said while leaning back against a dirty aluminum pole hosting the Plexiglas-encrusted bus shelter. "Nothing has gone my way for a while."

"Girls."

"Yeah, I guess you could say that. Or at least my luck is pretty poor."

"When you are young, that fight to get ahead and find the perfect girl is always present." I could not tell if he was interesting or a crazy old coot. He stood up and moved his arms around in a circular motion, his tattered dark blue chamois shirt, frayed at the seams, flopped about – too large for his frame. Dirty tan slacks on slender legs. Past grace and a certain style was on display when he relaxed. He stood erect; a well-groomed salt and pepper beard indicated a modicum of pride. This guy was no Rich. When he asked for a cigarette I knew why he spent the time to speak with me, and it put me at ease. In fact, I gave him another one for the road.

"When I was your age I used to dream about being a sports star. In my mind, play on the field equated to scoring off of it if you know what I mean." He didn't smile; his manner was direct and advisory. "As I aged and the girls I lusted after spent their time with other guys, I dreamed of getting in conflicts and kicking their asses." He laughed and took a long drag on his cig. "Once I was deep into my thirties and forties I fantasized about being the coach of a great team or the trainer who pushed a boxer to the top. When that nonsense got boring my thoughts turned to making a bunch of money to impress some girl and keep her forever. The dough would be my security blanket; keep me from having to work so hard for love."

"Do you think that is really true?"

"What's that?"

"That money will solve everything or at least draw the right people…I mean the person you love?"

"No, I don't think it works like that. But it does in some cases." Another long, slow drag followed. "It is kind of like those guys on the radio who get famous and then spout off about how you need to treat women badly to gain their affection. I have a feeling they pulled that shit after their money was already made." He laughed out loud and nodded, then a quick puff. I handed him a third cigarette because I knew he would be ready for a refill soon.

"Thanks son. Yeah, those guys are not telling the truth. It is pretty easy to act picky when you have power and money… but until you reach those levels, girl world is not that easy. And when you get old and crusty like me, women and you are just out of time."

"Oh come on, you aren't that old."

"Too old to care or do anything about it. You see, I can tell you that at this stage of my life, my opportunities have dried up…and that is too bad because spending time with a fine woman, someone that makes your skin tingle is just about the best feeling on earth." He sat back down defeated, shoulders slumped and moved to extinguish his first cigarette with his foot after flicking it on the ground. He kept matches in one of his pants pockets and he flipped the little container up in the air and caught it with the same hand.

"What these rich guys don't understand is that being with a fine woman or someone that makes you feel special is something everybody can enjoy, whether they have eighty million or eight cents. That is what the great blues and jazz artists understood. They played stuff down and dirty because they knew their audience members could relate. Have you ever heard any music by Robert Johnson?"

"No," I shook my head and tried to look mellow and mature, unsurprised.

"Man, schools today should get it together. There are lessons in music and literature and everybody can figure out the clues if they listen and understand that passion comes from effort and that waiting around to be rich, cool or smart is no way to pursue women. It is not the way to live life." The bus arrived as he was finishing his thoughts so I thanked him for his advice and handed over one more cigarette. Who knows how long he will be hanging out near that shelter?

After another bus transfer in West Seattle and a bit of a walk after the final leg, home sounded comforting. I purposely looked the other way when nearing Saji's Aunt's house. Blocking that part of the evening out of my mind was the best option. It was really late by the time   I navigated all the locks on the front door and made my way inside. The howlers were silent; but Mom's was up, her door was open and she felt like talking. She was still concerned about my father, who from her perspective was still AWOL in Pennsylvania. I am sure he was just taking advantage of a short-term job opportunity, but my attempts at building trust through conversation were going nowhere and I was running out of ideas. She met me in the hallway before I could get to bed and shared her concerns again.

"Have you considered writing a letter describing how you feel?"

"I already sent him two letters."

"When did they go out?"

"A few days ago…or at least the first one did."

"How about the second one?"

"I put it in the mail today."

I tried not to laugh, but I was unable to masquerade my smile as I sat on her bedroom floor. I had already brushed my teeth about three times to conceal my drinking. "But Mom, he hasn't even seen your letters yet…plus if you sent it to a temporary living place it might take a while for the pieces to even reach his room."

"I realize that, but I would like to think that he cares enough to call or write and tell me what is going on."

"You know how focused he becomes when he is busy."

"Yes, but ignoring us is unacceptable. An update and some feedback is all I want." Her sad eyes were making mine water. I had to say goodnight and told her I was too tired to provide any ideas. Of course, I really had nothing to add and I thought I would be fresh in the morning. My mother is so inconsolable in such situations that I think she takes the most negative position possible on purpose. Or maybe she really does feel like a rock at the bottom of the ocean. Either way, patting her on the head and going to bed did not make me feel any better.

My teeth were clean but I made another stop in the bathroom before bed to wash my face, which I had ignored earlier in my haste to cover evidence of alcohol. A lone sparkle, sitting just to the left of my nose, was illuminated in the weak lightbulb-missing ceiling light. I kept looking to make sure I was seeing the little guy. It sounds crazy but to me it was a sign – a small trumpet that could not be ignored. Georgina's cheeks had transferred the little gem and it was reminiscent of what my beautiful Torrie wore the sad night Nathan invaded her life and my heart. I decided at that moment to write a love note to Torrie, describing how I feel about her and what she means to me. I started, 'Dear Torrie'…then changed it to 'Torrie,' then 'My Love,' thinking that acting as a secret admirer would be a better idea than releasing my identity. After about three or four lines of complete shit I abandoned the idea. 'Torrie, I realize you have feelings for Nathan....'....'We do not know each other well, but you mean the world to me.' 'Every time I think of you my heart skips.' Describing how I think about her all the time, her body or her personality made me sound like a wacko. Every time I started writing how nice, polite and upstanding she is, it sounded ridiculous because I don't actually have a close relationship with T.

But as strange as it sounds...that sparkle was a message. It was a sign not to quit on Torrie. Her love must be won over a period of time. The tortoise and the hare and other long-range metaphors raced through my mind as my adrenalin made the late hour feel like a new beginning. The letter idea was terrible, but a better concept hatched after reflecting upon what the old man at the bus stop said. My new goal was to be even closer to Nathan and his woman, show her my personality up close and bide my time until she falls in love with me. This epiphany made me feel so good I bounded into bed with new vigor and fell asleep with a smile on my face.

Sunlight brought a new day and plan mimicking the energy I felt the night before. My favorite place on earth is the moist green landscape of the Olympic Peninsula; where my father and I go camping and fishing – even though I don't do either well. He does most of the work and I screw around and gather stuff. Other kids our age go camping and head out on trips together. I am going to organize a trip to the land of the big trees near the coast and invite fun people to join me.

13

Empty

When I called Nathan imploring him to join me and bring friends on a camping journey he was lukewarm about the idea at first. After I outlined how private moments would be plentiful he became interested. Fortunately, he was not on the Big 5 work schedule the following weekend so no impediments lurked. Torrie's schedule was always fluid so that would not be a concern. I did not want to bug him about her tagging along – that was a decision he would have to make himself – my goal was to facilitate. Nate was more interested in discussing our next mall project scheduled for Thursday. He wanted to make sure work would not interfere that day and I promised him I could manipulate my boss to make sure the middle of the day worked. My persuasive skills were terrible that Sunday, I was not thinking clearly, so I rolled outside to smoke, sit on the patio and contemplate another plan. Nathan was noncommittal. Then the phone rang.

"Ramy."

"Yes."

"You don't mind if Torrie and Chester join us do you?" A big smile on my end of the phone provided the silent answer.

"No, do you have to watch Chet next weekend."

"Yeah, since I don't work on Saturday or Sunday my mother asked me if I would watch him while she stays with a friend at a poetry retreat on Whidbey Island or some shit."

"Are you sure Chester doesn't want to hear some poetry?"

"He would probably run around screaming and freak out some of those old bitches." Nathan lowered his voice at the end of the sentence. Torrie was speaking with someone in the background. "But yeah, camping is a popular item over here so if you know the place we can provide a car."

"Should we invite some other people?"

"There is only so much room in the car chief."

"No, I mean people with wheels."

"Sure, fine with me. Hey, my mother is moving back into castle Foster so I need to get going because I am already late." I imagined Laney looking at her watch and shaking her head. I contemplated offering my services but somehow found the power to cease speaking as my mouth formed the words, 'I can help.' Since I expect to be the key landscape worker for weeks to come, assisting with the move-in is even too much for me.

"We have to talk about Thursday. Are you available later tonight?"

"Sure."

"Great, see ya."

After our chat I ventured outside to smoke and stand in the sun, meandering toward the curb in front of our house. As I stared like a jerk, the Road Pig rode up on a bicycle of all things – I was surprised the lime green ten- speed could hold his girth. He was wearing sunglasses and a tie-dye tank top and looked like a giant version of one of the guys in ZZ Top. He must be six foot five and shaped like an offensive lineman – not sloppy fat, just a big powerful guy. He pulled up in front of his fence and looked right at me.

"How's it going?" I had never heard the big man speak to anybody in my family.

"Pretty well, considering I am not doing anything productive."

"I do that all the time."

The big man stood up and launched his ten-speed over the fence. He was sweating in the hot sun and looked like he required about one deodorant stick per pit.

"I didn't hear the howlers last night, did you?"

"No, in fact, I have not heard them for a while."

"Those are some crazy SOB's...have you ever watched them?"

"Yeah, my friends and I used to sit on 19th and watch them come around the corner. We followed them for a while on a couple of occasions."

"My buddies and I watch them cruise the streets once in a while if I have some people over and the party goes all night, but I usually sleep through their parade." His manner was very pleasant – soft spoken and serious. Like a number of people I have encountered in life, his reputation overshadows reality. Everyone is scared of him because of his girth and his noise on the bike.

"Do you want a smoke?"

"No thanks, stopped doing that years ago. Non- alcoholic beer is my only vice now. You have a good one." He walked back inside and grabbed his bike with a meaty paw and headed for the garage. Just standing around, looking stupid and smoking certainly draws interest from adults. Perhaps there is an advantage to being young and confused in life. People on the outside – those who do not see you every day - wonder what the hell you are doing. Since my father left a list of chores focusing on summer projects, and I never know when he will return, it was time for action. I hoped my mother would leave the house, but as usual she puttered between her bedroom and the living room to peer out the window. She even spent a few minutes in the kitchen peeking around. Weeding, and there were some big honkers out there, was my first task, followed by mowing a dead lawn with a push lawnmower – I felt like I was moving air around. Then I washed the outside of the windows, which truly proved how dirty the inside of the panes looked up close. There were plenty more tasks ahead but with a hot sun on my back I started day-dreaming about admiring Torrie at the Peninsula.

"Yo, Ramos."

The unmistakable voice of Zip ruined my restful day. I was drying off the window in the front of the house with headphones on when he shouted my name. I turned around slowly and took a long breath.

"Hey guys." As usual, Tony was driving and the Zipper sat in the passenger slot, wearing some dark striped pants and a red rubber-looking shirt, like a motorcycle racer.

"Ya ready for this Thursday?"

I walked up to the car, kneeling down to speak with the guys at eye level. Tony was clearly stoned. He had a little smile on his face. Zip looked like he was ready to run through a wall, amped up, bouncing around in his seat, eyes juiced.

"Yeah, I told Nathan I would be available."

"Just checkin' baby. We need to make sure everybody is ready to go." He grabbed my left forearm with his right hand and gave me a big squeeze.

"What time and where?"

"Probably north this time; how about we pick you up along 35th?"

"I can do that."

"Is that your mom or something?" Zip moved his head in the direction of the house. I turned around and viewed my mother peering outside the now half-clean window.

"Don't worry, she's spaced out of her mind."

"Oh yeah, Nathan said something about that." His comment pissed me off but I forced myself to stay silent.

"What time on Thursday?"

"Can you meet us at 9:30?"

"Sure, any particular place?

"How about the bus stop at Barton?" I was annoyed with this suggestion because that stop is just up the road from Saji's Aunt's house but I wanted to get those two greasebags out of the neighborhood so I agreed. As usual, they sped off and unleashed a crazy U-turn in the middle of the street, tires squealing. After speaking with the Road Pig and discovering he didn't even drink or smoke I had visions of him lecturing me about safety. After cleaning up and venturing inside I braced for questions.

"Who were those people?"

"Friends of Nathan."

"From school."

An elongated pause followed as I contemplated the consequences of a long discussion about people from school and their intentions. "No, I am not sure where he met them. Next time he comes by you should ask him."

"I have not seen Nathan for a while. Is he still working at Big 5?"

"Yeah, I don't think he will ever leave that place."

"I hope those boys don't hurt themselves."

"They probably will at some point. Anthony is pretty reckless behind the wheel."

"Hmmm," she sighed, and then headed back into her room.

After our little interlude I focused on camping, patiently waiting for my mother to go to the bathroom. When she finally made her move I rushed into her and pop's bedroom and grabbed his fishing maps from the top drawer of the old wooden desk in the corner. I secured the bounty under my bed just as she stepped back in the hallway. Questions about my plan for camping would be a nuisance, and since there is no target date on the horizon for the keeper of the maps, who makes his own special charts and notes in small black lettering on them for future reference, I figured I would take a chance. Even if he returned soon he would be too exhausted to take a fishing trip for a while – he would spend all of his time yelling at me to finish more chores. When the television went back on in mom's room I started planning the journey. We would go to a little open campsite near Humptulips, this crazy little district on the Peninsula that has a name that has some Indian meaning, beautiful river or some shit. Imagining Torrie's expression when she reads the road sign on the way there made me laugh.

During the Spring I went out there with Pop and a friend of his named Marv Richards, who is pretty funny because he never smiles. Fortunately we took Marv's car, a Jeep, so we could all fit without sitting sideways. Richards is a strange driver, he always changes speeds when he sees something or while staring out the window. He kept jamming up to sixty-eight and then suddenly dropped to fifty. In the back seat it felt like I was going to fly into somebody's lap. When we stopped for gas Pop got out to chat while Marv pumped gas, which amused me because they didn't speak when we were on the road. Maybe he was nervous about the driving as well. Richards looks a little like Clint Eastwood but his eyebrows are bushier. Both he and Pop have a problem with friendliness so they both stood next to the Jeep glaring at people in their hunting jackets. They looked like two crazies that met in prison; instead of friends from the army. According to my father, Marv always plays poker with no expression whether he wins or loses. I don't know if this means he is good, but something about his ability to suppress his feelings impresses Pop, who shows emotion when filling up a glass of water. When they were both outside the car I had peace at last. It did not last long.

"John, did you pack all the bait?" Since he had already asked me four times, beginning at 4:30 in the morning, I was getting sick of the question. Pop was shouting at closed windows.

"Yep."

"What!"

"Yep!!"

By the time the car started rolling again they both felt like talking. "What are you lookin' at old woman?" Now Pop's attention was on some lady in another car.

"She thinks you're cute."

"Compared to that guy sitting next to her I am pretty goddamn cute. He looks like a Sea Lion."

"Yeah." After a great pause Marv begin speaking again. "If I looked like that guy I would shoot myself in the face."

"And that woman looks like the bait." Pop cracked himself up so he started cackling. "Are you sure that bait is cold?" He turned to look at me. I rolled my eyes.

"Jesus."

"Keep your lip to yourself boy. I have shirts older than you."

"Hey what is your oldest shirt?" This topic intrigued Richards.

"Twenty-seven years," he blurted out immediately. I was skeptical. It sounded like a number he just pulled out of his ass; I doubt he could calculate years that quickly.

"I've got you beat." Marv turned toward Pop after another long pause. "Thirty-two."

"Oh bullshit. You…[he started to chuckle]…you probably are just holding on to the first training bra you stole."

"At least I saw one. You were busy chasing around old women and grabbing their asses. Hey we better stop talking about bras or junior's gonna start masturbating back there." That crack made Richards smile.

I wish someone had been in the back seat with me so I could roll my eyes properly. Riding around with the poker buddies was not my idea of a good time. The best thing about the trip was that both of them cannot go an hour and a half without eating so we got to stop and snack and tear into our packed lunches long before arriving at the great fishing hole. My father brought four sandwiches, two bananas, two oranges and three cookies for lunch and he is so nervous he kept chomping everything along the way. As we unpacked our gear near the Humptulips River he turned to me and said, "Did you bring some cigs?" Then after he finished my pack I spent twenty-five minutes searching for a canteen he lost in the woods. Just when I thought my tasks were finished for the day he sent me up on a little mound near the beach to "clear out some space for our stuff." When he thought the brush was too close to his precious gear he instructed me to take his   little hand saw and cut back all the blackberries. Fifteen minutes later I looked like I had been in a fight with a bobcat and my blood was on the saw. "What the hell did you do to my saw?" bellowed my father.

Thirty minutes later Richards was perched about twenty feet below me on another mound near an indention in the river, a perfect low spot for dropping a line. A couple of guys in a small boat began encroaching on his territory. I knew the situation would lead to an uncomfortable conclusion when Marv started yelling and opened his raincoat, like he was flashing somebody. Underneath his coat was a large holster; something out of an old Western, and a revolver; it looked like a .357 to me.

"Why don't you guys fish in somebody else's hole?"

"I guess this is not a free river, huh Charlie."

"Did you notice me standing here?"

"Well there you have it…the self-appointed mayor of Humptulips right over here."

"That's right cocksucker, I am the mayor and I just made ruling. Get the fuck out of my fishing hole or you will be fishing lead out of your ass." As the two anglers started drifting further away one of them was shaking their head and the guy with all the commentary was making snorting sounds; he could not believe what was happening. Then my father decided it was time to chime in from his station further up the bank. He had probably been taking a crap or something.

"Why you uppity piece of shit, dry-ass cracker motherfucker. We've been fishing here for years and nobody has ever hogged the bank we're working like you fuckers."

"Call a cop."

"You couldn't catch a fish if it nibbled on your balls."

This was a particularly strange thing to say since the men had a boat full of fish, a bunch of really fancy gear and a general understanding of how to fish. After his last line Pop started coughing for about two minutes straight and tripped over the driftwood holding up his pole, he sounded like he was dying.

Finally one of the other guys yelled, "Happy Sunday to you too" and they never looked back again.

Marv kept glaring at both men, his bushy eyebrows turned in their direction like headlights. After two and a half hours of standing along the bank, which included a pleasant one-hour nap for me and endless coughing by Mr. Nature up the way, we left with zero fish because everybody was hungry again. If there is a fish god he or she is still laughing at us. After a delightful drive-in experience at Homer's Hot Dog Stand, 'Only the best since 1949′ we were passed abruptly on the highway by the same two guys with all the fish on the river in an expensive Porsche. When I glanced their way from the back seat my natural reaction was to shrink and look in the other direction. If they saw us in our sorrowful post- fishing state, my father and Richards shoving hot dogs in their faces and me staring out the window like I was heading to juvenile detention, they must have cackled their asses off as they sped by. I began wondering why Pop is so down on camping since he spends so much time screwing around during his fishing trips, but it was an inopportune time to discuss the matter. If they had caught *something* it would have been worth conversation.

After slumping down in the back seat for a while I looked in the rear view mirror and Marv had mustard in his eyebrows and Pop's gas was so bad that even he had to roll down the window.

"Did you shit your pants?" Richards asked the question so casually that it made me giggle.

"I think so."

That was the end of their dialogue for another thirty miles when they launched into a shared diatribe about men who wear earrings. Neither of them are in favor of the concept.

Remembering past journeys to the Peninsula made me laugh as I sprawled across my crappy little bed and wrote down names of people to invite on a scrap of cardboard picked out of the garbage. After several minutes of staring at the ceiling I realized maximizing time with Torrie required a more intimate party atmosphere, not a gathering dominated by obnoxious friends. I scratched out the names and began listed activities for next weekend. Rock skipping, fishing, bonfires, long walks, following animal tracks, checking out the old cemeteries in the area, picnics and home run derby.

I know, it sounds like a real sissy list gleaned from an after school special…or some dumb camp movie. I only left out s'mores and picking flowers. But this kind of crap is the only advantage over Nathan I possess – using my brain to itemize romantic experiences. I don't even think he reads that guy. He just reacts to everything most of the time and relies on innate ability. Hopefully, over time…it may take years…I will appeal to Torrie.

Spending time at the bowling alley that night sounded exciting because of recent experience, but there was a little more time before our local library closed for the day so I hiked over to the front of the place where the weekend powerhouse, Mrs. Wheeler, manned the entrance. In our neighborhood branch there is a turnstile that beeps and requires the person behind the desk to let you out so you do not rip off any materials. Most of the newer libraries are more normal, but my spot is so shitty, and has so few books, that snobs stay away. And if a kid is trying to get materials together for school they trek to another neighborhood so they can pretend that they are doing more research. I have the run of the place. Wheeler is really focused on people taking CD's so she sits at the front with her little gate buzzer and gives everybody the once-over. Her outfits are always high neck jobs that zip or button up to her chin, whether she is wearing a sweater or a dress. If they made outfits that covered your face and just left two eyes peering out at you like a hawk, Wheels would buy them. She knows me because I hang out in the corner and read pieces of a novel that I select for the day. Wheeler also remembers how many fines I have had to pay over the years; she is like a human computer.

"Good afternoon Mr. Ramos. Are you heading to your little corner this afternoon?" Wheeler is a little deaf, and since everybody in the library thinks you have to be quiet, when she blurts something out everyone nearby looks up like someone won a prize.

"Yeah, trying to sneak in a little reading before you close." I must sound like I am about eighty years old. After a little bit of lurking around a book titled, *The Newhouse Gang*, drew my attention. I settled in near the bay window in the corner where a bit of sunlight peeked through. There were little kids out playing on the lawn in front of the building, really hacking things up. I figured once Wheeler saw those kids she would go out there and jump on their shit. The Newhouse crew grew from a few guys in a Cleveland neighborhood who were down in the dumps. They tried to change their luck with a flower and garden show designed to pick up girls. They first tried to make their own band and after they realized they sucked, they got serious and moved to plants. As their scheme started unraveling one of the characters, Teddy, realized he really liked flowers and started a nursery. Of course, nobody picked up any girls. It is pretty obvious where this comedy is going; I probably do not need to finish this one. Several jokes centered on the guys pretending to be big shots and trying to fake people out on the street, in business meetings, at the local bar, etc. Everybody but Teddy had no clue what they were talking about and they were trying to sell people special landscaping services. The primary guy is Sal Newhouse, who sounded like a good friend to have. In books, friends are always up for doing something to keep the story moving. I like that world, one where time stands still and it doesn't take hours and days to convince someone to get off their ass and do something. I fell asleep for a few minutes and Wheeler kicked everybody out before she walked over and gently tapped me on the shoulder.

"Ramos."

"Yes, sorry…I didn't realize I fell asleep."

"You can finish that one next time you pay us a visit."

"Great, thank you." I meticulously tracked down the spot where I found the book. Wheeler is a real stickler for such things. She never smiles but I can tell she appreciates the effort. She opened the gate a good ten minutes after shut down time.

I felt like celebrating my camping concept with somebody so I called damn near everyone I know when I got back home. Chirp was working at Yummy Teriyaki. Nico was missing in action, his family had no idea where he was. In fact, his brother said, "Dude, I haven't seen him in about a week." Jasper was stuck in Wenatchee at a baseball tournament and he is in love with Myra Brackett, so none of us will see him until she leaves the state or his baseball coach kicks him off the team. His parents are worried. Everybody is concerned that old Jasper is not serious about his future or his baseball. But I bet they would make the same decision if they had a chance to hang out with Myra. Beach living is David Mack's summer vocation. He calls me all the time during the school year. Now he pretends to be a lifeguard at Alki Beach while he is really just spending his time scanning cute Filipino girls and working part-time at Artie's Burgers. Seattle beaches are so lame, and the weather is so shitty, that I could never understand why anybody would hang out at such places anyway.

"You should come down here J," was all he could muster when I reached him over the phone. "Yeah, it is too cold to swim but the view is nice and Artie is letting me walk around with a little tray selling hot dogs. He doesn't even have a license to do it, but I sold a couple of dogs to some cops so I don't think anybody is paying attention." I imagined standing with Dave as he walks around with his TV-dinner tray thing pushing hot dogs and that sounded about as much fun as playing with a bunch of little kids in a sandbox - so I passed.

Ricky Sugar suits up at the local Safeway but he spends every waking moment outside of work getting stoned and he always wants me to come to him. I had no interest in meeting him after his shift and being harassed about scoring some junk on his behalf. Plus, I don't have much money left and he always pays people back late. Todd Solvi is always a pain in the ass because he trumps everybody's ideas all the time. He waits like a vulture to hear your plan and then he dispenses a bunch of wisdom about how to refine or upgrade something. One time I asked him if he wanted to cruise to the Burien Drive-In and he spent about ten minutes hemming and hawing and suggesting another theater where the seats are more comfortable. What kind of a guy bitches about sitting in his own car? As I ticked off the pros and cons of calling Solvi in my head Mom's asked me to make her some coffee in our beat up red Braun. I don't know why she can't make her own coffee; she acts like my recipe is better. I think she just forgets how many scoops to put in. When I make coffee for myself I slop the water all over the place. When I pour it into the machine and Moms is watching I really take my time and try not to spill a drop. It is really strange how much I focus when people are monitoring me.

"Mmmmm," she cooed after tasting the coffee. She made a big deal out of my expertise but I was not fooled. I knew she wanted some company. We spoke for a while about my father's lack of communication, Nathan's family and their move back into their old digs and how shitty the Mariners were playing. I started fidgeting as I stood and spoke in our little kitchen. Eventually, I desired to head outside and spend a little time in the remaining daylight.

"Do you want to take a walk to the park?"

"No, I am not even dressed."

"I can wait."

"You go on, I can go another time." She missed the point; I was trying to get her out of the house. Daylight waned but it was warm outside and the ground at the park up the road, as much dirt as grass, was hard, unlike the Seattle squish that you step in nine months of the year. I walked the small perimeter of the area, kicking a few rocks out of the way periodically. It occurred to me I did not know the name of the park so I kept my eye out for a sign or a marker. I think someone tore it down or used it for firewood long ago.

After three circles around the little city block, which featured a handful of scraggly trees, some rocks, a bench and some lady walking her dog, I was underwhelmed by the scenery. An old dude listing on the bench's warped wood stared at me. Apparently, he does not get many visitors to his little place in the sun. Even the homeless guy sitting in the corner putting leaves in his sleeping bag was tracking my movements. I was in a goofy mood so I just started running back home as if chased by an imaginary pursuer. I even looked back with fear a few times and bowed my back as if the bad guy was lunging to grab me. When I reached visual safety around the corner I slowed down and laughed.

After walking the entirety of the street a few times, crossing back and forth, I walked to the other end of the block and viewed the park from another angle. I didn't feel like sitting down and relaxing; but privacy was paramount and the lady with the pooch was still frolicking about. The other clowns didn't bother me but she looked like she wanted to have sex with her dog so she wasn't going anywhere fast. It bugs me when strangers look in my direction. So I sat down on the curb after moving out of eyeshot again and drained a cigarette while a few cars passed by. One of them, an older Ford Ranchero, black with special gold trim, created by some weird Steelers fan or someone color blind, grooved by, blasting "Saturday Night Fever" by the Bee Gees. I don't why I find these little signals so important, but the music picked me up and I gained crazy energy. I felt like running some more or leaping up and doing some jumping jacks like a lunatic; like a little kid feels when a door is opened and he or she runs outside as fast as they can to catch the wind. I had to get out and do something. Right there on the curb I remembered the previous New Year's when I sat in Lindy's Diner for about four hours and watched other people depart, heading for fun as I blended into bright red vinyl seats.

The first two hours were spent facing a couple of old football coaches who were talking about some game from 1932 or something. One of them could not hear so he kept saying, "Huh," every time the shorter one said something. They both had caps and jackets and hunched over their hamburgers; drinking coffee until they probably wet themselves. When the short guy was not talking football he was talking about World War II and some battle he was a part of. "We handed them their balls in a sack," he kept bragging. Later when he was talking about some high school football game he coached he said, "Their balls were in a sack when we got through with 'em." The guy used the phrase about seven more times and he kept making it shorter, "I'll tell ya, their balls were handed to them." I longed for the old piece of garbage to fall asleep in his salad so his friend would go home and they would have nothing to yap about.

A couple of sisters a few tables over even got into a shouting match that night. That was pretty entertaining. One of them stormed out because the other one kept asking her why she broke up with her boyfriend. When she tired of the question she grabbed her coat, left her food and took off. Her sibling then spent about twenty minutes explaining she didn't have any money and telling the owner of the place she needed to go home so she could pay them. Everybody was on the same page when she left her coat as collateral but she still was nowhere in sight by the time I left. Okay, now I am really on a tangent, let me get back to the reason that experience was similar to my feelings near the park.

"Do you think I will find a husband tonight?" asked a beautiful Latino girl eating near the door and waiting for a friend to take her downtown.

"You've already found one honey," said a cop near the front door. "Although this one is too old for you."

"Mucho dinero," said the server watching this unfold. He smiled and rubbed imaginary money between his fingers. He obviously knew the cop because they both laughed. The young woman also laughed, looking as confident as she would ever be, in a dark lycra-looking shirt, a black coat and fishnet stockings that accentuated smooth shapely legs. Both the policeman and the server watched her as she slipped into the kitchen through swinging wooden doors, old west style. I was watching as well, she was an alluring girl. The cop had been helping himself to the coffee pot behind the counter and he said, "whooo," gave a quick headshake and headed out the door. His uniform looked too tight, like he was wearing his summer clothes and they could not contain his winter body. He also had a little milk or something, from the coffee he was sipping, on his mustache. Retirement was imminent.

"Whoa," someone yelled in the back. Other talk that was difficult to understand followed. "Contain your vagina girl!" was shouted at some point and the server peered over the swinging wooden doors facing the kitchen and shushed everybody. By the time she was finished showing off her legs, the young cook or waitress or whatever she is, came back into the dining room and headed out into the night. This time I really sized her up and she was wearing enough makeup to cover a building, but her outfit was still strong. When she walked out the front door and met a friend outside in the parking lot the server stared at them like he was missing a boat to a gold rush. I mean, he didn't appear to be in love with the girl, but he looked like a zoo animal hoping to escape to the other side of the glass. From then on it was really weird because he acted like he didn't want me to leave. He kept asking me if I wanted more coffee and water – I had to go to the bathroom about seven times. "You can stay a while," he kept saying, sad eyes below dark spiked hair and above a white striped colored shirt. Watching him made me feel so sad that I forgot about my problems, and vowed to never feel like that poor bastard on New Year's Eve, or any other time life felt like it was slipping by. I should really write this stuff down so I remember what my program should be in the future. Who knows? In twenty years I might not remember these things and then my time might be spent at the same crummy diner talking to some old fogy who doesn't understand that his balls are already in a sack. I did stay at Lindy's for another two hours, feeling sorry for the guy working and then I went home to a little television and some cake with my mother. These memories propelled my decision to head out and do something. I almost ran home to insure I could get out in the summer air as quickly as possible. I decided to go to a place where I could find some people.

By the time I reached Capitol Hill I was lethargic again, worn down after two and a half hours of bus rides, making a peanut butter and jelly sandwich for the road and rinsing off my clothes by hand and then waiting for them to dry in the rattling old yellow dryer that has been running on fumes for years. The last time the thing stopped working my father took it outside, turned it upside down, bashed it a few times with a mallet and plugged it back in. I am not sure if it works or if it just air-dries everything. My budget for the night was ten to twelve dollars; all indications were that Nathan would give me some cash for my assistance in his odd-ball operation before the next weekend and that would see me through until a paycheck arrived. The city was still shrouded in warm air so a yellow short-sleeve t-shirt, and dark brown pants that covered dirt well, were my weapons of choice. My feet hurt when my well-worn tan vans with white soles hit uneven pavement along the sidewalks of Broadway.

After the merchandise at Raffle's Records bored me, a group of skateboarders passed by making a ruckus. "I wish those little shitheads would make noise somewhere else," said a middle-aged guy behind me with his girlfriend or wife or something. As I pretended to glance behind me and get a look at the fellow, sometimes I do this by rubbing my mouth on the top of my shoulder and acting like I am using my shirt or jacket as a napkin, I caught a glimpse of Lem sitting across the street in front of a little coffee stand next to the parking lot of a bank. He was staring in the direction of the moon like a freak. I hesitated, paused again, sighed, and walked across the street.

"How come you aren't at work?"

Lem slowly turned my way and unleashed a big smile. He looked genuinely happy to see me, the lonely bastard.

"Yo, Ramos, what brings you to my seclusion?"

"You didn't answer my question."

"I quit the job at the grocery store."

"So you can sleep for a change?"

"And I can talk to interesting people like you."

"Hey why did you drop your meat the other night at Dick's? You freaked out Lisa Saji so badly she almost wrecked her car."

Laughing, "Dude I was so wasted that night, I barely remember anything." He put his head down, popped it up again with a slight grunt, laughed harder, right hand pressed against his abdomen. "Man that is pretty funny."

"So do you just hang out and drink coffee now that you are less employed?"

A smile, "Nah, I'm waiting for my sister."

"Mind if I hang for a while?"

"No, that'd be great. I'm just here watching the freaks go by."

"Yeah, I just witnessed some skate boarders' anger some adults across the street."

"That's nothing, they don't even have purple hair." Lem gave a disapproving look and looked like he had just swallowed something sour. His eyes narrowed and he started scanning the sidewalks for the profiles he described.

"I didn't know you had a sister."

"She was adopted. I was the only chosen one." Lem slung low in his chair. He gulped another slug of coffee like it was a drug keeping him alive.

"How old is she?"

"Jesus, I don't know. Seven or eight years older than me. As usual, she is late. I am supposed to give her a ride later so she can visit her friend."

"Isn't she allowed to go out on her own?"

"This is some scheme she is working on…I didn't pay attention to the details."

"Sounds juicy." I started smiling like a lunatic because I was suddenly in a great mood, no more walking around aimlessly. Sitting around talking to even some goof like Lem kept me from feeling self-conscious and glancing all over the place while darting around the neighborhood. I have never captured the art of relaxation. Instead I stare at things and smile all the time.

"Yeah, she runs around with guys sometimes and uses me as an excuse."

"What do you mean? So she dates multiple people? Who cares?"

"She is married."

"Really. Pretty scandalous."

"Yeah, but somehow she plays it well."

"Does her husband know?"

"Not to my knowledge."

"Huh? How can that be?"

"Shit, I don't know man; ask her."

We talked about sports, shitty jobs and how boring our lives are for about ten minutes and then a diminutive black-haired girl wearing jeans and a long-sleeve white shirt with a ruffled collar walked up to Lem. She was about as tall standing as he would be in the high-back chair if he didn't slouch all the time.

"Hey."

"Where the hell have you been."

"Sorry, I went for a run around Lake Union and I had to take a shower afterwards."

"You should have called me, I would have driven around the lake while you ran." She ignored him and turned toward the barista behind them. "I'm going to get some coffee, do you guys need anything?"

"Oh yeah, this is John. And this is my sister, Anya."

"Hi."

"Hi."

"He has some questions about your lifestyle."

"Shut up Lem."

"Okay, I will try and provide all the answers when I return from the coffee bar."

"What was that all about?"

"I thought you wanted to understand some things about her life?"

"Fuck off."

"She is very open; you can ask her anything. My family has no problem...."

"That isn't really your sister is it?"

"She was adopted. She was born in Ecuador."

"What are you talking about? You are totally insane."

"No, I am serious, my parents only had two genetic kids, me and my older brother. They adopted Anya a few years after Rob was born." Lem started laughing so I did not believe him. He is famous for bullshitting people at school. One time he convinced Tim Weller that he worked undercover for the Seattle Police Department and he was working at Sealth searching for drug dealers. His sunken eyes and rapid, loud speaking style make him sound older than his age, and he has old-man hair. I know that sounds strange, but his do is high and tight, like a cop or a firefighter would wear it. From a distance, he looks like a serious dude. You have to get up close and see his zits before you realize he is really a work in progress. Lem started smoking when he stopped yucking it up. I craved to burn one as well, but I feel weird smoking in front of strangers so I held off. The relative in question sat right between us, setting down her drink carefully. She spent about a year putting a bunch of flavoring and junk in the cup at the condiment bar before entering the table zone.

"Lem is claiming you are his sister...and I never know whether to believe him or not." There was a long pause as she removed the lid of her drink, reviewing her work.

"Sorry,…yes, we are brother and sister. I was adopted so obviously we look pretty different." Her dark eyes were flat and serious and I was embarrassed after asking the question in such a glib manner.

"Ramos also wanted to know why you date men other than your husband." I was infuriated but not surprised. I just stared at Lem, blew air out of my nose and shook my head.

"You are such a…."

"That's okay, I understand. Lem, you are acting like a shithead." Anya's comment made me laugh. She sounded like a sensible young woman.

"What do you want to know?" Her eyes now blazed, and moved away from her little brother and set on me. Her nose was positioned just above her wicked coffee concoction so she could digest the fumes.

I hesitated so Lem starting yapping again. "He wanted to know why you mess around with so many guys while you are married."

"I am not sure I would put it that way."

"How would you put it?" Lem sounded aggressive.

"You realize this is very confidential." Anya's stare was serious as she turned left and faced her brother.

"Ramos will not talk. He doesn't even know you."

"I am more concerned about your mouth." I laughed again.

"Okay…well I understand it sounds weird but my husband is kind of old fashioned and he is not into an open marriage, nor is he one of those people who can say, 'I don't want to know what is going on.' He is…"

"His name is Mark by the way." The interruption drew a sarcastic glance from Anya.

"Yes, Lem really likes my husband, and I love him, but to put my emotions aside completely and stay focused on everything else in life besides lust and love is very stifling."

"What do you mean?" Lem was releasing pent-up emotion, I was just curious.

"I have a problem with the fact that the moral world invades the physical world all the time."

"They are both the same."

"No…maybe I am not explaining this well. I am a spiritual person…."

"Yeah, you go to church with Mom and listen to all that Catholic bullshit."

"Now you are just parroting Dad." Lem shook his head and frowned and leaned back in his chair, looking genuinely offended. "That is a great example. When I am at church I might be atoning for sins or trying to make myself a better person… but I cannot truly understand the spiritual world without understanding the physical world and all of its complexity."

"What does that mean?"

"It means to view the world only as a place of rules, sins and barriers is to limit your ability to use your senses on this planet."

"Okay, but if you want to experience everything on earth," Lem smiled, "including banging guys besides your husband, why do you need to go to church along the way?"

"Because I like it and my mind expands as I read the literature and psalms, sing and learn from the people involved. Am I supposed to declare myself a sinner and disassociate from churches forever until someone declares that I am a good girl? I want to gain ideas and hear different perspectives; not sign up for one perspective because everyone else does."

"Okay, but how can you learn from people who would advise against your behavior?"

"Life is not that simple…I am sure there are a few people who sit through church services who feel the same way I do. Even though I grew up here, that is one aspect of America that I have never understood. People are so anal and judgmental compared to the rest of the world. I guess that is why our government feels like giving everybody advice all the time."

I was tired of the debate so I tried changing the subject. "What do you do?"

"I write for the *Shorewood Weekly*. In fact, I need to finish an article this weekend about land use policy and come up with an editorial that my boss will appreciate."

"Just a second Ramos, I have some more questions." Lem was smiling again, leaning forward in his chair, ready to strike.

"I do hope you are writing this down little brother so when you sin you can blame me for your odd behavior." Anya seemed unmoved by his concern. Her face was mellow and she kept sipping coffee.

"I am just going to forget about getting married." In response, Anya became animated.

"Then you are not even trying to experience everything and you will still encounter the same problems. People and their friends, and their friends, and their friends focus on relationships with the hope that they will progress into coupledom or a marriage. Everybody is supposed to pair off like we are all in a fucking Victorian novel. You are not able to date or sleep with a new person every week or month without appearing to be a sleaze. I just can't deal with that crap so I do what makes sense for me – which means living a private non-judgmental life and accepting that I am no saint."

"I thought the whole point was for people in a spiritual context…"

"You mean the person leading the sermon?"

"Yeah…what I was saying is the head church dude, priest, pastor, rabbi, whatever, aren't they supposed to help people establish values and understanding so you can cope with these feelings?"

"Okay, then why can't I cope while experiencing something wonderful and fleeting?"

"Do the people you are skanking it up with feel like you are jerking them around since you are in a relationship?"

"Most of them do not know and if they did, I am sure they would not be interested."

"That doesn't seem fair."

"It isn't fair at all…but I am unable to find someone who has the same perspective and a schedule that mirrors mine." Anya's arms were out and she was talking with her hands; her voice growing louder as Lem's questions piled on.

"Please understand, I do not feel very good about my life and that is why going to church, in a small way, makes me feel closer to myself, God and the people I love."

"But you used the term lust. How many people can you love?"

"I am not sure. But I feel like I can love multiple people and learn something from each of them."

"Is the chase or at least the beginning of a new relationship the most exciting part?" As soon as the question left my mouth I was embarrassed. I have no experience being in any serious relationship, nor do I have any experience with a steady girlfriend. What kind of a dumbshit would ask such a thing? Fear drained away when Anya calmly smiled and turned my way; leaving her frustrations with Lem behind for a moment, her nodding rhythmic as she contemplated the question. Anya is one of those people who really thinks about the stuff you ask her - you can tell, there is no bullshit. "Yes… yes, the beginning is when you feel full of wonder and excitement. You tingle and want to see the person every day. Spent moments daydreaming dominates your day."

"Then you get married."

"That's right Lem. And everything is just…the same."

"Have you spoken with Mark about this stuff?"

"Do you have any idea how heartbroken, angry and… sad he would be? Telling him or hurting him is the worst possible outcome…and I do want to spend time with him."

"I'm sorry, it just sounds like a sad situation to me…"

"But it's none of your business Lem," I interjected. My comment was a kiss ass deal but I was tiring of his questions.

"Thank you John."

"Okay, okay…but let's get back to the details that Ramos was asking about. How do you pull this stuff off?"

"Don't talk about it if the subject matter is painful…"

"That's alright, it is an awkward situation. Lem has saved me on a number of occasions." I glanced at Barnes, sheepishly looking at his toes, embarrassed because he knew I would view his Q and A as a cover-up since he obviously is part of the process and not the hard-edged moral tough guy he portrays. His conscience bothers him.

"Usually, I pretend to go to family or work events and Lem drops me off at home or picks me up if I say I am going to help our mother with something. That part is easy because Amanda is like a walking hurricane if there is a project on tap." It always cracks me up when someone calls their parent by their first name.

"Jesus, that's for sure. Last night she asked me to help her label a bunch of canned jellies she made earlier this year. After my hand got tired I pretended I had a job interview to get out of there."

"Mark doesn't even like coming over to the house unless we are having dinner because he knows our mother will get a family project going." They both laughed heartily. "Remember, when Uncle Sam left a day early because he was sick of mom asking him to look at the car?"

"Why do you think I am always out wasting time Ramos? I am hiding so I am not asked to do a bunch of crap at home."

"So you are not always above board when it comes to communication with loved ones either, are you?" Lem brushed off his sister's charge with a wave of his hand. "Come on, that is a different deal altogether." Anya just stared at him and returned to the easy target.

"Excuses do not work with Amanda if you are sitting around the house. She does not buy that you have homework or an article to finish." Then Anya became serious again. "This kind of stuff is easy to talk about," she moved her arms behind her back and then forward into a full extension, chest high, clasping her hands. After stretching she looked down at her coffee cup, now almost empty. "But there is no way I could live with my mother   all the time even though I love her. Strangely, I feel the same way about my husband. Mark is great; a really good person. He means well and I feed off his ideas and interests. Yet breaking away and touching someone else   or learning from another heterosexual male, what they like – their perspective on life – that is interesting. Honest feelings do not arise at home after awhile. You get in a rut and your life is not full enough; just a series of predictable patterns."

"Not if you have children or stay busy with a bunch of activities."

"That might work for you Lem, but I become bored too easily. My patience is limited and my mind wanders, and the dependency of the relationship is always present." Anya removed the unnecessary cardboard sleeve on her drink and wrapped her delicate hands around the stiff white paper cup, a Seattle classic, probably the most expensive, hearty paper coffee cup one can buy, featuring no design, completely utilitarian. She breathed deeply and felt the cup.

"Once you marry someone, the trust you share is that you can tell them most of your personal feelings. Not everything. Sex fantasies and lustful thoughts are out of bounds unless you want to fight and argue all the time. When you think you are failing or stumbling there is a warm body to speak with in bed or at the park, or a vehicle or wherever you share your thoughts, and you trust they will keep your communication confidential. Encouragement is truthful; it is not silly chit-chat that friends provide. Spouses, if they are normal, actually wish good things for you because they are proud and feel the flow of your success. If you hate somebody you can tell your husband that dilemma as well. They will listen and they are the only person close to you that will understand and accept petty jealousies. There is no handbook for this stuff…it just evolves and the older you get the more you are dependent on your partner. I am too connected to Mark to leave him. I have no idea what I would do."

"You don't have to…I mean, things might work out over time right?" I finally felt like I was a part of the conversation.

"Definitely…and my perspective has changed. I have realized that it is better to enjoy my life as a young person rather than focus on faults. And baby brother," Lem cringed when the phrase left her lips, "That is precisely why church does not bother me – I have to confront my fears rather than live in a state of guilt."

"You should get some advice from somebody."

"Wait, let me check." She reached into her right front pocket and pulled out her driver's license. "Yep, I am still Anya Barnes."

"And you are still Mark Knowles' wife."

"You two should have your own talk show." Anya laughed, bouncing forward in her chair, eyes closed. Lem scoffed and leaned further back.

"Josh said you didn't get enough cock before you married."

"Don't listen to your friends, they don't know what the fuck they are talking about. I am sure Josh thinks all women should be running around searching for cock." Barnes was talking about Josh Findler, who would be so excited to see Anya naked that he would probably pass out. Every time I see Findy he asks me if his hair is too short or if I like his new shirt. A guy who acts like that has no business giving advice. He is practically frightened to go outside by himself.

"You sound like you are pubing out." Anya just shook her head, exasperated by the side commentary. After a long pause she continued with adult talk.

"I have found the balance I require and that means treating Mark well when I am in his presence. My attitude is better, our sexual interaction is better; and doing things together does not leave me feeling pissed off – like I am missing something. Late at night I used to recoil and pretend to be asleep when he held me. Now I recognize that maximizing my time with Mark is the best option.

"How does it work?"

"What do you mean?"

"That is what Ramos wanted to hear about – how you meet these other guys."

"Lem, come on," I interjected.

"I don't know, if there is a mutual attraction...you just connect."

"But you have to act single."

"No shit, Lem. These little encounters allow me to get into a deep groove with a stranger and make me feel attractive and less needy, but I preserve my really wild side for Mark."

"That sounds like the opposite of what you would be doing."

"It's hard to explain, but having little connections with other people encourages me to really try different stuff with my husband. I even get new ideas sometimes."

"Oh, come on."

"No, really. My latest thing is to meet Mark at a wine bar or a sports bar and pretend not to know each other. After we start role-playing it gets really fun and we can tease each other in a sexual, flirtatious way that we miss on a daily basis." Now she was talking about some interesting stuff.

"Do you pretend to be yourself and vice-versa?"

"That is how we started, now we play different roles all the time. Last time I was a flight attendant who was only in town for one night. I usually make the choice and select a bio about me or some other character, he always just plays along."

"That is pretty lame."

"Sorry Lem, I didn't realize you were so wild. Another thing I did recently was take a picture between my legs with my cell phone." She paused for effect. "And then I sent it to him when we were both at one of his boring business dinners. Is that crazy enough for you."

"That is more impressive." Lem had a big smile on his face, and I think he was getting slightly embarrassed for the first time in his life. I started squirming in my chair, a little uncomfortable with the discussion.

"Then maybe you will like this…sometimes I wake him up by putting my nipple in his mouth. He likes that one. When we first started dating we used have sex in a window or a car but I was the only person anybody could see. The trick was showing me staring outside without a hint of what was going on behind the scenes." Anya giggled madly. She is as provocative as her brother – likes to stir things up. She was getting off on our discomfort and enjoying making people our age excited, a little drama queen. The Barnes parents must be pretty free flowing with their subject matter, or their kids just are just willing to talk about everything in front of anybody.

"And that is probably why Mark has no idea something strange is going on."

"No comment."

"Should we get going sis?"

"Yeah, I need a ride to Queen Anne, Thai Bistro." Off they went, toward Lem's Plymouth, parked a few blocks away. The loud beauty and the noisy beast.

I sat in silence at the same table for about a half an hour, there was no need to seek out more excitement after our conversation/interview with Anya. Strangely, her thoughts about relationships provided a new and deeper perspective on Nathan. Perhaps he is the enlightened one? I always worry about morality and listen to what adults tell us is the 'right thing to do.' Perhaps by not meeting more people and experiencing their company my social perspective is narrower than his? Is this possible? He seems like such an idiot sometimes but maybe I am the stupid one. I have always suspected that he is just taking advantage of good looks and opportunity – but he might just look at the world like Anya and have trouble articulating his beliefs. When my blank gaze settled on the murky vision of a distant bus shelter my internal clock signaled it was time to go home. There would be other social battlegrounds in the future, at which time I might even have a few more dollars in my pocket.

Listening to music was my only vice the rest of the evening, and my day on Sunday could not have been more boring: a little TV, some radio, library time and serious napping. Seattle's warm streak ended and a cool, fifty- six degree, breezy, cloudy rain layer covered the area. Since the Peninsula looks best when the weather is clear I began getting nervous about our journey. Hour after hour of rain smacking you in the face is no way to spend a summer. Monday was my big workday so I started smoothing one of my two dress shirts with our rusted old dent-shack of an iron. The other one, my collared blue shirt that might match the current store uniform, hangs in my room but it might be a lost cause. I realized ironing wouldn't solve the major defects and threads sticking out of that piece of junk.

My arrival at work was as uneventful as all other first days of school, jobs and everything else that requires forms, rules and directions before you have to do   anything. The company shows a little video on theft and the proper way to address customers that is so grainy that it looked like somebody's son owned a production studio and was working on a class project. Half the time I could not make out what the actors were saying. I never increased the volume or asked any questions because I was afraid they were going to make me watch it again. Things got spicy when Mr. Neuman showed up. He is the owner of the store and he spent about an hour and a half running around chewing everybody's ass – talking so loud that his confidential conversations were picked up by everybody in the store, even customers. His white hearing aids are about the size of quarters and they feature blinking red lights so he looks like a Christmas tree when he walks around with a scowl on his face and a mop of white hair. Whenever he looks his employees in the eyes they look down or glance at the floor. Part of the problem is horrible coffee breath. He is one of those guys that starts drinking the black stuff at about 4:30 in the morning and pounds it all day long. He also talks with big heavy breaths so everything comes out in a big black cloud.

Brian Lamb was still my big contact and he was excited that I showed up in tan slacks because the old guy probably beats him or something if the sales people don't wear tan or blue during "showtime," which is what the guys at the store call the floor. If you are sitting in the back screwing around with a soda or watching a video or a game on TV you are on deck for showtime. These guys are pretty corny. They all act like they are selling jets or something. This one dude, 'Big Mike," can talk about the specifics of a NIKE sole for about a half an hour. I pretended to listen to him while he corrected the guy on the video but after a while his commentary just sounded like gibberish to me.

"We need to hire some young folks who really move." Neuman was shouting in Brian's direction. "I want some *retail* guys, some *delivery* people, a few characters that ran for student government in high school. No more military guys; they are always waiting around for directions." After sharing his thoughts about hiring he walked up to some new packaging in the back that was full of teal and pink sweat suits. "Jes-us Christ," he muttered, shaking his head.

Then the old man delivered a speech. "Boys I am not impressed this month. Kick it into gear. When I was in Korea we had a saying, YOU can wait around for something to happen, or you can save a life. We are trying to save this store and I don't have any interest in watching you guys walking around playing pocket pool when you should be making it happen." I had no idea what he was talking about, but I nodded every time he looked in my direction.

After the boss left, Lamb started acting like himself again, looking at his pants in the mirror and telling me what to say and what not to say to customers. Then "Big Mike" started making fun of the owner, whose name is Earl. Apparently his family knows the old guy's clan and he said the store makes money and has for years. "He wasn't even in Korea. He is making shit up because his brother, Sammy was there." Then he talked about what a pain in the ass Neuman was when he mowed his lawn years ago. The old man would come outside with a ruler and check the height of the grass. "I always used to tell him that the setting on the lawnmower didn't change, but I think he likes acting like he is in control all the time. He probably goes home and kicks his dog around every day to show him who's in charge."

The day was not a total loss because after I replaced the slacks with jeans in a Starbucks bathroom, I jammed the bus up to Big 5 and Nathan gave me more money than I expected: $120 in cash.

"Are you serious? I didn't do much."

"You're the only one who has ever performed that job well; I knew you would be good." He looked tired, burned out from talking endlessly at work. In fact, he was as haggard as the guys I had encountered at my new job. I guess work boredom can be grueling after a while.

"You look like you could use some sleep."

"Yeah, I haven't been at home enough lately. Every time I see Chester he jumps all over me and wants to wrestle." My own interests overtook my concern. "Are you guys still planning on camping this upcoming weekend?"

"God yes, I want that little guy to run all over the place – get rid of some energy." I could tell Nathan was leaving out time spent with Torrie on purpose. His eyes were darting all over the place like he was searching for somebody – he was not relaxed and mellow for a change. His clothes looked better though, you can tell he is spending some of his winnings on threads, or wearing the merchandise. Crisp gray slacks, and a light blue oxford shirt, topped off by an attractive blue blazer. He didn't look like a shoe salesman and I wondered if Nate was working for the Rubin brothers on other projects.

"Are you ready for Thursday?"

"Absolutely. I was already briefed by Zip and Tony remember?"

"Okay." He was not listening to me. I skirted out of there and only focused on my new job for a couple of days. I worked part-time as I learned the ropes and God took a shine to me that week by giving me Thursday off. All I had to do was keep it together till my side job required my total attention a few days later.

14

Appearances are Deceiving

After my first experience at Nordstrom, I planned differently. Extra cigarettes were included to harness nervous energy. Hot weather, Seattle style, which means seventy-six degrees, had returned and the bus stop was empty, a pleasant scenario for me because I was plenty early. The two gangsta's showed early as well and look surprised that I was ready to go. I looked like a good boy and team player after my big payday. I have no idea who is handling the money in these transactions, and I do not want to know if you want the truth; so I am trying to impress everybody. The boys were not drunk or stoned this time so our little journey started well. After our normal pleasantries and Zip's questions about how I felt, my mind wandered and suppressed all desire to ask any questions about these guys and their social schedules. Unfortunately, my attempt to place barriers between work and play dissolved.

"You wanna come to a party this Friday John?"

"You mean tomorrow?"

"Yeah, I guess so. Man, I am losing track of my shit."

"Sure, whereabouts is this thing?"

"At this guy named Dimitri's house over by Northgate."

"Yeah, unless I have to head out of town early."

"Where are you going?"

"Just camping with some friends." I have no idea how close these guys are with Nathan and I wasn't about to talk about him or anybody else we mutually know. Fortunately, Anthony was expressionless – so I didn't get the old double team routine. He and my father would have a good conversation. We decided to solidify potential plans later. Since Alderwood Mall was our target, the traveling landscape was different and I didn't know where we were going half the time. I never break north from Seattle because I have no reason to go there and nobody I know ever heads in that direction unless they have to go for some school event or something. I dreamingly watched as we moved to higher ground. Soft green trees lined the freeway and everything was colorless, bland and in the way. Tony drove in the cross section of highways between Interstate-5, 405 and on some road called the Mukilteo Speedway, which was not speedy at all. "We are taking the slow way," said Zip at one point when tiring of changing the radio dial. These guys are always so early they waste time driving around. Maybe they think someone is watching us.

Traffic lights flashed and twisted in a slight breeze as we meandered past parking lots, gas stations and chain stores. All the intersections looked the same, bordered by SUV's, green, yellow, and blue versions. Some dirty, others clean and glittering in the sun. I tried to look inside each vehicle and the most dirty and poorly dressed people were driving the cleanest cars. As we turned east and headed toward the mall, our latest store of shame, the air was stagnant. As we combed through horrible traffic the little car failed to produce wind through open windows. Bored out of my mind, I started dreaming that we were all characters in a western. Instead of a shitty Honda, we were in a stagecoach behind strong-willed horses, in my mind they were Clydesdales, like those beasts in old Budweiser ads. But that is because I can't really picture a horse. Zip kept yelling, "Ya, ya," and tossing little spoonfuls of water from a pail. The liquid evaporated as it landed on the hot hides of the beasts. I was sitting in back chewing tobacco and pushing my hat down so the sun was shrouded from my eyes. A rifle sat in my lap, my gaze directed at the road already traveled.

"Ya see anything out there John?" Zip's comments indicated the shit was going to hit the fan soon. Tony just kept glancing left and right as he drove the horses. I was enthused by my fantasy. I wore a leather vest with long tassels hanging, dust kicked up behind the wagon. Moving forward on the car seat, I imagined standing hunched and peering out toward the edges of my patrol while the rugged, worn wheels of the vessel bounced along ruts and rocks. The sun was shrinking in the distance and we were short food and water. "We still have a hundred miles until town," said Tony.

"Hey, you there?" Zip was making eye contact with Tone in the front seat – they were both smiling and raising eyebrows.

"Sorry, I was spacing out."

"I just asked if you wanted anything to eat. We are going to hit a drive-thru in a moment up here – we're pretty early."

'No shit,' I thought. "No, I'm okay, maybe a Coke. I think I have a few bills."

Interrupting, "Nah, it's on me." Back on earth I was bored again, a little annoyed and uncomfortable with my surroundings, feeling like a kid being shuffled around with no actual knowledge of his schedule. They grabbed a burger and fries in addition to the drink; I guess they thought I needed the energy. I was licking my fingers by the time we reached the Nordstrom parking lot and my gut felt like a big rock anchoring the top of my body to the bottom. We parked about an eighth of a mile from the store and talked about directions and meeting after the heist. I was getting a little sick of the top secret planning. How many ways can I screw up acting like an innocent bystander in the wrong place at the right time? A Taco John's parking lot was our planned rendezvous after   the heist. I tried to forget my task at hand as I slowly stepped to the north entrance of the store. The dead feel of Alderwood early in the day was the opposite of active Bellevue Square, which is always full of gum-smacking teenagers and mid-day shoppers. People that look like they can pay for things make places more exciting. When a security guard with glasses and a serious expression on his face – some middle-aged slub – glared at me like his pants were too tight in the walkway between the front and mall doors, I started wondering whether Nathan's buddies had security contacts in places other than Bellevue. A bunch of drifters and a few fancy people from Whidbey Island, or some other dumb place, were walking around inside. Half of the people I watched just stumbled around doing nothing, the same thing I was pretending to do. The other half were darting around with large colorful bags of clothes and new handbags.

To kill twenty minutes I went over to the food court and sat down near some place called "Just Smoothies." After longing for a cool drink of my own, I ambled toward the pinnacle of customer service (Nordstrom) to make sure the girls were making progress. It did not take long to figure out they had been made and that our trip was going to be painful. They both were making a bunch of noise in the corner, giggling like a couple of whackos. "Those girls look like they are up to no good," said a wise-looking saleswoman near the register, about seventy yards from the thieves. She wore a blue suit and dark leather shoes, not a great outfit but one that made her appear serious, like she didn't take any shit.

"I think you're right," answered a younger associate who wasn't completely clued in, probably a cup of coffee away from normalcy. I needed to do something fast so I bashed into a big rack of clothes trying to knock down some hangers, or an entire tree of clothes. It sounded like a little girl banging a pebble on the sidewalk. The metal stand barley moved, a blouse fell off a hanger and the store people didn't even look my way. One of them even seemed to be reaching for a phone – so I made a direct line to the two idiots feeling nervous and pissed at the same time. I rubbed my head, which hurt after ramming into the giant clothes holder.

"Hey it's time to get moving…the counter people are watching." I was standing about fifteen feet away from them praying they could hear my loud whispering, but they kept yucking it up so I knocked a blouse on the ground, stooped down about three or four feet closer and said, "They are watching you," a little louder.

"Chill out fucktard," said one of the stick figures, obviously pissed that I was signaling an emergency. She wore a baggy top, long black pants with stirrups at the bottom and a purple headband that she probably found in the garbage outside the building. Her co-thief was so stoned that she started cracking up when the other bitch shouted at me. Her giant orange jumpsuit was something between a snowman and a prison outfit, probably full of clothes and weed – a felon stumbling around a store. Her eyes were sunken and glazed over; all she could do was smile. She is probably only seventeen or eighteen years old.

"Get moving or we are all going to get pinched."

Snorting, "Pinched? Have you been watching gangster movies or something?" A lone hand grabbed a wool hat and deftly jammed it into a massive purse, full of merchandise. I was sweating and looking all over the place. When I glanced back at the counter the younger woman was missing, thoughts of her summoning the police raced through my mind.

"We know security brains. Try not to shit your pants before you leave the store." Then she smiled and sauntered off, swishing her skinny ass and hips as if anybody was paying attention. A swift wind would have knocked her into a tree of clothes. My clammy hands and sweating neck made the room feel like 100 degrees.

"What a cunt," I muttered to myself.

"Can I help you with something?" The young woman near the register was right behind me. A glance over her right shoulder revealed clerk #1 was on the phone – looking in my direction. The woman on my tail turned around to see what I was staring at with such intensity. Her big brown eyes burned through me, wide cheeks and a small mouth expressed grave seriousness for such a young woman. I stammered as her gaze followed my every move. Only her bright red, ill-fitting suit, which looked borrowed from her mother, kept her from appearing super serious – she was someone in transition.

"Yeah, I need a belt, a brown belt, a size 34 I think."

"You're on the wrong floor." She smiled like a smart ass, her expression indicating she didn't really care what I was doing - but her co-worker did.

"Sorry, I came over here because I thought I recognized some people I used to go to school with."

"And I am guessing they were not the right people." A big smirk spread across her face.

"You got it."

Seven minutes later I was pissed as I exited the store in possession of the cheapest belt I could find – my winnings courtesy of Nathan will evaporate quickly at this rate. The section the girl walked me toward, so she could make sure I would really buy something, was next to the shoes and watching the guys who swap that leather made me daydream again. After walking into the wide hallway in the mall I sat down at a small wood bench next to an ugly fake plant. As I clutched my shopping bag I thought of perching on that stagecoach, rifle in hand. Coming hard from both sides, over a small hill, across drainage gulley's, were smaller, quicker wagons with no covers. Well-dressed shoe salesmen manned the wagons, carrying shoehorns, metal measuring tools and shoe polish. They started throwing this crap in our direction, hitting the top of the wagon and slipping a few items into the opening, narrowly missing me. I drew my rifle and fixed my gaze on the bow-tie-wearing freaks in the wagons just as a container of shoe polish glanced my right thigh.

"Shoot those bastards," yelled Zip behind me. As I locked eyes with one of the shoe boys driving the horses he looked frightened and moved down, lamely trying to hide behind his transport. I suddenly turned around and shot Zipper in the face, reloaded and shot Anthony in the back of the head as he reached for a pistol. As blood flowed and the spooked horses jumped in the air, wobbling the wagon, I stumbled and fumbled until I pointed the rifle downward and jumped out of the moving target, falling down in the process, but managing to keep the weapon from going off. As I stood up, dust from the other horses covered me but I was spared an onslaught from the shoe boys, who were dumbstruck by my actions.

"Need some socks to go with that belt?" The young clerk's mocking voice shook me toward reality. She was just walking by in the hallway.

"Nah, I'm fine, thanks. Where is the bathroom?" She slowed and walked backwards to address the question. "Down here to the left, I am heading there myself."

"Thanks." I pretended to walk in the same direction until she disappeared around the corner. It was time to head over to Taco John's. Just as I reached the parking lot Nathan called me.

"Yep."

"Hey, what is going on over at Alderwood?"

"Did somebody call you?"

"Yeah, like three people."

"If they get that excited over nothing, I would hate to hear what happens if they ever actually get in trouble."

"Just tell me what happened so I can tell everybody to chill."

"The two girls…"

"Macy and Sydney?"

"I guess, I don't know, I mean it is not like I talk to these people before showtime."

"Okay, okay."

"They were making so much noise and spazzing out so badly that the women working at the store started looking and talking about them – in fact, I wouldn't be surprised if they called security."

"We know security."

"I know that, but somebody from the outside must be able to harass you guys or you wouldn't need me in the first place."

"I understand your point, but the girls are saying you were messing with their program."

"What am I supposed to do? Just watch everything and keep my mouth shut or let someone know if people think they are up to no good?" There was a long silence. "Two people working at the store were pointing and whispering about them."

"I know you are right…these idiots are pretty green and they don't know what the fuck they are doing."

"They think they are being secretive and they are unbelievably obvious." I emphasized 'unbelievably,' sounding out the word to make a point.

"Well, no big deal. I just wanted to find out what was going on. I better get back to work."

"Sounds good, I am going to meet...."

Interrupting me... "Okay, don't need to know, talk to you later."

These people have all watched too many movies. Sometimes they do not want to talk about someone over the phone; then someone gets their ass out of joint and they start freaking out. I was glad to be done with the call and continued walking to meet Tony and the Zipper, hoping the two twits from inside would not be there sucking down burritos and complaining about me. As soon as I entered the joint I wished I hadn't. All four of them were there, and Jen, who looked at me like I was puke on the floor.

"Hey guys."

"We can't have you causing scenes when we're doing our thing. That could have been a fucked up operation in there." The same bitchy girl inside the store was dogging me in front of everybody. I am sure she had been buttering up everybody with her stories since she walked in the door.

"I agree, that is why I wanted to talk to you – the women by the register were pointing at you guys."

"Man, you have no idea..."

"Hey, come on you two, keep this mellow." Tony, the boy I watched randomly invade a family home in silence, was suddenly a voice of reason. I stood, exasperated, sweating and really pissed while four of them filled a booth, staring in my direction. Zip sat in a lone chair at the end of the table.

"And if you go crying to Nathan one more time..."

"I didn't call Nathan, what the fuck are you talking about?" I was really getting agitated.

"How come he is on my ass then?"

"I have no idea, I think he called *me* because you were bitching...in fact, call him now! I am not the whiner here."

"Fuck you, you know what you are…" she stood up like she was coming to kick my ass. Jen, who was sitting next to her, stood up, blocked her path and told her to chill out. Then Ms. Tough Ass started talking softly about all sorts of things under her breath like she was going to intimidate me. "He don't know me…don't know what I'm capable of. Had enough of his mess. I'm gonna bust his ass." Since she weighs about eighteen pounds I have been more scared. I have a feeling the granny at the bus stop would keep her gun in her purse and just beat the crap out of her. Tony and Zip seemed amused by the our little shouting match, which made me feel better because the last thing I wanted to deal with was a bunch of questions from those two on the way back. After everybody settled down the crack thieves left with Jen, who was also pleased that she forced a confrontation over nothing. When they walked out the door she was griping the yappy one's arm and guiding her out to somebody's car. While I munched on a bean burrito and sucked down Mountain Dew, Zip starting talking while Tony stared out the window.

"Man those two were pissed when they got back."

"I'm not surprised, they made quite a scene."

"Do you think they can do the work?"

Zip was crouched like a panther searching for prey as his friend sat at the end of the worn booth with a toothpick in his mouth. It occurred to me that he thought he was in a gangster movie or something. I just don't understand people sometimes…he acts like everything is sewn up and that we have all the pieces in place – the security guys, the right people grabbing stuff – people who will not talk, and then once someone gets a little heated everything is a crisis.

"Yeah, everything will be fine, this is only the second time I was around these people, and I just think it takes time." Expressionless faces peered back at me. "I just get worried when it seems like people are figuring out our system…and those two women were not faked out by anybody." More staring. I knew I was rambling and I could not stop.

"I don't think we will have any trouble in the future… they might be pissed today but I think they will stop bitching about me when they realize that I am on their side. As long as they never speak with anybody everything should be fine."

"I just hope the next time is more organized. We can't afford to fuck this up," countered Zip. Tony nodded as the words left his mouth. I looked at my shoes. So as I expected, all the guys who said this was the perfect situation were sitting on their asses, listening to bullshit from witnesses, not even aware of what I saw. I was getting more frustrated by the minute. On the way back Zipper kept jawing about how we should meet two times a week to go over plans and make sure, "We are all on the same page." Tony just kept driving and commenting on people he thought were funny looking in other cars.

After I escaped from those two whacks, I spent the rest of the day trying to figure out how to escape their party invitation. My worrying was unnecessary because I never heard from them after they dropped me off. Friday was busy, plenty of work at the shoe store, running around looking for sizes that were not in stock. Everything was mellow on the social front. Nate called at six to ask if I wanted to leave that night so I ran around packing like a maniac for an hour. Just when you think you are a light packer someone calls and messes with your program and all you do is run around looking disorganized and screwed up. My mother kept coming out of her room, television blaring, watching me make sandwiches, check laundry in our aging dryer, grab toiletry stuff and search for an old worn map.

"Be careful."

"We will. Everybody just wants to get on the road so we won't be too tired to drive." My mother knew my rap was bullshit, but she was making the remark she was supposed to as a parent and I was responding with my own line of kid nonsense. I was ready at 7:15, Nathan's projected arrival time. An hour-and-a-half of waiting and two phone calls with new projected launch times resulted in me watching the Mariners lose on television on my mother's bed and the growing realization that the great trip might never happen. Ma never misses a game and being near her was comforting. I even fell asleep for a few minutes while sprawled out at the end of the old creaky bed. Moms kept eating popcorn while propped up against the light wooden headboard. Every once in a while she would guffaw as another Mariner batter whiffed or hit something right at one of the A's. They really suck. Finally, the King and Queen arrived a few minutes after nine. Only Nathan came inside. He greeted my mother with a big smile near the front door. She peeked out and waved from her bedroom doorway in green sweats and a plaid red shirt. "Good luck," was her only comment. I found her words awkward so I just gave a little grin and shut the door. I knew as soon as we got off the porch she would scamper over and check the lock three or four times and peek out the window as we were leaving.

To protect against foul odors I scrubbed my pits about three times each so I could sit in the backseat with my arms up on the high-back chair. I even put on some cologne, some strong-smelling stuff called 'California' that I nabbed in my father's cabinet when my mother was in the can. Pits ablaze, I popped my duffel bag in the spacious backseat, stretched out and moved into position in the middle of the long cushion, with a big smile on my face. I jumped in the car just ahead of Nathan, who was fooling around with the fishing poles, sleeping bags and a tent in the trunk.

"What's going on guys?" Torrie turned and flashed a big toothy grin in my direction. Her eyes locked on me for a second before she turned around to face the road. She has such perfect teeth and skin tone, a glow follows her when she turns her head, perfectly shaped. She smells just how you would imagine a beautiful girl to smell – not flowers or perfume, fresh, like a breeze blowing honeysuckles in your face – an empowering feeling, a breathless situation. I closed my eyes for a few seconds, digesting how lucky I was to be near her during a weekend getaway.

"Hey J, you okay back there?" Nathan was eyeing me up and down, he could tell I was hyper and wide awake, an irregular persona for me.

"Yeah, just glad to be out of the house. My father is on the road and my mom wants to talk all the time."

"Hey, what is the address to pick up Chester?" My time as the sheriff of the backseat was about to end.

"I forgot to check for a little kid's sleeping bag Nate."

"Torrie's parents had one – so we are good. Did you bring your map?" We chatted about the location near the landing near the river and how much I was looking forward to relaxing over the weekend. Then I started babbling about the rain forest, talking about vivid green moss on the ground and trees as tall as skyscrapers. By   the time I finished my speech the place sounded like heaven and I was nervous that the weather would be so crappy that we would not even be able to view the river through the fog. Torrie seemed generally interested in my story. She started talking about how her family had visited a remote part of Lummi Island a few times, but I had no idea what she was talking about, someplace up north by Bellingham.

"Jesus, Ramos, you make this place sound like the tropics or something. Your father always just made it sound like some secret fishing hole."

"I know, I will calm down. It just brings good memories, ya know?"

"We're taking your word for it."

"I'm sure it will be fun." Torrie believed me and she unleashed a complimentary giggle to prove it.

"As long as I can drink I will be fine," added Nathan.

When Chester invaded the backseat he positioned himself in the middle, my place. Third wheel storyteller time was over as the little man with the big voice took control, asking questions, bouncing in the backseat and darting his head all over the place, looking out the window. First, he sprinted to the car after spying us from the front porch with Mrs. Hollingbeal. I did not see Chuck, the pebble thrower, anywhere and Laney was out of town, and living at home again. Chester just enjoys spending time with the Hollingbeal's and always begs to visit. His little blue backpack bobbed as he ran and a red cap with a big C on the front covered his head. The car door was still locked when he grabbed the handle and pulled on the metal like he was saving mankind – thrashing and forcing with every ounce of his body.

"Hey mellow out, this is not your car."

"Don't worry Nathan, its no big deal." While the two lovers soothed each other I got off my ass and unlocked the door. Nathan reminded his brother to check locks before attacking doors, a lesson that captured his attention for about a block and a half. I am not sure if all kids have some sort of deficit disorder or if Chester is just special, but he is always moving, grabbing, darting, puffing out his little cheeks and thrusting his arms toward the sky. He also likes to stretch - I think he picked that habit up from Nate.

"I don't have any money, but I sure am hungry!" Chester's yell and call to action made us laugh.

"Chester, are you telling me Mrs. Hollingbeal didn't feed you?" The little man was pushing me so far behind Torrie that she forgot I existed. Bouncing hands were moving up and down along the top of the backseat and his head kept moving right and left, like he was watching a tennis match in the front seat. His focus on Torrie was intense, he was smiling and staring and when he jumped up, or rose in the seat, his ass was in my face – not a good feeling. A bathroom and snack stop just south of Olympia was on the agenda, we all needed a break, the little guy was tiring us out. Nathan chose Denny's over Shari's and my request to check out downtown was voted down. No one else understood that our moisture-filled drive would culminate with an evening along a river bank. Unless the moonlight charitably found a clearing, discovering a suitable campsite would be difficult. Leaving late had screwed everything up.

"You want your home fries?"

"I think so Chester. But you can have a few if you wish."

"Man, don't give him your stuff, he will take it all." We all laughed as the little man sheepishly slunk into his chair, embarrassed in front of Torrie, who was keeping his attention along with mine. Little dimples deepened when he smiled, a reddened face accentuating his cheeks. As I finished my eggs, depression set in because my hope of getting close to Torrie was evaporating at the hands of her boyfriend, an obvious scenario, and his adorable little brother who constantly kept her interested in his affairs.

"Do you want a milkshake Chester?"

"YEAH, can I?"

Torrie was paying for everybody – gas, meals, and even Chester's snacks – whenever we stopped. Considering Nathan was supposedly picking up heavy cash from his little mall operation I was surprised. I tried to pay when we stopped for gas but Nate waved me away.

"Her parents have plenty of money bro."

"Yeah, but *she* doesn't."

"It's alright, it makes her feel good and I give her cash." I did not trust Nathan so I continued offering. He is really a cheap sonofabitch sometimes. After meandering through the gloomy, dark Black Hills the road dropped into flatland near Elma. After another ten miles the tiny lights of Montesano passed by. A sign stating, "Central Park" was next, at the top of a wide road with a Jersey barrier in-between that curved around until a few lights along the Hoquiam River were visible in the distance. The neighborhood sign used to confuse me when I was younger because I would hear somebody talking about Central Park in New York on the national news or something and I had no idea why anybody would be talking about some dinky place in the Northwest.

Cresting over the hill, Torrie slowed the car as large rock formations hovered above. Huge nets were slung over the hillside, keeping pieces of the rocks from falling on cars. Steel rods diving into boulders are visible in the light of street lamps. It looks like a giant hammered nails into the hillside. A light rain dusted the car, a normal occurrence in that part of the state. Even summer nights cannot escape moisture in Grays Harbor country. The weather prospects looked good in the newspaper so I prayed for a west wind that would push the bad stuff toward the ocean. As we crested over another vista, steamy discharges rose from the river and sawmills below. I could smell the air; reminiscent of wet sawdust. It brought back memories of living on the Harbor as a young child. The lights of cities below, Aberdeen and Hoquiam, excited the other three passengers in the car, but I was too informed to get excited. The fun stuff lay ahead, in the deep forest. We chugged through green lights and one-way streets in desolate towns as lights from the hills flickered on the river as she meandered snake- like, covered by rotting piers and dark green and gray bridges. Human activity only showed when we caught glimpses of shift workers walking briskly toward neon tavern signs. Local princesses in jeans shorts, probably gorgeous years ago, stood outside smoking. A few hot rods zipped by, thrusting exhaust into the midnight air.

"What do people do for fun here?" Torrie sounded worried.

"They beat their dogs." Nathan's comment didn't help.

"Why would they hurt doggies?"

"He's just kidding Chester," Torrie said as she smacked Nate in the arm.

"Come on, that's uncalled for," was Nathan's retort. Chester laughed.

"Remember guys, we are not hanging out in Aberdeen and Hoquiam."

"Thank god." Nathan was cracking everybody up and I was just grateful we were getting close to the borders of these gloomy towns. Our campground would be more enticing. Since I had talked up the beauty of the area I did not want Torrie's impression to be of greasy rednecks in the middle of the night and it wasn't like we were going to meet any of the finer local citizens the next day over coffee. As lights faded, we traversed the final bridge along the last urban turn of the river; a quaint grouping of little wood houses lined the road out of town. Bright moonlight shone as the city withdrew and skies opened, clouds separating.

"Man it's like Halloween here every night." Nathan sounded nervous. He is always super cool. His sudden personality shift cracked me up, a real departure from the Nate I know. He was looking all over the place, trying to get acclimated to the surrounding woods and gloomy highway. Chester was snoring, his head jammed between the door and the back seat. I glanced to make sure his lock was depressed. Sure enough, everybody in the car had a locked door but Nathan.

"I wonder what those people are doing right now?" Torrie's gaze fell on a little white home reflecting light from the moon. Frayed curtains slung across a picture window set to implode in a strong wind. Concrete steps in front were crumbling. Dark shadows moved in the living room as we waited at the last red light on the edge of town. A log truck sputtered to a halt heading in the other direction; a freight train in the night. While traveling at high speeds the vessel shook the little houses sitting on planks and lumber, survival boards designed for river flooding. There were no actual foundations. As we ventured further into the night only fluorescent road lights, high globes perched on long wooden poles, lit our path. Nathan kept asking me if I knew where we were going and every time Torrie told him to pipe down so Chester could sleep. As we meandered along Highway 101 and turned onto Ocean Beach Road I warned everybody about sharp curves and migrating deer but only road-induced dips and roller coaster twists made them take me seriously. A stunning moon and bright stars, shrouded by the lights of the city, showed the way. Our gyrating suspension did not wake Chester and I was grateful. The kid has a lot of energy and would have asked me a million questions about where we were – he is just like his brother that way.

More logging trucks passed as we bounced along a highway dissecting forest on both sides. There was the occasional rolling clearing, probably farms dotted by trees and resting animals; but nobody could tell in the dark. The further we traveled toward the rain forest and the coast the less we saw. Foreboding iron gates framed gravel driveways and "no trespassing" signs proliferated. Every third road was blocked by concrete barriers or felled trees; old logging roads where hunters get away from their wives or do some target practice. Yellow signs were the markers I watched since one of them held the key to the campsite in the dark. Warm moisture was changing to cold but we were making good time on the windless road as we reached our next point of demarcation, Copalis Crossing, a little three-way stop.

"Turn right here."

"Where?"

"No, I mean turn right."

"Jesus, are we reaching the end of the earth?" Torrie laughed at Nathan's crack. A rotting sawmill and rusting trucks polluted the junction and even I had to concede it looked abandoned and spooky. We meandered another seven miles until I spotted my marker, a fluorescent road sign full of bullet holes – Pop and I have been locating the road this way for years. One time the sign was knocked down while we were fishing one weekend and a crew was putting up a new one as we left, and sure enough, the new sign was full of holes the next time we came. I wasn't confident in our location until I saw the hollowed out Ri_b_ on the marker. Apparently, targets are hard to come by on country roads. There are no other driveways for about three miles so I had to convince Torrie to turn the car around in the darkness and head toward the holes. She was so nervous about driving in the ditch along the narrow road that it took about a year for her to maneuver while Nathan laughed and Chester woke up like he was breaking out of prison.

"Wha, wha, wha, what's going on!"

"The car is moving little man."

"Where are we?"

"Ask J, he is taking us to some river."

"What did you wake me up for?" His voice was wobbly and unsure.

We all laughed as Chester screeched his head back and forth in all directions, looking out in horror at black forest and an aging road with faded striping. When he realized massive fir and hemlocks lined the trail he smushed his face against the backseat passenger window behind his brother, wrenching his neck like he was viewing skyscrapers.

"Wow, do you see those trees?"

By the time we turned left on Ribby, a large nutria crossed the road sending Nathan into apoplexy. He wiggled his feet around, jumped up in his seat and pointed. "Whaaa! What the hell is that thing?" I explained the travels of the giant rodent, a rat-like beauty that made its way to the Northwest from swamps in Louisiana by way of South America or some shit. Pops loves to see nutria and he scared the crap out of me one time by placing a dead one near my pillow when I was taking a nap near our little fishing hole.

"Jesus, what is that monster?"

"It looked like a giant rat," said Torrie, who did not scream. She probably figures even the rodent will think she is hot.

"They do not move very fast and they are pretty gentle, but they are scary-looking," I conceded.

"Do they attack people?" Chester's eyes were so wide they were taking over his forehead.

"Nah, they just get out of your way."

"Do they smell?"

"Probably. They look smelly."

My relaxing weekend was turning into a gothic horror show for the city boys. The only person who remained calm was the delightful Torrie, who told Nathan he was acting like a baby. I sighed, imagining the workload awaiting me. Putting up a tent and camping with a bunch of novices is not my idea of a good time in the middle of the night.

"When I used to go to Camp Seabrook we used to see deer," said Torrie.

"Yeah, but you didn't see monster rat-boars." I tuned out as they discussed the creature in detail.

Torrie drove ¾ of a mile past tall gray hayfields and rusting tractors. Heavy equipment was stuck in soil, covered by moss. Layers of mud rose between stranded items, idle until future property owners rescue them from the muck. A small wooden sign nailed to a tree labeled "Public Fishing Hole" was my signpost.

"Turn here," I bellowed, startling everybody. Nathan craned his neck viewing giant trees lining the impending gravel road and Chester's head was on a swivel. They looked like a strange mechanism in action, Nate moving up and down and the little guy turning side to side.

"Go slow," I warned as we bounced along the potholes, kicking loose gravel and sputtering along. When the contours of the path dipped and sprung up, the car slid and resurrected her traction when climbing out of large craters.

"Does this road ever end?" asked Nate after only half a mile. He thought I was lost.

"No, we will know we're there when we fall in the river." Torrie laughed and Chester yelled, "Good gracious," which made all of us crack up.

"There really *is* a campsite after a mile and a half," I said, trying to be reassuring.

"You mean a mile and a half from here or from the beginning of the road?"

"The beginning."

We bounced all the way to the flat beachhead near the calm waters of the Humptulips, a famous destination for King Salmon years ago. Amazingly, only two tents occupied space, we had our choice of spots.

"Is that the river over there?" Chester's question was ignored.

"Don't drive in Torrie!"

"She won't, don't worry," I said.

"I can't swim!" Chester was freaking out again.

"We are going to be a long ways from the river."

"What do you think of your joke now Ramos?" Nathan had a big smile on his face.

"It wasn't my best."

As Torrie walked around with Chester, explaining the Humptulips would not sweep him away during the night, Nathan made friends with the tent dwellers, who had a campfire blazing. Three boys, two girls, a big truck, two motorcycles and a bunch of empty beer cans surrounded the fire. The distractions left me alone to build tents, a huge pain in the ass. Fortunately, there was no wind and working alone made the job easier. By the time I finished unloading the car and checking everything, Torrie and Chester were roasting marshmallows at the river camp and Nathan was pawing and straddling a big dirt bike. I didn't feel like talking so I just sat down on an old log that washed ashore long ago and listened as two motorcycle stallions told Nathan how to jump bikes; and a guy with a beard and two girls in jeans and sweatshirts drank beer and shared tales with Torrie and Chester about growing up in Shelton. I kept listening until beard man offered me a beer. As I sucked it down, Nathan heated up.

"Did you get our tent set up yet?"

"Yes, can I get you something to drink?" I asked sarcastically.

"Nah, but you can make me a sandwich; I'm pretty hungry."

"Ease up Nature Pipes." Nathan was wearing a tight t-shirt that read 'Natureripe.' Beard man got the joke and laughed so I decided to introduce myself. 'James' explained they were all students at Olympic College and that one of the dirt bike boys, Neil, grew up in the area and was familiar with the fishing hole. The other dude, 'Sam,' played baseball for Olympic. He and Nathan were having so much fun talking motorcycles I thought they would start making out. The two chicks, Megan and Cheryl, were with the bike guys, and beard man was a lone jokester. Everybody kept drinking except Torrie, who was trying to convince Chester that people were drinking soda pop in cans because she was worried he would tell his mother about Nathan's babysitting skills. I am sure Laney knows the real story anyway. We were all getting pretty silly around the campfire, telling stupid jokes and babbling like fools. The girls kept giggling and whispering and James, who is obsessed with movies, was glassy-eyed. If he could have stood up, he would have fallen down. He was just listing back and forth, making little burp sounds, "urp, urp, urp."

"Do you think there is a Jedi toilet?" He was looking at me.

"What the hell are you talking about?"

"A Jedi toilet. You know, Star Wars duuude." By this time the motorcycle guys were trading back and forth on a bike with Nathan and kicking up dust as they zipped along the river bed pulling big wheelies on hard sand. Chester was fascinated, Megan and Cheryl were bored and gossiping about other friends over the noise. Torrie was hounding Chester, which made it difficult to speak with her. First, they played catch with a wiffle ball in the light of the fire; then a Frisbee and then baseball man jumped off the bike and got out a ball and some old gloves they could use. You could tell he was pleased with himself after reaching into his team bag and holding up the stuff with a big toothy smile. A baseball cap and the high collar on his North Face pullover squished his stocky face.

"Poop in Jedi toilet I will," spoke James in his best imitation of Yoda. I laughed and everybody else stared. He continued to project the ways of Yoda.

"Do you think Yoda takes showers or just hoses off?"

"I think he bathes in plant serum."

"What are you talking about dude? Plant serum is not awesome. Shower in blood I should." Sam and Nathan came back to the fire while Neil urinated in the bushes.

"Smelly bottom I have."

"Gross James," slurred Cheryl.

"Yeah, what *are* you talking about? You are so weird," added Megan.

"He's talkin' about Yoda bitches," announced Sam.

"Nice. You guys are really classy."

"Mean to girls Yoda is. Special Jedi bathroom Yoda has." For another two hours or so similar banter around the campfire continued until Chester crashed and everybody else slowly followed. I was the last person to enter a tent, and before I retired, I started another one of my stories under the influence. It was hard to decipher later.

A silent river passed by the boy with all the answers. Friends loved him, cycles sat outside his tent and he slept in the arms of a beautiful suitor. Nothing could stop him. He was destined for greatness, a football star or a trainer of wild animals, a born leader. Who would he inspire? Once a petty thief in Delridge he now stays away from dangerous work and does his planning behind a desk. Most amazing is the fact that this boy, this American star, never gets caught, and he probably never will. A simple smile and enthusiasm for people and their activities is his weapon. It is like my friend always said. He never gets caught because he doesn't want to. Will anything be different thirty or forty years from now? I doubt it. Those blessed with good looks, charm and confidence find their way.

I stopped writing after losing my pencil in the sand. I didn't have much paper left in my notebook anyway. I grabbed a blanket and slept outside the tent. When I awakened I had to jump around a little bit to get my blood moving. James was already up and starting another fire. I shared some water with him until the sun hit him in the face and he went back into his tent and sacked out. I had already fished for a couple of hours by the time the other three broke out of their dark lair. Two small bullheads were all I had to show for my efforts but it was a beginning. The other crew, started circling the fire and building it up while drinking water and soda. I missed my father's heavy black coffee. Smoking kept me wired and focused. Around eleven, Nathan started giving little Chester lessons on the bike and Megan and Cheryl started telling Torrie how beautiful she is, compliments she lapped up for a while with a big grin on her face. I grilled my fish for everybody above a little fire pit I set up and Neil and Sam played with the other motorcycle. Even James came outside for the party. His head was screaming from the night before so he didn't say much.

Cheryl was even kind enough to bring out some fruit and crackers to go with the fish. After lunch everybody milled around independently and I decided to keep an eye on Nathan and Torrie's activities. After rubbing his full belly Nathan took T's hand and led her down a trail cutting through groves of alder. I knew they would be slow so I gave them space before roaming in their direction. I don't really follow people around, so sneaking around behind Nathan and Torrie felt strange. Sandy, soggy ground made visible footprints so I inched along until voices and giggling became inaudible…and then silence. It dawned on me that they might be making out or playing grab- ass and I didn't want to look like a creeper so I decided I would act startled as if I ran into them. Fortunately, the shrill sounds of motorcycles racing along the gravel road, about ninety feet away, overwhelmed every sound in the area. Neil and Sam were blasting away and Chester rode behind Mr. Baseball. I saw them through the trees. Red helmets and red and white jackets peeked through. Dust and dirt kicked up when the humming motors revved even louder. As the bikes raced toward the country highway Nathan unleashed some big 'whoops,' and yelled as the threesome zipped by. His shouting helped me draw a bead on his distance ahead and the language I picked up was hostile.

"Nathan, I didn't come out here to watch you and your friends ride motorcycles."

"Those guys are not my friends."

"Those hick girls they're with are hard to talk to."

"I'm just tryin' to relax."

"Can you ever relax with me?"

"Fuck," Nathan sighed and yelled simultaneously.

"I'm glad you take this so seriously."

I perked up and moved ahead in a crouched position. The din of the bikes returned as they reached gravel, headed back to the campsite. Torrie walked deeper into the alder in a huff and Nathan did not follow. I shadowed her for a while. She paused when encountering a little pond in a recess in the forest. Taking little steps, she stooped and picked up some pebbles and tried to skip them across the water with the full force of her body. It was a pathetic performance, T couldn't turn her slender feet in the dirt and her body was barely twisting. Low- rise designer jeans hugged her shapely hips and tapered into perfection along the contours of her legs. A red sweatshirt covered the rest of her beautiful body. She pulled her hair down, stuck the band in her pocket and stretched while looking skyward. I slowly moved toward the pond, intending to speak to her, my mouth forming silent words. I was not sure what I would say, but as long as I made plenty of noise and did not startle her, I figured soothing conversation and compassion would be appreciated.

"Thwack!" A snapping twig caused me to jump behind a tree, my heart beating so loud I could hear it in the forest. I glanced away from Torrie while crouching down in time to view Nathan moving briskly through the trees. He didn't say anything until he stood next to Torrie and grabbed her arms. I gently crawled away on all fours until blocked by thistles. Then I walked in long loping strides while hunched over; like early man. Once out of earshot, I meandered through the forest and came out by the campsite just in time to watch the three boys pile into their giant Dodge truck and head off to town for more beer. "We'll be back in an hour," one of them yelled. 'Make that an hour and a half,' I muttered to myself.

Chester was fiddling with the bikes and the girls were watching him so I kept silent, trying to avoid babysitting duty. I finally discovered a little meadow in the woods, laid down and, took a snooze. After about twenty minutes one of the bikes awakened me. It sounded like a distant lawnmower. The revolutions were all screwed up, like someone was tuning a motor in a garage. Then the engine raced and a lone scream, "Noooo!" The intonation sounded shrill; I figured it was Nathan and that he was either pissed at Torrie or Chester was screwing around with the bike on his own. I wandered back to the campsite. There was nothing to see over there; Megan and Cheryl were walking in the distance along the water, bending over and inspecting found treasures. So I figured I would head back to the gravel, taking my path through the woods. Birds were chirping, the bike had stopped and light peaked through the forest. A beautiful setting for a walk, fishing, or just screwing around. A sing-songy voice indicated I was close to Nathan and T so I started walking with a purpose, taking bigger steps and crashing into fallow sticks and kicking up brush. I did not want to sneak up on Torrie anymore, I owed her that much.

Drying leaves and needles crunched against dirt as I soldiered on, until I suddenly stopped and held my breath after detecting sobs from my boy Nathan. Like all males, his cries were deep, lumbering spits and sniffles with little bursts of breath, unlike a girl's cry, which is a wail, designed to get your attention. Something was wrong and I didn't know whether to run toward him, sneak away or tip-toe in his direction. I just started creaking along with tiny steps, making as little noise as possible. Sunlight slipped through cracks in the trees bringing waves of energy and a peaceful scene in the forest as a little clearing near the road lurked ahead. I slowed my breathing and slipped behind large trees, brush and stumps on my way to a suitable hiding place, ducking down and straining to see what was going on with nervous anticipation. Near the clearing, I noticed two fallen trees, crossing paths, opening up a little window between massive trunks. Taking big steps and landing on my tip-toes, I moved behind the lowest ancient log and peered above her with a direct view of the road and the commotion about twenty yards ahead.

"Oh my god…please tell me this is a dream." Nathan's sobbing made the birds cease chirping. His crackling, breaking voice rose up and down in inaudible cries. He was shaking and gasping for air.

Chester's perfectly round head was gruesomely dented. Dry blood covered unblemished, perfect skin. He was motionless near a tree that took the brunt of his force as he came unhinged from the motorcycle in a gothic horror scene. Leg and arms apart, instantly knocked senseless. Once soulful eyes were empty; glazed in a frozen state, magnified by an open-mouthed stare. His expression indicated his spirit could not fathom his body had perished. The machine was in pieces, the front wheel rested ten feet from the Western Cedar that claimed the life of a promising boy. My heart slowed to a crawl, nerve endings tingled. Everything was in slow motion; breaths came in sucks and gasps. I sat down using every bit of energy in my body to balance myself on the forest floor. Nathan was naked and stripped down, he was inside Torrie but motionless except for bursts of sobbing and little body shakes – she did the work and her gentle rocking and rubbing of his chest was comforting rather than sexual. Everyone I wanted to be close to was in trauma. Shock consumed my brain waves, momentary stillness when comprehension was unavailable to me.

Nathan shook under Torrie between sobs and wails, all the while holding his side with his left hand and keeping his right arm wrapped around his brother's legs. He did not want to let them go. As his body stuttered to orgasm, she disengaged and pulled up his torso and held his face to her bare breasts.

"I will always be with you baby. God will protect Chester." Torrie's ability to form words was amazing, I was frozen. She had a beautiful smile on her face as she comforted Nathan, I slunk away, only to return through the woods after everybody was dressed, emotionally naked. I was only capable of making grunts and sobs, which Nate returned. Ten minutes later they loaded the prone boy in the front seat of the car, between them, so they could both touch Chester while Torrie drove and rubbed Nathan's neck. I remained at the campsite while they spent time in town at a hospital and a morgue. Laney took the train to meet them and eventually Nathan picked me up the next morning. By that time the baseball crew had left and I was alone and numb, too shocked to think about myself for a change. Nathan kept talking about what his brother would never experience and saying, "It should have been me man….it should have been me." I was speechless and kept nodding my head in agreement like a jackass. Torrie's parents picked up Laney and comforted her on the way back to Seattle, where a service was held the following Wednesday. The ceremony was more solemn than anything I have ever witnessed, and I have been to a few funerals. There is something about a kid dying before he even begins to experience life that just rips your heart out. After the service I began feeling like speaking again and realized my life was getting shorter by the day. Over the next twenty-four hours I tried to comfort both Nathan and Torrie, groping for normalcy, wishing for social equilibrium.

When I stopped by Torrie's house the following day she was distant as hell and kept saying, "You should talk to Nathan. I have never seen something so sad." She had no interest in hearing from me. Her eyes did not meet mine and her cheery, smiley demeanor was gone. My opportunity to truly get to know her was gone. She steered me to Big 5 to locate the man. When taking a walk outside, after explaining Laney pushed him to stay busy by working, Nate just started sobbing and couldn't stop. He kept leaning against me and the brick façade of the building, incapable of finishing a sentence. I was torturing him, reminding him of the worst day of his life, so I booked out of there and walked around for a while. Several things raced through my mind. Should I speak to the Road Pig about his dog? Tell him the real story. Was it time to get out of the department store spy business? Would that be loyal to Nate? As I trudged to work the following day I realized nothing would change. My summer would be full of free landscaping services and sad conversations. Just like "the daily" all over again, I do not want to do anything too risky. Man, I wish Chester had never climbed on that bike.

9 79888 6151527